THE
CRYING
SEASON

ALSO BY D.K. HOOD

Don't Tell a Soul
Bring Me Flowers
Follow Me Home

D.K. HOOD

THE CRYING SEASON

Bookouture

Published by Bookouture in 2018

An imprint of StoryFire Ltd.
Carmelite House
50 Victoria Embankment
London EC4Y 0DZ

www.bookouture.com

ISBN: 978-1-78681-543-9
eBook ISBN: 978-1-78681-542-2

This book is a work of fiction. Names, characters, businesses,
organizations, places and events other than those clearly in the
public domain, are either the product of the author's imagination
or are used fictitiously. Any resemblance to actual persons, living or
dead, events or locales is entirely coincidental.

To Gary, for his endless cups of coffee and reminders to eat.

PROLOGUE

Last fall

"Run and don't look back."

Shots peppered the undergrowth, and splintered trees showered Paige Allen with bark. She strangled a scream and gaped at the crimson patch spreading across the front of her fiancé's shirt. "I'm not leaving you." She grabbed Dawson's arm, willing him to move.

"Go!" Dawson stared at her with unfocused eyes and blood trickled from the corner of his mouth. "*Please… go.*"

Terrified, she willed her feet to move and rolled into the bushes. She could hear someone crashing through the trees then more shots rang out. Dawson's body contorted as bullets pierced his flesh. He took two unsteady steps forward then fell face down on the trail. His fingers clawed the dirt in a feeble attempt to survive, then he lay staring at her with unseeing eyes. She knuckled the sob threatening to escape her mouth. *Oh my God, he's dead.*

In the distance, she could hear something big moving toward her through the undergrowth. In disbelief and unable to move, she glanced down the track but no one came into sight. What was happening? Terror had her by the throat and it hurt to drag air into her lungs. She peered through the dense vegetation, looking for an escape route. *I have to get out of here.* Teeth chattering, she scrambled deeper into the forest, moving far away from the trail. To survive she needed to be silent but each twig she stepped on cracked like a whip.

The sight of Dawson's blood-splattered body and his dead staring eyes flashed across her mind in horrific reruns, slowing her responses. The wind rustled the trees, lifting the leaves underfoot and creaking the branches. Each noise sounded like the footsteps of the killer. She ran in blind panic, weaving through the trees and tripping over roots.

Her sense of direction descended into chaos but she ran on, dragging her feet through the thick bushes. As she broke out of the trees, a sob escaped her throat. "Oh, no." She had run in an arc and was now back on the trail twenty or so yards from Dawson's body.

She turned on her heel and bolted up the path toward the mountain. Someone had killed Dawson. The man she loved had died like an animal in hunting season; run to ground and shot. Tears streamed down her cheeks and the salty flow leaked into her mouth. She had to get away and tell the cops. Desperate, she scanned the area ahead for a hiding place and found a huge boulder bathed in shadows off the main trail. If she could make it a few more yards without the gunman seeing her, she could hide.

The bushes tugged at her hair and tore at her clothes with each step. Panting, she made the shelter of the rocky outcrop and took a quick glance behind her. The bushes on one side of the trail quivered and the crunch of boots on the forest floor sounded like a stampede of buffalo. *He's coming.* A figure thundered through the narrow pathway then stopped and kneeled beside Dawson's body. Dressed in army camouflage with matching face paint, he turned to look in her direction and she held her breath. Her pulse thumped in her ears so loud, she thought he would hear it. Without one ounce of compassion, the man dragged Dawson into a sitting position against a tall pine tree then turned slowly in her direction.

Sheer terror gripped her, making it hard to breathe. She had to get help. With shaking limbs, she pulled out her cellphone and ducked deeper into the shadows. The light on the screen lit up the dark space like a beacon then slipped from her trembling fingers and smashed on the rock. She gaped at the scattered remains in disbelief. *I'm alone; no one is coming to help me.* The footsteps came closer, slower and more deliberate, stalking her.

She stared at the small opening between the sheer rock face and the boulder. If she reached the other side of the massive stone, she could run in the opposite direction. Surely, he was too big to follow her through the narrow gap. Trembling, she eased around the edge of the boulder.

Too late. One large hand grabbed her by the hair and lifted her then threw her onto the ground. The man stared down at her and a wide grin split his face.

"What are you doing on your lonesome out in the forest?" His voice was strange, distorted.

Paige spat the pine needles from her mouth and staggered to her feet. Anger and revulsion gave her courage. "Are you crazy? You shot Dawson."

"He can't help you now. Tell me, can you count to ten, sweetheart?"

Noticing the amusement in his eyes, she took a step backward and swallowed hard. The man gave a low chuckle then raised his rifle and pointed it at her. She gaped at him in disbelief. "What do you mean by that?"

"One…"

Paige turned and ran, crashing through the undergrowth. She found the trail down the mountain and took off at full pelt. No sound of footsteps came from behind her. She could escape. Heart thundering, she leapt a fallen log. Mid-flight, pain ripped through her back as if one of her lungs had burst with the effort. She forced her legs onward but the forest dissolved into a kaleidoscope of green. Falling, the ground came up to meet her, pushing the air from her painful lungs. Flat on the sandy trail, she blinked as a wildflower came into perfect focus then faded into black.

CHAPTER ONE

Present day

Monday

Deputy David Kane ducked out of the way of a beer bottle cartwheeling and spewing foam in all directions. The bottle flew over one shoulder and smashed into the wall, showering his back with glass. Instinct on full throttle, he spun around in time to grab the swinging fist of a burly man in his palm and twist his wrist, bringing the arm up behind the man's back. He swept his assailant's feet, sending him down hard on his knees. The man howling in pain did not resemble the usual rough type who frequented the Triple Z Bar. Kane dragged the man to his feet then slammed him against the wall, taking in his expensive jacket and hiking boots. "You planning on spending the hunting season in jail?"

"Go to hell."

Kane pulled the man's hands behind him, read him his rights then dragged him outside and secured him to an old hitching post. "I'll see if I can arrange that later." He sidestepped the growing mound of broken glass at the entrance and headed back inside the bar. *One down.*

His work as a deputy in Black Rock Falls was very different from his time as a sniper followed by five years' service in DC's Special Forces Investigation Command. He had had no other choice but to leave DC after a terrorist planted a bomb under his car, killing his wife and leaving him with a titanium plate in his head. Off the grid in the not-so-small backwoods town of Black Rock Falls should have been a walk in the park. However, the dynamics of his life had changed dramatically on discovering his boss was an ex-undercover DEA agent. Sheriff Jenna Alton, with a new name and face, was hiding in plain sight in witness protection, and Black Rock Falls was anything but the quiet little town he envisaged.

An argument had erupted between his prisoner and two local men over the carcass of an eight-point buck, then escalated into an all-out brawl. The red-faced owner stood behind the bar brandishing a shotgun; his mouth was moving but his words were lost over the noise. Men fought each other like animals, using chairs, tables, and pool cues as weapons. A woman wearing a short skirt and high heels jumped onto a man's back and raked down his face with polished nails.

A miasma of beer and sweat hung in the smoke-filled room. Kane sidestepped a punch from a man wearing a red bandana tied around his balding head. He pivoted on one foot, aiming a kick to the huge belly swinging over his pants, and his boot sank into Jell-O. When the man buckled, Kane shoved him into the pool table then ducked and weaved through the fight, heaving bodies out of his way to help Deputy Rowley.

The young deputy was in a brawl with two men and others had moved to join in. Rowley was holding his own but an idiot with blood streaming down his face and holding a chair high in the air was heading his way. Kane drew his Glock and fired three shots into the roof. The room fell eerily quiet and the angry crowd turned to look at him. "Get out of here before I haul you all downtown."

The mass exodus was swift, and he holstered his weapon then stepped in front of the two men who had been attacking Rowley. "You *do* know it's an offence to hit an officer of the law, right?"

"He tried to arrest me for stealing the buck." The man gave him an indignant look then tried to straighten his torn shirt.

"You can add resisting arrest to the charge." Sheriff Jenna Alton's raven hair glistened under the lights as her annoyed scrutiny moved around the bar. Unruffled and in complete control of the situation, she moved to Kane's side and when she looked at his prisoner her mouth turned down. "Cuff him and bring him in." She indicated toward the other man with a nasty cut under one eye and bleeding like a stuck pig. "Him too." She read both men their rights in a clipped monologue.

"Yes, ma'am." Rowley's mouth twitched at the corner as he pulled the zip ties out of his pocket. He turned to Kane. "Did you get the big one who came at you with the bottle?"

"Oh, yeah." Kane smiled. "He is cooling his heels at the hitching post out front."

"And squealing about his $2,000 Stetson he misplaced in here." Jenna gave him her patented "I don't give a shit" stare and shrugged. "Says he'll make a complaint to the sheriff about you through his lawyer. Apparently, I'll skin you alive." She cleared her throat. "More paperwork."

"Who is gonna pay for this damage?" The barman's angry stare rested on Kane's face and he still held the shotgun.

"Lay down your weapon – now!" Jenna glared at him and the owner complied sheepishly. "Who started the brawl?"

"I'm not sure but those two and the city dude were throwing bottles and chairs."

"Okay." She turned to the other men. "Do you have jobs, property, or cash to pay for this damage? You have the opportunity to settle now before it goes to court."

"Nope." Torn Shirt wet his lips. "Only my car and we can't walk home; our cabin is in the mountains. The buck is ours legal. We have a Vehicle-Killed Wildlife Salvage Permit. I'm within my rights."

Kane snorted and secured Torn Shirt. "Is that your car outside with the buck tied to the hood?"

"Sure is."

"The buck out there has a bullet wound and some other damage." Kane raised an eyebrow. "Care to explain?"

"He ran out in front of my vehicle. You check for yourself. Its leg is broken and I have a damaged headlight." Torn Shirt looked at Jenna pleadingly.

"I have a Vehicle-Killed Wildlife Salvage Permit too." The owner gave Kane an optimistic look. "I'll take the buck for my own consumption as restitution for their part of the damage but I want a cash settlement from the rich dude you arrested outside."

"That seems fair to me." Jenna looked at Kane. "Fix it."

"No way! I found it legal. It don't belong to anyone. I don't know why that crazy man started a fight." Torn Shirt smirked at Kane over one shoulder. "Ain't no law about picking up roadkill. My permit is up to date and paid for."

Kane turned to the proprietor. "Take the buck. As he said, 'It don't belong to anyone.'"

"Sure, it's better than nothin'." The bar owner headed out the door.

"That ain't fair." Torn Shirt gave Jenna a puppy-dog stare. "Sheriff, you tell that son of a bitch he can't do that, it ain't fair."

Oh, this is going to be fun. Kane bit back a grin and raised one eyebrow at Jenna.

"Okay, but it won't be good eating after you leave it out in the sun for weeks." Jenna gave Torn Shirt a tight smile. "You could remain in jail until your court case."

"Oh, man." Torn Shirt bit his bottom lip as if considering.

"Well, what's it to be?" Jenna's eyes flashed as she glared at Torn Shirt.

"I ain't got much choice, have I?"

"You had the choice not to fight in the first place. I'm going easy on you." She turned to Kane. "Get them into the back of my vehicle. I'll drive your rig back to the office." She held out her keys.

"Yes, ma'am." Kane swapped car keys with a smile. Jenna called his black SUV "the beast" after the upgrades. It was fast, very fast.

With the three men secured in Jenna's vehicle, Kane watched her drive away then went back inside to examine Rowley. He would have a shiner but looked okay. "Get some ice for that eye before we leave and ask the barman to look out for a Stetson, and to call if he finds it."

"Yes, sir."

With Rowley holding a bag of ice to his eye, they hurried back to Jenna's rig. The men secured behind the bulletproof glass argued the entire trip back to the sheriff's office. Torn Shirt and the man with the cut under one eye gave Kane their information without a problem before he handed them over to Deputy Cole Webber who took them to separate interview rooms, but the man who had attacked Kane glared at him, eyes blazing.

Kane pushed him down into the seat in his cubicle. "Name?"

"Ethan Woods. Those men took off with an eight-point buck I'd bagged."

Kane sighed. "Did you tag your kill or report them as poachers to an FWP officer at the check station?"

"No." Woods shot him an angry glance.

"The question on my lips for an experienced and I hope licensed hunter would be, 'Why?'"

Woods' face reddened and he gave Kane a look cold enough to freeze Black Rock Falls. "I want you to call my lawyer."

"Sure." After entering the name in the arrest report, Kane looked him over. "Are you injured?"

Woods gave him a stony stare. Oh boy, he was complying with his right to remain silent. Kane shrugged. "Duty of care, sir. We have the paramedics coming in anyway. If you need them to look at you, let me know." He leaned back in his chair. "Lawyer's name?"

"James Stone."

Kane's day was deteriorating by the second. He groaned inwardly. The Black Rock Falls lawyer had been a pain in the ass. Apparently, before his arrival, he and Jenna had dated a couple of times and it didn't work out, but Stone wouldn't take no for an answer. Kane had spoken to Stone and implied he was involved with Jenna to convince the man to back off. Since then the cooperation between the sheriff's department and Stone had ended. Sucking in a deep breath, he made the call, and from the way Stone went into action the moment Kane mentioned the prisoner's name, he figured Woods must be some big-shot client of his. He could almost picture Stone dashing to his car to get to the sheriff's office before he disconnected. Smothering a grin of satisfaction, Kane moved his attention back to Woods. "I'll take you to an interview room to wait for your lawyer."

"Did you find my Stetson?"

Kane had dealt with people many a time who believed law enforcement were the scum of the earth and their money could buy them out of any situation. The attitude Woods was giving him came from years of privilege and getting his own way, likely old money. He shrugged. "I've asked the barman at the Triple Z Bar to look out for it."

"That's not good enough." Spittle flew from Woods' mouth. "Get back down there and find it."

"No can do. I make a point of staying out of places like the Triple Z Bar unless there's a ruckus. If somebody hands it in, we'll let you know."

Woods' face turned a peculiar shade of purple. "Those lowlifes will steal it and you know it. I paid them good money to track for me and they deserted me out in the forest, said they'd hunt down the buck I clipped."

"You should have hired professional trackers." Kane looked down at the man's enraged face and smiled. "Don't you know if you lie down with dogs, you're gonna get fleas?" He gave him a light push toward the interview room. "This way."

"I demand you go to the Triple Z and find my hat." Woods threw him an indignant stare over one shoulder.

As Kane ushered Woods past Deputy Rowley, he grinned. "Seems like Mr. Woods has given up his right to remain silent and refused medical assistance. Inform the sheriff, will you, please?"

"Yes, sir."

CHAPTER TWO

Jenna glanced up from her computer screen as Rowley knocked on the door. "Problem?"

"No." Rowley looked at her through a swollen, streaming eye and gave her Kane's message. "Woods is in interview room three."

"Okay." She pushed to her feet. "The paramedics are on their way. Go sit down and keep ice on that eye. I don't want you doing anything until you've been checked out."

"Yes, ma'am, but I'm fine."

She moved closer, peered at him, then frowned. "You don't look so good and I'm worried about you. Let me see your hands."

When he lifted his bruised and skinned knuckles, she shook her head. "Oh, Jake, they're not fine and neither are you. Will you at least sit here in the quiet for a while?" She pulled out a chair in front of her desk. "I'll ask Maggie to bring you some ice and send the paramedics to check you over. Let me know if you need anything."

"Sure, thanks, but I'm okay." Rowley turned his hands over and sighed. "I've hurt myself worse than this working out."

Jenna ignored him. Rowley had not complained once since the first day he walked into the office as a rookie. He was dependable and efficient, and she was proud to have trained him, but this time she had to put her foot down. She went straight to the counter to speak to the receptionist, Magnolia "Maggie" Brewster. "Rowley is a bit banged up. I have him in my office. Can you get him some ice and keep an eye on him until the paramedics check him? I'm sure he has a concussion."

"Right away. You know, I can't figure out how Deputy Kane came back from that brawl without a scratch." Maggie rolled her brown eyes skyward. "I don't believe he would send Jake in alone."

Jenna bit back a smile at her indignation. "No, Kane was there in the middle throwing bodies in all directions. I think Kane knows how to duck." She glanced toward her office door and lowered her voice. "Kane cleared a path through the fight and I followed. Rowley jumped straight in fists flying." She leaned closer. "I figure he was having the time of his life."

The door to the sheriff's department swung open and James Stone stormed inside with an expression of doom. He marched toward her, gripping his briefcase like a shield before him.

"Sheriff Alton, you have my client, Ethan Woods, in custody."

How did he get here so fast? Jenna took in his casual clothes and hiking boots. The lawyer usually arrived wearing an expensive suit and polished leather shoes. "We do but he has already waived his rights."

"I don't believe it." Stone gave her a cold stare. "Take me to him. What's the charge?"

Jenna lifted her chin. "He attacked one of my deputies with a bottle and incited a brawl at the Triple Z Bar." She led the way to the interview room. "Then there's the buck."

"Buck?"

As they entered the room, Woods sprang to his feet.

"James. Thank God you're here. This idiot arrested me." Woods waved a hand at Kane, who looked up from his notes.

"You're lucky I'm here. I planned to take a trip to New York this week." Stone placed his briefcase on the table and pulled out a seat then gave Jenna and Kane a dismissive wave. "I'd like to speak to my client alone."

"Sure. Press the buzzer when you're finished." Jenna glanced at Kane. "You can bring me up to date with the other two prisoners. I gather they're not being represented at this time?"

"Nope." Kane stood and his cold stare moved over Stone, but he followed her out the door without another word.

In the hallway, she stopped and leaned against the wall. "What have we got?"

"Leroy and Abel Finch. They are brothers who own a cabin in the mountains near Bear Peak. Their licenses check out and are current. There is no evidence to indicate they are poachers, no infringements with Fish, Wildlife and Parks." Kane glanced at his notes. "I have no proof of who started the brawl. The buck has a through-and-through wound so no bullet even if we took the time to do ballistics. It does have a broken leg, so it could have staggered out onto the road before Woods had time to reach it. Woods did say they left him in the forest to chase down the buck." He shrugged. "It's hearsay at best."

Jenna tapped her bottom lip, thinking. "I'm not sure the charges of striking a law officer will stick. I figure they'll have witnesses coming out the woodwork to turn around the charge to police brutality. If it sticks, all the judge will give them is a fine. I'd rather lock them up for the night and let them go with a warning."

"That sounds like a plan. I'll go talk to them next." He tipped his head toward the interview room with Woods and Stone talking animatedly. "What about Woods?"

"We'll see what he has to say. I figure he'll offer to buy his way out of trouble and we can send him on his way. How much damage do you think they did to the Triple Z?"

"I figure if Woods offered the owner five grand, he'd be dancing naked in the street with joy." Kane's mouth quirked up into a smile. "Most of his tables and chairs are from yard sales, then add a few glasses. A day to clean up the mess and I think he would come out ahead." He flicked a glance toward James Stone. "His lawyer is probably charging him more than that an hour."

"Okay, we'll see if he'll do a deal." She sighed as Deputy Webber came into view looking glum. "It looks like I'm going to be busy for a while. Can you deal with Woods?"

"Sure, I'll cut him a deal to pay damages and let him go." Kane grinned. "It might take the edge off Mr. Freeze for a while. He is one lawyer I detest dealing with; he is such an arrogant ass."

"I couldn't agree more."

When Webber marched toward them, Jenna could tell by his expression that something was wrong. She turned to meet him. "Problem?"

"Maybe. A couple of hikers found a human skull near the reservation border. I asked them to wait in the front reception area. Rowley is still in your office with the paramedics."

Jenna considered her options. "Bring them down to interview room four and send the paramedics down here as soon as they've finished with Rowley to check the Finch brothers. If the brothers are okay, lock them in the cells. I'll speak with them later."

"Yes, ma'am." The deputy turned on his heel and hurried back along the passageway.

Can my day get any worse? Jenna sighed and pushed a hand through her hair. The brawl at the Triple Z slid into obscurity. She looked up at Kane. "I'll go interview the hikers."

"Sure." He rubbed his chin. "A human skull, huh? You want me to call in Wolfe?"

She shook her head. She counted herself lucky to have the medical examiner, Deputy Shane Wolfe, on her team, and discovering he had served in the marines was an added bonus. "Not yet. I'll see what they have to say first. I hope it didn't wash down from the reservation. There are some ancient burial sites there and they don't like people walking on their sacred land."

Footsteps heralded the arrival of two paramedics. Webber followed behind with a young couple. Pushing down the need to ask the extent of Rowley's injuries, Jenna entered the code on the door then ushered them into the interview room. She took a seat and rested her hands on the table. "I'm Sheriff Jenna Alton. Can I have your names and contact details for the record, please?"

"Jim and Bailey Canavar out of Kansas."

Jenna took in the couple's appearance. Jim Canavar, a tall man with glasses and wearing clothes that looked too small for him, was a stark contrast to the young woman beside him: very attractive, shoulder-length raven hair, with manicured nails and wearing branded outdoors clothes. She shouted money with a capital M. Pulling her attention away from them, she filled the details in the report. "Do you remember the exact location of the skull?"

"Yeah, I took down the coordinates and took some photographs." He glanced at his wife. "It scared the hell out of my wife when she went to take a pee."

"I'm sure it would." Jenna wrote down her email address and passed it to him. "Did you touch the skull or disturb the area, Mrs. Canavar?"

"No, I saw it just off the path then ran back to tell Jim." Bailey gripped Jim's arm and looked mournful. "I didn't even want him to take photographs. I don't want them in our honeymoon shots."

"I'm sure he will delete them but before you do, please send the coordinates and image files to this address. I'll pinpoint the area." She waited for him to comply then smiled. "What brings you to Black Rock Falls?"

"We're on our honeymoon and staying at the Cattleman's Hotel. We drove up to the parking area at Deadman's Creek then hiked all day, planning to camp in the forest then come down in the morning." Jim shrugged. "The wardens told us it wasn't a designated hunting area but we could sure hear the guns blazing in the distance. I'm pretty sure the trail borders the reservation but we found the skull on this side of the boundary just off the main trail." He raised one eyebrow. "I figure it's a murder victim."

"We don't have any open missing persons' files at the moment but I'll be sure to check with other counties." Jenna smiled. "It's likely it washed down from an ancient burial site in the rain."

Her email pinged a few moments later and she opened the files. A gruesome image flashed onto the screen. The skull with tufts of black flowing hair stared at her from bottomless black sockets. She swallowed the bile rushing up the back of her throat at the unmistakable sight of a bullet hole right between the eyes. With the front teeth missing and a crack from jaw to cheek, the open mouth might as well be screaming homicide.

CHAPTER THREE

Jim and Bailey Canavar waited at reception in the Cattleman's Hotel. As Bailey enjoyed staying at this five-star hotel, Jim had the chance to slip away on his own to go hunting, but his wife wanted to cut off that avenue of pleasure. He had renewed his hunting license just in case. He might have lived in Kansas for the past ten years, but as a born and bred Montanan, he visited the state many times. Black Rock Falls was in the middle of nowhere but the hotel had a bar and first-class restaurant. He loved roughing it outdoors but his bride had found the idea of hiking and camping in the woods akin to sleeping under a bridge. At least by combining one or two days hiking with the equivalent luxury of the Cattleman's Hotel, he would keep her happy for a while. When the person in front of him in line stepped away, he moved up to the counter.

"How was your day?" The receptionist, dressed in a suit and tie with a gold badge displaying the name Nigel on his lapel, smiled at Bailey. "Did you enjoy the hike?"

"Not particularly." Bailey did her usual pout of displeasure. "Finding a skull ruined my entire day, maybe my entire honeymoon."

"A skull?" Nigel blinked a few times then leaned on the counter. "Do tell."

Not sure if the sheriff would approve of them blabbing the information around town, Jim lowered his voice. "We found a human skull up near the border of the reservation. We've just returned from the sheriff's office."

"Oooh, how exciting." Nigel gave him a conspiratorial wink. "You *do* know Black Rock Falls is becoming famous for serial killers." He grinned. "People love to hear the stories. We have strange goings on from way back, haunted barns, and did you know around these parts people go missing and are never seen again?" He waved to the advertisement for a crime thriller on the back of a tourist handout. "They're even writing about us now. It's great for tourism."

"Really? There is no accounting for taste." He was familiar with the area but scrutinized the maps on the counter. "Can you recommend another trail, nice and quiet, we can try? Someplace we can make camp overnight."

"You said we could have two days in the hotel." Bailey flicked a lock of hair over one shoulder. "That was the deal."

"Yeah, honey, we'll stay here a couple of nights then head back up the mountain. The weather might not hold, then we'll be staying here again."

"Okay." Bailey let out a long sigh. "At least all this walking is good for my figure."

"And I have just the place." Nigel opened a map with a flourish and pointed at a winding road into the mountains. "You can drive through the mountain here and follow the road to this parking lot. It's a new one and has a convenience store with a gift shop on-site. The family who owns the place runs a couple of cabins for hikers out back."

"I was looking more for a camping site, something well away from the tourist areas." Jim pointed at the map. "Where does this trail lead?"

"Ah, yes, Bear Peak. There is an old trail up there. It's half a mile from the parking lot and a bit isolated but there is a plateau some ways up and it has a nice secluded place to camp. Great views from up there too."

Jim grinned. "Thanks. That sounds perfect. I like isolated." He smiled at his wife. "I think a nice hot bath then a fine dinner will put you in a better mood plus there will be plenty of time for you to go shopping and visit the beauty parlor while I gather what we need for the trip."

"I'm in a better mood already. I'll head on up to our room." Bailey smiled at him, brushed past a man standing beside her and drumming his fingernails on the counter, and made her way to the elevator.

CHAPTER FOUR

Perfect would become his word of the day. His attention moved over Bailey and his smile fixed in place, covering his inner turmoil. Nothing beat the thrill of watching a woman—particularly a spoiled, obnoxious young woman like her—running for her life in the forest. How satisfying it was to watch their horrified expressions when they realized no matter how far they ran or where they tried to hide, he would find them and they would die.

He took a map from the counter and a pen from an ornate holder, marked the trail leading to the campsite, then folded the map neatly and pushed it into his pocket. He noticed Nigel was staring at him. "Could you book me a table in the restaurant for dinner at eight?"

"Yes, sir." Nigel picked up the phone.

He turned away from the counter, pulled out a small black book from his inside pocket, and searched a coded list. He ran the tip of his finger down the page to select a few suitable names. A shiver of excitement rushed over him. He loved the chase and finally the kill. No other adrenaline rush matched the exhilaration of running down a woman and killing her slowly. It was addictive and next time the thrill wouldn't be his alone. Next time, he'd have a special guest.

CHAPTER FIVE

Tuesday

Jenna slid from the cabin of Kane's black rig and surveyed the new parking lot at the top of the mountain. Mayor Petersham had spent a great deal of money clearing a landslide blocking the road to the popular fishing spot. Although fishing and hiking were two attractions, the town's history of brutal murders lured sightseers by the thousands. With tourists bringing prosperity to Black Rock Falls, having the road open again was a sound economic move. A new owner had refurbished the old cabins and lived on-site, offering a convenience store, which sold everything from hot coffee to ammunition.

Jenna took in the spectacular views; at her back, mountain peaks rose up to form an impenetrable barrier, dark against a brilliant blue sky, and waterfalls sprang from the many fissures in the black rocks, feeding into a lake, which spilled down the mountainside in a thunderous roar toward town. By turning a few degrees, she could take in a vista of the pine forest and down to the wide-open spaces leading to the town of Black Rock Falls.

A cold wind lifted her hair; soon winter would arrive and life in town would change dramatically but for the next few weeks, the crisp, fresh mountain air drew hunters and hikers galore. She turned to Kane. "This has changed since we were last here. I'm glad we don't have to ride up that steep track beside the falls to reach the crime scene."

"From what Wolfe said, it's still about half an hour on horseback." He walked to the back of the horse trailer then turned and his face broke into a wide smile. "It sure is pretty up here. I'd love to explore it some more, maybe hike along some of the lesser-known trails and camp overnight."

Jenna gaped at him; surely, he was out of his mind. "Camp up here? You'll freeze to death."

"Nah, not these days." He cocked one eyebrow and went to open the tailgate of the horse trailer. "People survive fine in the Antarctic. It's about taking the right equipment and clothes."

"Well, count me out. I don't call freezing my ass off fun." She turned and opened the back door of Kane's rig, and Duke, Kane's bloodhound, flopped onto the road. She grabbed their backpacks and heard Kane chuckling. After closing the door, she walked to where he stood holding the horses. "What's so funny?"

"Not a thing." He took his backpack from her then swung into his saddle in one fluid movement. "I just thought, after being stuck in the office week in and week out, you'd enjoy a break."

"I do and it's just as well we have Walters to hold the fort while, we're up here." Jenna pulled on her sunglasses. "I'm sure glad he didn't retire altogether."

"I figure he likes taking charge." Kane nodded toward the others. "They look way too happy."

Jenna took in the sunny smiles of Deputy Jake Rowley, who moved his horse beside Kane, and Deputy Paula Bradford, who following close behind. Jenna frowned. "For deputies about to scout an area to search for human remains, you all seem a little too keen. What's going on here?"

"Nothing, ma'am." Bradford tossed her blonde ponytail over one shoulder. "It's just nice to be out in the fresh air after the auditing we've been doing all week." Her mouth curled into a smile as she glanced at Kane. "Anytime you want some company on a camping trip, count me in. I just love sleeping rough."

"Me too." Rowley chuckled.

"Roger that." Kane threw Jenna the reins to her horse. "Ready, ma'am?" He whistled to Duke and the bloodhound bounded out of the bushes to greet him.

"Sure." As Jenna struggled to climb into the saddle, she noticed Kane's mouth twitch with amusement. Okay, so the last time they had ridden, after insisting she was just fine mounting a horse without a leg-up, he had not offered again. The truth was, after another vicious workout with him in the gym, every muscle ached and she would have accepted his help. Trying to act nonchalant, she heaved herself into the saddle then looked at her grinning deputies. "What now? Do you need a group hug?" She turned to Kane. "You have the coordinates; lead the way before we all get mushy."

"Yes; ma'am." Kane made a clicking sound with his tongue, and the black horse, named Warrior, moved forward into the forest.

The trail ahead was wide enough for two horses and Jenna moved her mare close to Warrior. "Why is it every time we come into this beautiful forest, someone has died?"

"Forests cover over a million acres of Montana, and when you consider over 2.5 million people die a year in the USA, the few fatalities that happen in this vast forest are negligible." He flicked her a glance. "Murder and death happen, but it shouldn't take away from the beauty of a place like this. I sure am grateful to not be working in a city."

Jenna stared at him in disbelief. *It's like riding beside Google.* "It is beautiful here and it changes so much every season."

"Like I said, we should take a weekend and spend the night up here before the snow comes." He pointed to the mountain. "There are trails alongside the mountain, places to climb up onto plateaus to see right across Montana."

The idea of a real break would be wonderful but shopping in Manhattan was more her idea of fun. "I'd come with you but just us, or it's no different to today."

"You saying you want to be alone with me?" Kane wiggled his eyebrows at her.

She gaped at him. "I'm alone with you most of the time, Kane. I just don't want to take work with me on vacation, if you know what I mean?"

"So, you'll come?" Kane grinned.

Jenna loved their easy friendship and laughed. "Okay, if we can fit it in before the snow." She glanced at the two deputies in animated conversation behind them. "Did you find out anything interesting about the area where the skull was found?'

"Yeah, this trail is on an old map, which makes me wonder how long that skull has been here." Kane glanced at her. "The recommended trails are chosen to make sure they are well away from the hunting zones. From what happened at the Triple Z, I think it's time I checked out a copy of the current Montana Fish, Wildlife and Parks hunting regulations."

Jenna considered his words. "I'm sure Wolfe will know. He is a walking encyclopedia on local law."

Duke, who had run ahead nose to the ground, let out a loud, whiny bark. The bracken opened and he came toward them, long ears swinging, yapping like a puppy.

"He's found something." Kane dismounted and handed Jenna his reins. "Good boy. What is it?"

The bloodhound bounded off into the undergrowth disappearing into the trees. Jenna scanned the area and could only see the long shadows of trees and brown and green bracken. "It could be a bobcat or a bear?"

"Unlikely. Duke doesn't usually react to wildlife; a bobcat or bear maybe if it was a threat but most times he runs in the opposite direction." He chuckled. "Self-preservation is at the top of his list." Kane looked at her. "Do you want me to take a look?"

"I'll come with you." She slid from her saddle and turned to call to Rowley. "Wait here with the horses. Duke has found something."

"Yes, ma'am." Rowley gave her a wave.

Jenna glanced up at Kane. "I hope it's not another body."

The bond between Kane and the hound had been instantaneous. Jenna had never been a dog person but Duke's big sad eyes and the way he bumped his head on Kane's leg in greeting had changed her opinion. After Kane had rescued him last summer, Duke certainly appreciated his love and attention. The bloodhound worked with him as if they had trained together, and what was so strange was Duke seemed to understand every word he said—even covering his eyes with both paws when Kane mentioned the word "bath."

Just then, Duke came back, crashing through the scrub with bits of forest debris stuck to his coat. He gave an excited bark, bounced on his front legs, looked at Kane, and whined almost mournfully. Jenna moved to Kane's side. "You talk dog, what is he saying?"

"He's found something and it's not a dead animal." Kane led the way down a narrow path between the trees. "His first owner must have given him extensive training. I know he tracks scents but this is the second time he has reacted like this, as if he is trying to tell me something. Last time we found a grave."

A shiver ran down Jenna's back as she followed Kane down the rough trail. She clambered over tree roots and pushed through brush that tore at her clothes. The leaves on the variety of bushes had turned a rich copper. Underfoot, twigs, leaves, and pinecones littered the ground, making the way hard to negotiate. She scanned the area but the forest was densely packed and trees in all stages of life blocked the light, leaving the odd shaft of sun to dapple the forest floor.

When the wind rustled the trees, dust and seeds appeared to dance in the sunbeams. It was both eerie and beautiful, almost magical. She heard a squawk and stopped walking to stare into the canopy in time to see a bald eagle take flight. The birdlife in the mountains and surrounding forests was incredible. *I should feel safe here but no one is safe with a lunatic stalking the forest.*

"Jenna."

Kane's voice got her attention and she stared at his serious expression. "Have you found something?"

"Over there." He indicated with his chin. "We have a homicide." He bent and patted Duke. "Good boy." He waved a hand at him. "Seek." The dog wandered off into the bushes.

She peered through the tree trunks and swallowed hard. Tied to a tree with yellow nylon cord sat the skeleton of a tall man, held together by the remnants of a thick padded jacket, thermal underwear, T-shirt, and jeans. His mold-covered hiking boots had tipped over, leaving the tattered fragments of blue jeans covering the end of the bones, and both hands appeared to be missing. In an effort to remain calm, she sucked in a deep breath then moved her attention back to the skull. Looking into the face of a victim was the hardest part of a murder investigation. The expressions of victims haunted her and made her determined to find them justice.

An arrow complete with fletching pinned the head to the tree and around the shaft, the skull had fractured like the crazing on an old piece of porcelain. She swallowed the bile rushing up the back of her throat. Pine needles and leaves had collected on the top of the skull and foliage grew from eye sockets, giving it a surreal, grotesque appearance. She moved closer and squatted in front of the corpse.

"Don't touch anything; that could be blood on his shirt. It looks like bullet wounds—hard to tell but it would be shredded if an animal had eaten the flesh post-mortem."

"Bullets. I've seen similar corpses during my tour of duty." Kane wiped his mouth with the back of his hand as if disgusted. "What it looks like is someone used this man for target practice. This is overkill."

CHAPTER SIX

Horrified by the remains, Jenna forced her professional side to take in the details before her but it was difficult to confront the results of torture. This was the medical examiner's field of expertise, and as no personal property lay scattered around the body, she would leave everything to him. Duke's bark startled Jenna and she straightened to welcome the return of the dog. "What is it, Duke?"

"He has likely found something else." Kane frowned. "Coming?" He headed in the direction Duke had taken.

"Yeah." Jenna followed him away from the trail and into the forest.

The bloodhound had taken them close to the rock face and the temperature dropped considerably as if cold seeped from the mountain. Not fifty feet from the crime scene, Duke barked again, and ahead Kane ducked as he pushed bushes aside to look at something.

"What is it?"

"It's a backpack... no, two back packs."

She took the pair of surgical gloves Kane handed her and pulled them on then bent to examine the two bags half-hidden under the forest debris. She lifted a purple and pink backpack from a bed of leaves. "I would say this belongs to a woman or kid."

She turned it over, and after a little persuasion, one of the zippers slid open to reveal a wallet. She pulled out the wallet and opened it with care to examine the contents. "There are bills in here, so this wasn't a robbery." She lifted the driver's license. "Californian driver's license, Paige Allen, aged twenty. She has shoulder-length black hair."

She looked over at Kane and frowned. "Maybe this backpack has a connection to the skull?"

"I have Dawson Sanders, twenty-four, same state. He has five hundred bucks and change." Kane pushed the wallet back into the bag. "I figure they had a campsite somewhere; this bag has essentials for one day's hiking. Did you find a cellphone or satellite phone?"

Jenna shook her head. "Nope, and what idiot goes hiking without a phone?"

"No one and there are other inconsistencies." Kane's eyes narrowed. "Why hasn't the body been disturbed by animals? If the skull belongs to the woman, I would figure wildlife disturbed her remains, which, with the number of carnivores in the forest, is usual. His should have been scattered too; it doesn't make sense."

"No attempt at burial either. This is the 'use and disposal without feelings' you've described to me as psychopathic behavior." Jenna removed her gloves with a snap. "Remind me to check the billboards next time we leave town. I'm starting to believe we have one saying 'Psychopaths are welcome in Black Rock Falls' posted along the road somewhere."

Jenna took the coordinates of the body and the backpacks. "We'll mark the area but leave the bags here. Wolfe will need all the information we can supply." She shrugged out of her backpack and delved inside to find the police tape then passed a few bright-orange flags to Kane.

After securing the sites, she patted Duke on the head. "You're an asset to my team. We would have overlooked the remains without you."

"Maybe not." Kane had a map of the old trails on his cellphone and showed it to her. "I downloaded these maps, to plan my own hike. This overgrown track is on a list from some years ago and leads to a spot near where the Canavars found the skull. I was going to suggest we search for remains in this area."

"How long has that old map been handed out?"

"Five or so years but looking at the style of hiking boots on the victim, he hasn't been here for more than a year." Kane's brow winkled. "I have a pair in the same style and that was last winter."

Interesting. Jenna pulled on her backpack. "Do you think Duke will be able to find their camp?"

"Maybe—I'm not sure how much scent is left in the couple's belongings, but he did find the backpacks."

"Okay, I'll get Wolfe to take a look at the bags and remains then we can fan out and search the immediate area. There might be something in the backpacks for Duke to use for a scent." She turned to walk back to the horses. "I know you're planning to explore the old trails but if something goes wrong you have people in town to look for you. Why do you think this couple came up here? It seems a bit strange for a couple out of California to wander so far off the usual tourist tracks and without a cellphone between them."

"I have no idea but I figure if this couple went missing a year ago, we should have been notified." Kane moved ahead then stopped and held a large branch back for her to pass. "Unless they didn't tell friends or family where they were going, and that would seem a bit strange."

"Maybe they don't have a family." Jenna lifted one shoulder. "But someone must have missed them. Problem is, people don't want to get involved."

"Yeah, but these people must have jobs and places to live, bills to pay. Someone must have noticed them missing." Kane rubbed his chin. "At least we have names. I'll search the database when I get back to the office and see if anyone lodged a missing person's report."

Jenna followed the path to meet Rowley and Bradford. What Kane had mentioned about seeing similar scenarios during his tour of duty had piqued her interest. She had a top profiler in Kane and valued his expertise. "You said you've seen this type of murder before, so what's your take on the killer?"

"It's too early to tell but I'm not jumping in on a psychopath profile just yet." Kane moved to her side and stared into the distance. "I could give you a few different motives. For instance a love triangle, the killer stalking the couple and taking revenge on the guy for taking his girl." He shrugged. "Or perhaps a military veteran living in the forest and having flashbacks of his tour in Afghanistan. Some suffer so bad they see people as the enemy and act accordingly. He could still be here living off the grid in one of the caves. There are hundreds of places he could be using all along the rock face."

Jenna stared into the distance, contemplating his words. "Yeah, that makes sense. I guess we can add thrill-kill to the list."

"Anything is possible at this point." Kane shrugged. "The billboard notwithstanding, we seem to attract the crazies."

Jenna nodded in agreement. "You sure have that right."

When they met up with Rowley and Bradford, the deputies were sitting on a log chatting. She had been right to team the rookie, Bradford, with Rowley. They had become friends and worked out together at the local dojo. Deputy Webber, another recent recruit, was experienced but had requested to work with Wolfe. He had voiced an interest in forensic science and was proving to be an asset to her deputy slash ME. She recognized the benefits of having a partner on the job, and her two new deputies sure helped the department to run smoothly. She strolled into the clearing. "We found a body and two backpacks. We'll head to Wolfe's position then do a search of the area. There has to be a camp close by, so keep a lookout." She walked to her horse and heard Kane behind her.

"Leg up?" Kane cupped his wide palms and offered them to her.

Relived, she nodded. "Yeah thanks. I'm a bit stiff from our workout this morning."

"My fault, I didn't leave us much time to cool down before we headed out, but you have to admit, getting up a half hour early for a workout keeps the stress levels down." He smiled. "A spell in the hot tub tonight will help."

Jenna nodded. "The walk eased the pain but I'll keep that in mind." She gathered her reins. "I've always tried to squeeze in enough time to work out no matter how hard the case, and I encourage my deputies to do the same. It's part of my training I value a lot. Apart from being fit enough to handle the long hours it does help me focus."

"There is always time. The way you have the team organized, someone is always working on the case." Kane smiled. "We run like a well-oiled machine."

Hoisted into the saddle, she waited for the others to mount then followed Kane along the trail, searching in all directions for any sign of a camp. At first, she had imagined the skull might have been someone lost in the forest many years ago, and being surrounded by thousands of trees now, she realized how frightening that would be. Becoming disorientated in Stanton Forest would be easy. Apart from knowing which direction was up or down the side of the mountain, everything was much the same. Pines as far as the eye could see and a wall of mountains. Without a GPS, the only directional advantage was gained by taking the trails closer to the waterfall and following the noise, but here somewhere in the middle she might as well be in any forest on any number of continents.

The image of the man tied to the tree flashed into her mind. So many questions surrounded him. What had brought him and his companion to this deserted part of the forest? The killer, as Kane mentioned, could be a military veteran, living off the grid and believing everyone was the enemy. He could be lurking somewhere close by, believing they were a military patrol. The idea made the hairs on the back of her neck stand to attention. She turned in her saddle to address her deputies. "Keep alert. We don't know if we have a killer living close by."

There would be no need to speak to Kane; he would already be scanning the area, searching for any movement. One thing for sure: once a marine always a marine. She glanced around, looking for any trace of habitation, and sighed; in the space of one year, the forest could swallow up a campsite. Bears could tear down a tent and scatter belongings in all directions. The killer could have ransacked the camp as well. Really, finding anything intact would be a miracle.

Not ten minutes later, she heard horses whickering then Wolfe's blond head came into sight above the bushes. He turned and held up a hand like a traffic cop. Three horses, not two, were waiting patiently in a small clearing. Two she recognized as belonging to Wolfe and Webber, who owned the third? Had someone stumbled onto the crime scene? Wolfe had not contacted her in hours, and this part of the forest was not on a recommended trail. Deputy Webber was nowhere in sight, nor was the person who owned the third horse. Her instincts went on full alert and she noticed Kane stiffen and rest one hand on his weapon. *This can't be good.* She cleared her throat and dropped her voice to just above a whisper. "Okay, dismount. We go on foot from here. Spread out, and keep alert. It seems we have a visitor."

CHAPTER SEVEN

He took lunch at the Cattleman's Hotel and his attention settled on Bailey, dressed in a garish, bright-pink jogging suit. They would be leaving after breakfast on Wednesday morning and taking the old trail through the forest that Nigel had recommended.

The area was familiar to him. In fact, the deeper into the forest they went, the better. They would be closer to his secret cave, and the likelihood of seeing anyone else would be remote. He liked to spend time enjoying the chase, although the thrill of stumbling over other hikers only added to the excitement.

When Bailey's haughty tone of displeasure rose above the low hum of conversation in the restaurant, he lowered his gaze to his plate. So spoiled and used to getting her own way, she used her ample charms to get what she wanted. He moaned and rubbed his temples. Her whining voice was driving him insane. He needed a distraction before he lost his cool, and his mind filled with her running through the forest, tripping over then trying her feminine wiles on him. She would beg him not to shoot her or slit her throat. He bit back a laugh. She would be confused when he gave her a reply in the negative. No one dared to refuse her; she thought she was too damn precious. *Not to me.*

Killing her would soothe his brain. He could not allow her to continue to pollute the world. It was time for him and others of like mind to rid the population of these matriarchal, emasculating women. Women were on this earth to serve men and give them children, period. He closed his eyes and could feel the handle of his weapon against his palm. See the muzzle of his gun pressed hard against Bailey's forehead. He would watch her bewildered expression as he squeezed the trigger real slow and put a bullet right between her eyes.

Sharing the thrill had come along by accident. He had discovered the dark web some years ago. Untraceable and safe, he moved like a ghost in complete obscurity in a place where everything, including a person's life, was for sale—at a price.

CHAPTER EIGHT

On Jenna's whispered command, Kane slid into the bushes. He could hear her behind him moving as silently as possible through the dry undergrowth. He used the trunk of a wide pine and turkey-peeked around the corner. Wolfe's short wave to ward them off could be two things: Either he was in trouble or he did not want them contaminating a crime scene. Not being a man to take chances, he reacted the same way as Jenna and moved forward with caution. He patted his leg and Duke came to his side. He found it strange the dog had given no warning.

"Can you see anything?" Jenna had pressed her back against a tree.

"Nope." He scanned the area where he had last seen Wolfe but nothing moved. "Orders, ma'am?"

"Move out with caution. I'll watch your back."

Kane turned to look at her. "Roger that. Keep Duke with you; he'll make too much noise."

He slid between the close-growing trees using the shadows as cover and moved to Wolfe's last location. To his relief he heard voices and rounded a clump of bushes to see three men crouched down and examining the ground. Two he recognized as Wolfe and Webber but not the third. "Wolfe, are we clear to enter the area?"

"Yeah." Wolfe stood and his mouth quirked up at the corners. "Sorry, man, I should have shouted out but Atohi found something and I was engrossed."

Kane turned to look back in Jenna's direction and called out, "Clear."

He took in a tall, lean man with black hair flowing past his shoulders. The man, a Native American, walked toward him, his brown intelligent eyes dancing with amusement. He was about thirty, wearing a thick hunting jacket, plaid shirt, and jeans.

"You must be Dave Kane? Atohi Blackhawk." He held out his hand. "Man, you came in here without a sound. I'm impressed."

Kane shook his hand. "Nice to meet you. Have we met before?"

"Ah, no. Shane dropped by the res to ask about sacred burial sites close to the boundaries. He mentioned you moved like a ghost. I'm a tracker so I came back here with him to check out the skull in case it was one of ours. I had a poke around and found a few interesting items close by." Blackhawk smiled. "I'm happy to help out when needed."

"We'll be glad of any help you can offer." Kane heard footsteps and turned at Jenna's arrival. "Ah, Atohi Blackhawk, Sheriff Jenna Alton." He waved a hand toward the other deputies. "Jake Rowley and Paula Bradford."

"Nice to see you again, Atohi. What did you find?" Jenna moved to his side.

"A cellphone and more bones." Blackhawk frowned. "I'd say the animals got to the body—they are spread all over. We only found a few of them."

"I see." Jenna wrinkled her nose. "What do we have, Wolfe?"

"From the size of the pelvis, a female; from the teeth, she was in her late teens, early twenties." Wolfe's fair brows narrowed. "I would say the bullet wound in her skull is the cause of death but I've found what is consistent with knife wounds across two of the bones we found. I need to take a closer look to determine if this happened post-mortem or not." He rubbed his chin. "The cellphone is toast.

The screen is broken and it's soaking wet. I doubt I'll be able to pull anything from it at all."

"We found a body on the way here; well, Duke found a skeleton. From the clothes and size, I would say it is male. It is pinned to a tree by an arrow through the forehead." Jenna rested both hands on her hips. "Then Duke found a couple of backpacks. We have ID and Kane figures they must have a camp close by—they only had one day's supplies with them."

Kane called the dog to his side. "Duke is becoming an asset. We would have missed the skeleton; he is some ways off the main trail." He glanced at Wolfe. "If the skull belongs to the woman he was travelling with, then I'd say he was killed first. She dropped the backpacks and ran for her life and the killer caught her here." He turned to Blackhawk. "Where did you find the cellphone?"

"About twenty feet in that direction." Blackhawk pointed toward the mountain. "It was close to a boulder at the foot of the mountain. Don't worry, I didn't touch anything. Wolfe took photographs and bagged the items. I found a button as well."

"I think she tried to wedge herself behind the boulder, she probably dropped her phone and smashed it." Wolfe's expression was grim. "Any signs of torture on the male victim?"

"I'm not sure, there's not much left and what is there is held together by clothes." Jenna pushed a strand of hair behind one ear. "Apart from the missing hands, it appears to be intact." She glanced at Wolfe. "Why are their hands missing?"

"Small bones are difficult to find; they are easily carried off by birds or rodents." Wolfe shrugged. "Finding them in a forest this size would be near impossible."

"I'm wondering why the male victim's bones haven't been scattered by animals." Kane let out a long sigh. "I would say he was shot as well; his shirt looks like there are bullet holes in the material."

"Let's not jump to conclusions." Wolfe frowned. "Decomposition causes stains of all descriptions on clothes, but being untouched by animals is unusual."

"The only thing I can think of that keeps animals away is gasoline." Blackhawk's eyebrows drew together. "Maybe the killer planned on burning the body then thought better of it."

"Yeah, if he started a wildfire up here, he wouldn't be able to outrun it." Kane stared into the thick, dry undergrowth. "I can't imagine anyone would be stupid enough to even contemplate such a thing."

"I can test what remains of his clothes for residue." Wolfe lifted his chin. "If he is covered with gas, our killer might have used it to ward off animals. He might have liked to visit his victim. Many of them get a thrill out of watching a corpse decay."

"How disgusting." Jenna grimaced. "Although, I guess I shouldn't say that as it's a crucial part of your job. Kane's told me all about the forensic body farm you visited."

"I wouldn't make a very good ME if I couldn't identify the different stages of decomposition." Wolfe looked abashed. "I happen to find the different variants, including insect infestation, animal intervention, and the effects of temperature, extremely interesting."

"Just the image I need before lunch." Jenna's stomach clenched. "How much longer do you need here? We'll need to get to the other crime scene ASAP."

"I'm done." Wolfe turned to Webber. "Collect up the equipment and get it packed away on the horses." He glanced at Jenna. "Unless you want to see where we found the skull and other bones?"

"No, that's fine." Jenna indicated with her chin toward Kane. "We'll go on Kane's theory and go back to the male victim and work back in this direction—but first we'll eat." She turned and headed toward the horses. "Rowley, Bradford, with me, and keep alert... We have a killer in the mountains."

Kane watched her go and turned to Wolfe and Blackhawk. "I think he's long gone. Although, Duke didn't make a sound before we spotted you."

"That's because he knows Shane and Cole." Blackhawk smiled. "He is smart enough to know who is a friend by their scent."

"Maybe but he doesn't know *you*, does he?"

"Duke and I are old friends." Blackhawk rubbed the dog's ears. "He was born on the res, and his owner was a cousin of mine who lived in Black Rock Falls. We trained him together." He sighed. "I went to the animal shelter to collect him when my cousin died but someone else had taken him. I'm glad he ended up in a good home."

Kane decided not to explain where the dog had been between owners and nodded. "Great, maybe you can let me know the range of his skills sometime?"

"Yeah, I'd like that and we'll have plenty of time to chat. I'll be around for a couple of days, maybe more. Shane has hired me as a tracker."

"Oh, I'm sure we'll have a lot to discuss. I'd like to know more about the history of Stanton Forest."

CHAPTER NINE

After eating lunch, Jenna surveyed the area Wolfe had secured and glanced over his images then ordered her team to head to the next crime scene. The time they had in the mountains in late fall was limited. Snow already coated the peaks of the mountain range and a cold wind rustled through the trees. All vegetation apart from the majestic pines had shed their leaves for the onset of winter, and underfoot multicolored leaves littered the way. Finding evidence at this time of the year would be near impossible. It was as if the forest was hiding its secrets beneath a cloak.

With Kane leading the way, deep in conversation with Blackhawk, she moved her horse closer to Webber's. Cole Webber had turned out to be a solid albeit quiet member of the team. His attention to detail impressed her but it was as if he hid inside a protective shell, not allowing anyone to get too close. She had to admit, the job had gotten in her way of getting to know the deputy better. On the ride to the next crime scene, she would remedy that error. "How do you like partnering with Wolfe?"

"I like it fine." Webber's mouth twitched up in the corners. "I'm not sure how he keeps so much knowledge inside his head at one time." He clicked his tongue at his horse and moved closer. "At first, I wasn't too sure about examining human remains and I admit to spewing a couple of times in the past at autopsies, but the way he explains everything makes it a whole lot easier."

A cool breeze brushed Jenna's cheeks. She pulled up the zipper on her jacket and glanced up through the canopy of green to catch a glimpse of the sky. To her relief, a blue cloudless expanse greeted her. *No snow today.* She nodded in agreement to Webber's reply. "Yeah, he knows his stuff. When he first arrived, I knew he had some level of experience in forensics and computers but not the extent of his expertise. Having our own ME after using Mr. Weems, the mortician, for years makes life easier." She glanced at him. "Are you thinking of studying to become his assistant?"

"Yeah, not as in getting a degree at this stage." He looked pensive. "Not that I wouldn't want to go back to school for the qualifications I need, it's more about time and money."

Jenna nodded. "I'm sure we can work something out."

"Thank you, ma'am." Webber touched his hat.

She turned in her saddle to greet Wolfe as he maneuvered his horse toward her. "I guess you have questions about the second victim?"

"Yeah, a few. How far off the main trail did you find the man's body?" Wolfe eased his horse closer to her. "Are you sure it's not a hunting accident? The couple could have stumbled into a designated hunting area. It should be easy to check, I'm sure the FWP keep records."

"Kane said he figured the killer used the victim as target practice and I agree. I could plainly see a hole in the sternum through the tattered shirt. We left everything in situ and only disturbed the area around the backpacks. From the image of the woman's skull, I would say without a doubt this is a double homicide."

"The skull leaves little doubt. I've called in a forensic anthropologist, Jill Bates from Helena." Wolfe gave her a small and very unusual almost satisfied smile. "I sent her some images of the skull and she wants in on the investigation. We're lucky, she wasn't busy."

Jenna nodded. He appeared in a good mood but then anything to do with dead things brightened his day. "Will you need her to examine the bones before you remove them?"

"I could call in a team from Helena, but as the skeleton is intact, as long as I follow protocol and film the removal, I doubt anything will be overlooked." Wolfe shrugged. "I am experienced in the preservation of a crime scene in this situation and Jill insisted I go ahead. We can examine the remains more thoroughly in the lab."

Jenna's mind drifted back to the gravesite they had discovered earlier in the year and the time it had taken for a team of forensic anthropologists to collect all the evidence. Wolfe had been there working alongside them from day one. "I'm sure the investigation is in safe hands."

"Thank you, ma'am." He smiled.

After snaking through the forest, the track opened out onto the clearing beside the main trail. The hair on the back of her neck stood to attention knowing a man met a gruesome death not yards away. She turned to Wolfe. "The body is on the left off the main track, about twenty feet heading toward the mountain."

"Roger that."

"This is your area of expertise." Jenna dismounted. "How do you want to proceed?"

"I'll take a look at the backpacks first. If they have supplies, then we can assume the crime scene is the beginning of their journey, which would mean we could search for the campsite on the way back down the mountain. Obviously if they have no supplies, they could be heading toward the camp."

"Okay." Jenna pulled a bottle of water out of her backpack and sipped. "I guess you'll need Webber to assist you with the remains and everyone else can fan out and look for clues."

"If you search from the crime scene and back to where the couple discovered the skull, you might find the way the woman ran from the shooter. I'll view the remains and get them ready for removal." Wolfe slid from his horse and went to her side. "I'll need photographs and live footage of the scene as I move the remains. Who has a steady hand?"

As if he needs to ask. "Kane." She raised an eyebrow. "I'll search the immediate area with Bradford. Rowley can team up with Blackhawk."

"That sounds like a plan." Kane had moved to her side without making a sound. "Do you want me to show Wolfe the backpacks, ma'am?"

"Yeah, I'll organize the search. Make sure you are wearing your earbuds so I can contact you. Webber is assisting Wolfe with the removal of the remains."

As Kane and Wolfe disappeared into the forest with Duke on their heels, Jenna's deputies gathered around her. "Okay, listen up. I want you all wearing earbuds so we can keep in touch. Webber, you will be assisting Wolfe, so unpack the equipment for a body retrieval. The rest of us will work a grid back from the crime scene to the position of the next body. There are dark areas so use your flashlights if necessary. Look for anything, scraps of material, hair, bullet casings. Wear gloves, take a picture with your cellphones of anything you find before you remove it and bag it. Make sure you label every evidence bag with location, time, and date." She took a deep breath. "If you discover any bones, animal or human, leave them in situ and notify me immediately. Do not, I repeat, *do not* interfere with any bones." She glanced around. "Questions?"

When they all stared at her in silence, she gave them a curt nod. "Okay, grab your gear and get ready to move out."

The deputies moved to the horses, and although they were not more than a few feet away, a feeling of unease spread over her. She had seen the results of a number of vicious crimes in Stanton Forest and had not forgotten any of them, but all had been closer to town. Here, miles from civilization, with no cellphone to call for help, it did not take an overactive imagination to envisage what it must have been like running through the thick undergrowth with a killer close behind. On a slow walk, she had tripped a number of times negotiating the rough terrain, gnarled tree roots, and fallen branches. The idea of running blindly through them would be terrifying. She chewed on her bottom lip, determined to discover who had killed the young couple. *Why do these lunatics keep choosing Black Rock Falls?*

CHAPTER TEN

As Kane led the way to the backpacks, he surveyed the ground, hoping to find some small shred of evidence to link to the killer. Behind him, Wolfe walked slowly, often pausing to peer intently at something. Kane stopped and turned to Wolfe. "I considered offering Duke some of the clothing in the backpack to see if he can track the woman. Do you think a scent will still be around after so long?"

"Doubtful. I would say it's been at least a year since the woman died, and not many scents would survive the snowfall; even here with the protection of the trees, when the melt comes the entire area is pretty well washed clean." Wolfe pushed back his hat. "I'm hoping I find some evidence under the body. Killers often make the mistake of leaving evidence under a body. I hope we find something useful."

"How long will it take to move the remains?"

"Not long—it's one body, and not an archaeological dig. From what Jenna said before, it appears to be intact. It wasn't buried, so this will make it easier." Wolfe waved toward the backpacks. I'm glad you took some photos of the area before you went in. Get some shots of the bags from all angles. I'm interested to see what has grown on and around them; it gives me a better idea of how long they have been here." He sighed. "I'm hoping I can get something from the cellphone records; a date and time would be very useful but from what I can see the damn thing looks like a burner."

"A burner?" Kane scratched his cheek. "Who would take a burner on a trip like this?" He pulled out his cellphone and took the required photographs, snapping every item Wolfe removed from the backpacks.

Wolfe was bending and placing items from the backpacks into evidence bags. "Food, energy bars, and water. They were moving away from their camp." He straightened, handing off the bags to Kane. "We know they're not from the local area, so how did they get here? I'm sure a vehicle left abandoned on the road would have sent up a red flag for the rangers. They would have made a search of the area and there would be a record. Make a note to call them in case they found one. It could have been towed to the impound lot."

Kane shook his head. "Nope, we have the keys to the lot and it's empty as far as I'm aware."

"Did you search the remains for keys?"

"Nope. I thought it better not to touch anything. I did find the wallets inside the backpacks, which I thought strange. I keep mine in my back pocket, nice and safe. The woman maybe, but I can't imagine why they kept both sets of ID in the backpacks." He frowned. "Unless they planned to swim somewhere, but there isn't anything close on this side of the mountain."

"The Canavars found the skull off the main trail in the bushes." Wolfe turned and looked back the way they had come. "Are the remains of the man on or off a trail?"

Kane pointed in the direction they had traveled. "On an old trail. Back the way we came and to the left. I found the track on an old map listed as an auxiliary trail or animal track that runs along the foot of the mountain. There is a plateau to climb to if they planned on taking in the view but it's some ways away."

"Why would a young couple risk getting lost up here or eaten by wildlife?" Wolfe bent again to collect soil samples and pieces of vegetation from the area.

The same worry had drifted through Kane's mind when asking Jenna on a similar trip. "I figure they needed to get away from civilization, just the two of them." He shrugged. "I know how to survive out here, and for me it wouldn't be a problem. I'd come with a satellite phone and plenty of supplies dropped off along the way, plus I'd make sure I arranged to contact someone at least once a day." He took another evidence bag from Wolfe. "Perhaps this man had similar training?"

"Or he was an idiot," Wolfe held up a couple of the evidence bags and frowned, "looking at what he had with him." He sighed. "Okay show me the remains." He hoisted a huge backpack over his shoulders. "We'll grab Webber on the way, I'll need his help."

"How is he working out?"

Wolfe let out a snort and gave Kane a pensive look. "He is a fine young man, keen, works hard but has eyes for Emily." His expression changed to borderline angry. "I know she is studying hard and will be going to the University of Great Falls soon but I can't stop him visiting her there. I want her to finish her degree and work with me before she gets pinned down with a family."

"Whoa, he is way too old for her." Kane stopped walking and gaped at him in astonishment. "That worries me and I'm not her father."

"Yeah, and she is a headstrong woman as you well know." Wolfe gave a strangled half laugh. "She takes after me, I'm afraid."

"I wouldn't say a word to her... She has your stubborn streak." Kane straightened. "I'd tell him you're not happy with the situation at the moment because of her age. Give him a reason to pull back a bit, maybe ask him to consider waiting until she finishes her studies. That will take years. He wants to work with you, so I figure he'd comply." He smiled. "With luck, she might meet someone closer to her own age at college."

"I'll live in hope."

At the clearing, Webber was at work collecting the crime scene kits from the packhorse. Kane moved to his side. "I'm glad you think ahead."

"Time is our enemy right now; removing the remains then getting back to the road before dark will be difficult." Wolfe glanced around. "I've been hearing gunshots in the distance. Just how far are we from the nearest hunting area?"

"Probably a mile or two." Kane stowed the evidence bags into one of the saddlebags on the horse. "Sound carries up here and echoes on the mountain. We are out of range of most rifles."

"How far to the remains?" Wolfe walked to his side. "Grab what you can, Webber. We'll carry the rest."

Kane picked up a couple of the bags. "Just through there." He pushed his way through the bushes. "Come on, Duke, keep up."

The dog let out a yap of reply and followed him, peeing on trees along the way. As they got closer to the remains, Kane picked up a rancid smell on the breeze he had not noticed earlier. He slowed his step and did a visual scan of the area but found nothing moving within the mottled shadows.

"Has the temperature just dropped or is it me?" Webber trailed along behind them, lugging the equipment.

Kane glanced back at him and smiled. He could remember having the same feeling of dread entering a crime scene and had squashed it many a time. The morbid feeling would pass with experience. "It's just you. Most likely apprehension at seeing a man pinned to a tree with an arrow."

"Keep your mind focused on discovering what we can do to help him now." Wolfe's cold expression moved to Webber. "We are his only hope to get revenge on the sick bastard who killed him. Once we can prove this man's name, he is no longer 'the victim' or 'the remains.' Do not forget someone took his life and what we do from now on determines *how, when,* and hopefully *why* he died."

"Sure." Webber did not look convinced. "Do you think he's watching us, like a ghost?"

Kane slapped him on the back. "If he is, maybe he'll give us a few clues." He turned to Wolfe. "Through those trees is a path; the remains are down there about ten feet along."

"Okay, we should drop the equipment once we hit the path, suit up, then move in with just a crime scene kit for now. Check the area for anything we can use."

They arrived on the pathway and moved slowly in a line searching for any small clue. When they reached the remains, Kane heard Webber's sharp intake of breath. Kane turned to look at his ashen face. "We believe this is Dawson Sanders, age twenty-four."

"That's not an arrow." Webber moved closer. "It's a bolt from a crossbow: carbon with a brass insert. They are expensive and that size could take down a bear." He peered at the bolt with interest. "It has an illuminated nock. So why leave it behind?"

"Yeah, I think we might need more of an explanation, Webber." Wolfe flicked him a glance.

"Carbon bolts with brass inserts or a mixture of carbon and aluminum are expensive; the illuminated nocks make it easier to recover the bolts. The nock is the orange part on the end and it usually glows, so this has been here for some time. Most hunters recover their bolts." Webber glanced at Kane. "It seems strange to leave it behind in a crime. It would likely carry the owner's prints."

Kane met his gaze. "That is vital information. I had no idea you were an expert on crossbows."

"Yeah, it's my hunting weapon of choice." Webber smiled. "Silent but deadly."

"Unfortunately, we would be lucky to find any viable prints after a year or so." Wolfe sighed then pulled a camera from his backpack and handed it to Kane. "Film everything, the pathway, the area around the body, and the body." He turned to Webber. "You take the photographs and remember there can't be too many images of a crime scene. If you both start with Mr. Sanders, then I'll examine his remains."

Kane was familiar with the camera and zoomed in on the body at every angle before walking slowly up and down the path. When he returned to Wolfe, his friend dropped to his knees, lifted the ragged shirt, and peered at the skeletal remains. He kept the camera steady.

"Interesting." Wolfe bent closer. "The damage to the thoracic spine is inconsistent with the damage to the ribs. I believe the killer shot this man in the back, and from the entry angle, the victim was standing at the time. The nicks on the ribs would indicate the shots entered him in the lower thoracic spine and travelled at an angle of approximately twenty degrees, exiting just below the clavicle on the left side. There are no bullets within the body cavity, so we're looking at three through-and-through wounds." He turned and looked down the trail. "There is not enough damage for the intention to kill outright with one shot. The point is, how far away would the killer need to be to put three rounds in a man walking along this trail?"

Kane took in the terrain and mentally tried to recreate the murder. A shooter would need a clear line of sight between the trees. To hit a moving target in the woods would take a reasonable degree of skill. As vegetation changed with the seasons, it would be close to impossible to gauge the position of the shooter with any accuracy without a laser scope. "That would depend on the weapon. From the angle you mentioned and the approximate height of the victim, he would have been walking in a northerly direction. To obtain the trajectory you are describing, the shooter would have been downhill, or likely kneeling or lying down. Many hunters build blinds, and set up inside. If the wounds are through and through, the bullets must be somewhere close by."

"Yeah, and by the size of his jacket he had a broad chest, so the bullets wouldn't have traveled very far once they left the body." Wolfe's forehead creased into a frown. "I'll check the soil under the body but if the rounds had been hollow points, they would have ripped his ribs apart."

"Webber, check the immediate area."

"Yes, sir." Webber gave him a curt nod, pocketed his cellphone, and moved slowly up the track.

Kane glanced around the scene again, not convinced they were in the correct position. "Problem is, we are assuming he was shot here. From his injuries, could he have crawled to the tree?"

"Doubtful. One of the shots would have pierced his heart, the other two his lungs. I'd say he died within seconds of the third shot."

"So, he could have been dragged here from anywhere along the trail?" Kane rubbed his chin. "We'll expand the search, looking for blinds and bullet casings from at least twenty yards in the southerly direction, although I doubt we'll find anything after so long. We should have thought to bring a metal detector."

"There would be hundreds, maybe thousands, of casings in the forest." Wolfe shook his head. "Hunting goes on just about all year long. For now, check the immediate area. Time is getting short and I need to get the remains back to the lab. Keep filming everything I do." He stood. "I want close-up shots of the neck and head. I'm going to remove the head; if this bolt is approximately twenty inches long, it's not embedded too deeply in the trunk of the tree."

As Kane zoomed in, a cold wind brushed his cheek. What Wolfe was doing came close to the macabre. He forced his mind to concentrate but memories of the targets he had killed in the line of duty played in a loop like one of those annoying ads on TV that drove him crazy. He wondered how many of them had rotted away alone in a deserted place like Dawson Sanders. *At least the ones I killed didn't suffer.*

CHAPTER ELEVEN

He moved along the trail with a bag of trail cams slung over one shoulder. Preparation was the key to a good hunt and he prided himself on being well ahead of the game. He smiled, feeling satisfied he had found the perfect place.

He spent time preparing the trail by moving a few logs here and there to block an escape and clearing the old pathway to encourage the prey to run in the right direction. He wanted full view of Bailey at all times via the trail cams. Best of all, if a hunter or anyone else wandered along and stumbled over the cameras, they would not give them a second glance. So many people used them, from nature studies to tracking game movement.

Humming as he worked, he stopped to attach a trail cam to a tree. He set it up and checked to make sure it worked. Run on a motion sensor, each camera sent an image to his cellphone and he could access a live feed and upload it to the net or anywhere else he chose. By using live feeds, he would know exactly where to find the women. He loved to watch the reruns; the chase was different every time, and the pleading and begging in the moments before he finished them gave him an adrenaline rush. He had so much entertainment stored on backup drives he could relive his kills at any time. This was the second part of his preparation; next he would construct blinds along the way to conceal his presence before the kill.

He checked the images on his cellphone to make sure no one could recognize him from any angle. It was not worth risking his identity even in the preparation. After making his way back up the pathway, he turned and walked slowly, scanning the areas where he had attached the trail cams. Satisfied he had hidden them all out of sight, he collected his bag then headed back to his camp to collect the necessary equipment to build the blinds.

He had found the cave years ago and it served him well. A rock formation and a line of trees concealed the entrance, but to be sure, he had constructed a sturdy gate and a portable electric fence to dissuade bears. Exhilaration and power tingled through him the moment he slipped into the cave. He inhaled, enjoying the thrill of the stale odor, and turned on the lantern hanging from the wall. "Almost done. Maybe you'll have a new friend to keep you company soon."

He scrutinized the skeletons wrapped in plastic sitting propped up against the wall of the cave. It excited him to visit them and he often returned to relive the moment they had become part of his family. He had chosen each one of them and not all his kills made it into his collection. Here in the cave, the memories of watching them die with a mixture of surprise and shock filled his mind in brilliant clarity. He sucked in the thrill like a drug and lived off the high for weeks but regarded these kills as priceless and a testament to his ingenuity. He made his inspection, walking along the row, and bent to push a tuft of hair back inside the plastic. "That's better."

Some of them leaned over as if whispering a secret to another, and dark, soulless eyes followed his every move, but they liked it here. Every one of them returned his smile.

CHAPTER TWELVE

Aching muscles plagued Jenna with each step through the unforgiving terrain. She assumed that by pushing her body during the early-morning workouts with Kane, her muscles would have accepted horse riding, but they had plotted revenge and the climb uphill had done her stiff legs no favors at all. What made it worse was Kane rarely showed any signs of fatigue, although he suffered cruel headaches from the plate in his head and often hid his discomfort from her. In truth, he never complained. She had swallowed a couple of paracetamol with her lunch and would keep going no matter what. Showing weakness in front of her deputies was not an option. *Sometimes being sheriff sucks.*

"I think I've found something." Bradford pointed to something metal peeking out from under the forest floor. "I'll take a few pictures."

Jenna gave herself a mental shake. "It looks like a belt buckle." She pulled out a pair of gloves and pulled them on with a snap. "I'll take a look. Get an evidence bag ready."

After taking a pen from her pocket, she bent down and lifted a few leaves from the end of the buckle then stopped. The buckle shone through the debris but it was not the leather belt attached that had halted her movements. The belt was in a tight loop with one long end disappearing into the undergrowth, and in between, she made out bones. She had seen enough skeletons to recognize them as human forearms. "Stay back." She stood, waving Bradford away, then took a roll of crime scene tape out of her pocket and wrapped it around the tree to mark the area.

"Are they human?" The color drained from Bradford's face.

"Yeah, pretty sure. From what I can make out, these are more bones belong to the female skull the Canavars found. Wolfe will confirm but I figure we have two bodies in total. The male tied to the tree and the partial remains of a female, spread out over this area." Jenna opened the mic on her earpiece. "Kane, I've found more remains. I'll secure the scene."

"Roger that." Kane's voice came into her earpiece.

Jenna pushed back the revulsion of what her find implied. "Looks like two forearms secured with a leather belt. They are small, so it could be the missing parts of the woman Wolfe and Blackhawk found." She sighed. "I only lifted a few leaves. I don't know how much is under there but it is close to a tree. Maybe he had her tied up here. Ask Wolfe what he wants me to do."

It seemed to take ages for Kane to get back to her and then when a voice came in her ear it was Wolfe.

"From the evidence collected and until proved otherwise, I'm assuming we have the remains of Dawson Sanders and Paige Allen. Of course, this is just for our own reference, until I can verify the identities by the dental records and DNA. We have Sanders' remains in a body bag. I have taken soil samples, so I'm pretty well done here. Once we have stowed these onto the horse, I'll come to your position."

"Roger that. I'll send Kane the coordinates."

Jenna contacted Rowley and Blackhawk, and a few minutes later they came through the trees toward them. She noted how Blackhawk guided Rowley well away from the path she had taken. When they reached her side, Blackhawk peered at the remains. She moved to his side. "Did you find anything?"

"Not yet but those bones have been carried here. Can you make out the marks on the bone and the leather belt? They're animal teeth marks and it likely dropped them here to feed its young. See the marks are different sizes?"

"Yeah, now that you mention it, I can make that out." In an effort to keep the image of the poor woman being some animal's dinner well and truly out of her mind, she turned to him. "I'm waiting here for Wolfe. As we have the position of the skull and now this, will you be able to work out which way she ran?"

"Nope but we'll keep to this animal trail. It's more likely if the killer had a woman with her hands tied, it would be easier to drag her along a path rather than through the forest." Blackhawk turned without another word and headed into the trees.

"Do you want me to go with him, ma'am?" Rowley's dark eyes rested on the remains for a few seconds before moving to her face.

"Yeah, stay with him and let me know if you find anything." Jenna pulled out her GPS and sent her coordinates to Kane. She waved Bradford to a fallen tree. "We might as well sit down and rest up until they get here."

Jenna shrugged off her backpack and pulled out a bottle of water. She removed her hat and tossed her hair, glad of the cool breeze. The weather, although sunny, was getting colder by the day and yet hikers came from all over to trek through the forest. She had noticed how Bradford moved with ease over the rough terrain and seemed to have unlimited energy. The rookie was settling in well; she listened and, from what Rowley had told her, was becoming very good at martial arts. "Homicides are difficult. How are you coping? Any problems?"

"No, not at all, ma'am." Bradford removed her hat and set it on the log beside her. "I like Rowley as a partner as well. He is very easy to get along with. I'm doing okay with the unarmed combat side of things but I'll never match Deputy Kane's skill on the shooting range."

She hid her smile. "Not many can, I'm afraid."

"I asked him to give me some advice and he was very helpful but he said I should be able to strip down a Glock and reassemble it with my eyes closed." Bradford gave her an "is he for real?" look and shrugged. "He told me I should be able to do that with any weapon I own."

"It comes down to practice." Jenna shrugged. "Stripping it blind is something I can do, and I would say Rowley and Webber can as well." She sipped her water. "Knowing your weapon is very important. I'm glad Kane took you to the practice range. He mentioned he wanted to see how you were progressing. Don't be surprised if he invites you to the gym. Webber works out at one in town and Kane drops in there from time to time to put the others through their paces. I guess he's been waiting for a report on your progress from Rowley."

"I've never met a deputy like him before; he is more like a drill instructor." Bradford chuckled.

"Who is like a drill instructor? Me?" Kane's voice came from behind her.

"Yes, you." Jenna turned and glared at him. "Dammit, Kane, do you have to creep up on people? We are at a murder scene, in case it slipped your mind." She welcomed Duke's return by patting the dog's head and going about removing the burrs from his coat.

"I wasn't creeping, ma'am." Kane gave her a brilliant smile. "If I had been, I'd have said 'Boo.'" He flashed Bradford a satisfied smile. "Oh, come on, Paula, a drill instructor? I'm not that bad, am I?"

"Well, I guess not." Bradford's cheeks pinked.

"I'm just a perfectionist and want to make sure you're capable of handling any type of weapon." Kane dropped his backpack and let out a long sigh, then his attention settled on Jenna. "Wolfe and Webber are right behind me, ma'am." He dived into his backpack for his bottle of water.

Jenna pushed her water back into her backpack and stood. "I see them now." She glanced at Bradford. "Go and help them with their gear."

She turned to Kane. "How did it go?"

"We have the remains packed away and enough footage to make a movie. Webber found one undetermined bullet casing. Wolfe will be able to tell us more after he gets the victims back to the lab."

CHAPTER THIRTEEN

After listening to Wolfe's hurried report on Dawson Sanders' remains, Jenna led him to the bones she had found and waited with interest for his comments. "I can't find anything else in the vicinity; do you think these were buried?"

"Most likely carried here and consumed by animals." With gentle care, Wolfe removed the bones then placed them in a bag. He gathered soil samples then glanced up at her. "Dawson Sanders was wearing a belt so we have to assume this belongs to Paige or the killer. It could be a vital clue. If these bones belong to Paige Allen, we know the killer tied her arms behind her back before death. There would be no other reason, and if that is her skull, the killer subjected her to a vicious attack before killing her."

"Blackhawk figured the marks on the bones are of animal origin." Jenna pushed on her hat and stared at the thin white bones. "He is with Rowley and they are searching in the direction of the skull's location."

"It will be difficult to find the complete skeleton of Paige Allen; animals could have spread parts all over." Wolfe passed an evidence bag to Webber to label. "Unfortunately, cadaver dogs will be no use either; they search for the smell of rotting flesh."

Jenna's earpiece crackled and Rowley's voice came through.

"We've found more bones." He gave his position. *"They look small. I figure we've found the missing parts of Paige Allen."*

"Roger that, we are on our way." She scanned the pile of equipment and her deputies' exhausted expressions. It had been a long day. She turned to Wolfe. "Head to the coordinates with Kane and Webber. We'll follow behind with the rest of the gear."

"Yes, ma'am."

"I need to duck behind a bush before we go." Bradford waved a hand absently toward the undergrowth.

"Sure." Jenna turned, surprised to see Kane coming back down the trail. "Is something wrong?"

"Not really." Kane's eyes searched her face. "You look all in and I'm starving. I have two huge steaks in my refrigerator. Would you like me to cook for you tonight?" He smiled.

Jenna let out a contented sigh. "That would be wonderful. I'll pick up some hotcakes from Aunt Betty's on the way home. I could eat a horse."

"Deal." Kane picked up one of the bags, and with a whistle to his dog, he hurried off in Wolfe's direction.

Jenna hoisted on her backpack then picked up one bag of equipment. "You okay, Bradford?"

"Yes, ma'am." Bradford came out of the bushes, straightening her clothes, and then bent to pick up the other bag. "Do you ever get used to the murders?"

Jenna shook her head. "Not really."

"I was hoping you'd say yes." Bradford sighed.

Jenna could see Kane in the distance and quickened her pace, eager to discover more information on what had happened to Paige Allen and Dawson Sanders. Two young people enjoying a hike in the forest. She came up with a few different scenarios. The killer did not fit into the same classification as some of the others she had dealt with during her time in Black Rock Falls and they had no missing persons' reports from any of the neighboring counties.

The last killer they had investigated targeted teenage girls, not young couples. The MO here was different to the killer in Black

Rock Falls last summer, and it made her wonder if a jealous lover was responsible; or could it have been an opportunistic kill? It would be interesting to hear what Jill Bates, the forensic anthropologist from Helena, discovered after she examined the remains.

In the meantime, she would discuss her thoughts with Kane over dinner, although he preferred no shoptalk when they spent their downtime together. This case was so intriguing, she could not wait. His insights would help her decide which way to take the investigation.

"Where do you want the bags, ma'am?" Bradford moved to her side.

Dragged out of deep thought, Jenna smiled at her. "Over there with the other gear." She followed and dropped her bag then removed her backpack.

The wind had picked up and she glanced skyward. The last thing they needed was rain but above only a few white clouds blocked the sun. After pushing her way through the bushes and avoiding a patch of poison ivy, she moved to Rowley's side in a small clearing. "What do we have?"

"The majority of Paige Allen's bones, apart from the hands." Rowley's forehead creased. "Wolfe believes she wasn't murdered here. We searched around and discovered some clothes about ten yards down the trail. I asked Wolfe before collecting them, and he said to go ahead."

"Okay."

Interested, her attention moved over the bones spread over the ground and sticking out like mushrooms from the forest floor. When Blackhawk walked to her side wearing a sorrowful expression, she noticed a pair of jeans in his hands. "What is it? What have you found?"

"These clothes are almost intact. They haven't been torn apart." Blackhawk slid the jeans inside an evidence bag and passed them to her. "The underwear is inside as if they were pulled from her feet first. An animal would shred them to get to the flesh." He gave her a concerned frown. "We found her boots as well and they are still laced up." He motioned toward Rowley. "He has them."

"Ma'am." Rowley held out an evidence bag containing a pair of hiking boots. "We were very careful not to disturb the area but these were thrown under a bush." He pointed into the woods. "I think Wolfe needs to take a look over in that area. One of the trees has a few holes in it on one side; too many for a random shooter."

The breeze had turned into a howling wind and cold seeped through her clothes, chilling skin damp from walking. "Okay, thanks. Leave the evidence with Bradford and go tell him." She went to her backpack and bent to pull out her jacket. The sun lost its heat around two in the afternoon, and this high up the ranges, the temperature could drop below zero at this time of the year.

"Do you think he raped her?" Bradford was staring at the clothes inside the evidence bags. "From the damage he did to her face, he was a mean son of a bitch."

Jenna pulled up the zipper on her jacket and turned to Bradford. "Unless he left his DNA on those jeans, we'll never know. Unfortunately, the remains will tell us little in this state. We can only hope the killer made a mistake and left a fragment of evidence behind. If he has, Wolfe will find it, and by now Kane will have an outline of a profile for the killer." She sighed. "This case is different from any I've handled before."

"Deputy Kane suggested I familiarize myself with some of the old cases, and none of the killers seemed to kill for fun." Bradford picked at her fingernails as if the topic disturbed her. "The bullet wounds and the arrow through the head look like the killer was enjoying himself."

"Yeah, you're right." Kane walked up to them with an unreadable expression. "This murderer kills for fun. In all the other homicides we've investigated, we discovered the killer had suffered trauma in their past that triggered their behavior. This one is dangerous because we don't have a pattern of behavior yet. Unpredictable is the hardest to catch. I'll need to look for similar crimes and see if this killer has struck elsewhere before I profile him." He turned to Jenna. "We have a probable crime scene. Wolfe is still collecting evidence."

Jenna nodded. "Show me."

"Roger that." He glanced back at Bradford with an expression etched in stone. "Stay here with the evidence. I'll send Rowley and Webber back then you can start hauling everything back to the horses."

Jenna followed him into the bushes and touched his arm to get his attention. "It's getting late and cold. I can't believe you want to come up here for a hiking weekend… We'll freeze to death."

"Nah." He turned and grinned at her. "We'll walk the trails during the day and spend the night in a cabin. There are at least six plateaus in the area I planned to visit. There are views up here you can only see by foot. Or we can cheat a bit and bring the horses." He held the bushes back for her to pass. "I promise you'll be as warm as toast. We have to do it soon though, before winter. There is no way I'm coming up here once the snow comes, cabin or no cabin."

"Okay, we'll talk about it some more over dinner." She surveyed the scene and glanced at Wolfe. "How long do you figure these bones have been here?"

"A year or so." Wolfe meticulously collected soil samples after removing the bones scattered at the base of the tree. He dropped onto all fours and peered closely at the ground then taking a brush from his bag feathered away the dirt. "Well, look what we have here. A diamond engagement ring and there's an inscription inside."

"What does it say?" Jenna moved closer and peered over his shoulder.

"Paige and Dawson forever." Wolfe dropped the ring into a small plastic bag and sealed it.

"They are the same names on the driver's licenses we found in the backpacks." Kane's eyes narrowed. "If that ring is real, it would have cost a fortune."

"So we can rule out robbery as a motive." Jenna let out a long sigh. "At least we have something to go on. With the identities of the victims we'll be able to locate relatives and find out when they went missing."

"Just a minute. For now, we are assuming the remains belong to Allen and Sanders, and they probably do." Wolfe brushed the leaves from his pants and his cool gaze lifted to their faces. "All we have are bones and I do not intend to sign off on the identity of either victim until I have positive proof. This means dental records or a DNA test." His attention settled on Jenna. "The female victim's bones have been scattered over some distance. In truth, we're only surmising this is one person; it's easy to jump to conclusions."

"That's fine by me." She nodded then turned her attention to Kane. "If the remains are Paige Allen's, how do you figure the murder went down?"

"It would have been brutal."

Jenna stood to one side and watched as Kane recreated the murder.

"Going on Wolfe's deductions, the woman was likely shot in the back same as the other victim." Kane's brow wrinkled into a frown. "We have to assume from the distance between the two crime scenes she was running from her killer. She falls to the ground and the killer ties her hands with his belt and props her up against a tree." He moved to a tree with a distinctive bullet hole. "We have no idea what she endured before he killed her."

"No, not without a body." Wolfe shook his head. "We have nothing conclusive to indicate rape but I believe the killer removed her clothes and there is every indication they were dragged from her. The indentations on the bones need closer examination, but I believe we have both animal and knife markings." He moved closer to the tree, indicated to the bullet hole, and lifted his concerned expression to Jenna. "From a preliminary examination of the remains, she had blunt force trauma from maybe the grip of a pistol then he shot her between the eyes at close range. The damage to the skull is extensive. The bullet traveled through the skull and embedded in the tree."

Jenna could visualize the horrific last minutes of the poor woman and ground her teeth. Alone and helpless, she probably witnessed her fiancé's murder then ran for her life. She dragged in a deep breath. Death had come again to Black Rock Falls. She raised her chin to look at Kane. "I gather it will be some time before we'll have an approximate time of death but what can you tell me about this killer?"

"It depends if we find more victims." Kane leaned nonchalantly against a tall pine. "If the two victims are the extent of his murder spree, and taking into account this crime scene and comparing it to the death of the other victim, then this could be a one-off crime of passion."

Jenna nodded. "Yeah, I've seen quite a few domestics and the man always attacks the woman's face."

"It's common in homicide as well." Kane rubbed the dark stubble on his chin. "This was particularly vicious, so a jealous lover, ex-boyfriend would be someone we need to look at." He sighed. "If we find more victims, we're talking about a whole different ball game."

"Okay, so worst case scenario?" Jenna swallowed the lump in her throat. "I have a real bad feeling about this murder."

"A thrill-killer who hates women or a particular type of woman." The nerve in Kane's cheek twitched. "Unpredictable and happy to bide his time until he gets the perfect victim—think Bundy. He liked college girls: long brown hair, similar body type. This type of psychopath is your typical nice guy but he is intelligent, cunning, sly, and as slippery as an eel. I would say Caucasian, late twenties to mid to late thirties, or maybe older if he has been doing this for some time." His lips flattened into a thin line. "If this is the profile of our killer, the male victims are collateral damage and no woman who resembles our female victim is safe in Black Rock Falls." His attention moved over her. "As we're talking, five six with shoulder-length black hair between twenty and thirty-five… That includes you, Jenna."

CHAPTER FOURTEEN

Later that afternoon, he walked to the Weapons, Fishing and Ammunition store. He peered across the road at a couple walking by hand in hand and snorted in disgust. To think a man could tie himself willingly to a viper like her. The way she tossed her hair and fluttered her eyelashes at every man they walked by was no better than hearing her long red nails scrape down a blackboard. Why men committed themselves to years of mental torture, he could not imagine. He had to admit the woman was attractive, but looks fade and it was likely she would be in another man's bed before the year was out.

With a grin, he lifted the rifle and aimed it at the couple through the window, lining them up. No sport on earth matched the rush he experienced hunting humans, and it lasted because he could watch the reruns anytime he chose. Oh yes, he used the trail cams to record every delicious moment.

The shopkeeper's voice speaking to another customer brought him back to reality and he lowered the rifle. Not that he planned to purchase anything. He had never been a foolish man, and buying a rifle in town then using it to kill someone would be beyond stupid.

He had little preparation left to do. His guns waited in his cave, loaded and ready. Earlier, he'd set the trail cams in place, spread over a wide area, just in case Bailey managed to get away from him. He had covered every contingency to provide a good hunt. His client would meet him at an appointed spot, no names would be exchanged, no trace left to connect him to her murder.

He strolled to the counter and smiled at the assistant. "Nice, very nice, but I'll think it over. I'm not planning on hunting again until spring. I've been too busy of late." He handed him the rifle then strolled from the store.

He glanced up at the sky; the forecast for the morning was clear and cool with expected carnage. A chuckle spilled from his throat. He could almost taste blood in the air. *I can't wait.*

CHAPTER FIFTEEN

After dinner, Jenna flopped on Kane's sofa and rubbed her eyes. Exhausted did not come close to how she felt. Her bones ached from riding and hauling equipment from one crime scene to the other. She took the cup of coffee from Kane and smiled. "I'm exhausted. I thought I would fall asleep standing up in the shower."

"You didn't have to help me tend the horses." He sat beside her and placed his two large feet on the coffee table. "Although I did appreciate the help."

Jenna shrugged and the small movement tugged at her sore muscles. "It's my horse and I'm responsible for her. From now on I'm helping you muck out in the morning as well." She stifled a yawn. "I actually enjoy grooming her; it's a small piece of normality in a crazy world."

"Yeah, I feel the same." He gave her a contented smile. "I know you wanted to discuss the case tonight but I have nothing to add to what I said at the crime scene. I think we are in a holding pattern right now, stuck between a crime of passion, at least a year ago, and a thrill-killer who might strike again."

"Wolfe will be able to tell us more when he and the forensic anthropologist examine the remains." Jenna sipped her beverage. "I guess our idea about taking a couple of days for a short vacation is off the cards now?"

"Maybe not." Kane's grin flashed white. "It's been at least one year since the murders and Wolfe has a lot to do before we can start investigating. We only want one weekend and could head away from this side of the mountain and follow the trails that wind up into the ranges. Yeah, it will be cold, but we have thermal underwear and the cabins have fireplaces. You've been through a lot worse in basic training, I'm sure."

Oh, the coffee he made was so good. She stared at him over the rim of her cup, savoring the taste. "I was much younger then but apart from being exhausted from the gruesome murder we had to deal with today, I do enjoy being in the mountains. It has a tragic beauty." She sighed. "Inside, I know what has happened there, but somehow it's as if the scenery is trying to make up for man's mistakes. It's different every time I go there—the trees are the same but the colors and variety of flowers and wildlife amaze me."

"I concentrate on how peaceful it is up there." He reached for his steaming cup. "It's like the beaches where many men died in battle. The sea has washed away the blood, leaving no trace of the tragedy. Same here, the forest grows over the damage as if hiding the memory of what happened." He sucked in a deep breath. "The sea and forests see death every day, animals and fish eat each other. To them it's survival, to us it's murder."

"How poetic." Jenna drained her coffee and pushed to her feet. "Thanks for dinner but I must be getting home. I'll put my cup in the dishwasher and see you in the morning. As much as I would like to stay and chat all night, I don't really want to sleep in your spare room again."

"Leave the cup, I'll walk you home." Kane whistled to Duke then headed for the door. "Duke needs to go outside before I turn in."

They strolled across the grass to her front porch and she opened the door, punched in the code on her house alarm, and turned back to Kane. He had a habit of waiting until she was safe inside the house. "Thanks for walking me home."

"My pleasure."

His lips quirked up into a tentative smile and he turned away. "I'll see you at five if you still want to muck out the stables with me. It won't take long and will be a good warm-up for our exercise routine."

Jenna could not help a smile spreading across her face. She had seen this gentle side of Dave Kane break through his tough exterior before and enjoyed another glimpse. "Sure, I'll be there to help, and tomorrow is my turn to cook breakfast."

"I'll look forward to it."

She watched him amble slowly back to his cottage with Duke at his heels. *Maybe the iceman is melting.*

CHAPTER SIXTEEN

Wednesday

The following morning Jenna walked into the morgue with Kane to find a blonde woman in her thirties dressed in a white coat bending over the skeletal remains they had retrieved the previous day. The woman glanced up and smiled as the door whooshed shut behind them.

"Ah, you must be Sheriff Alton and Deputy Kane. Shane has told me so much about you, I feel I know you already." She removed a surgical glove and offered her hand. "Jill Bates."

I hope he hasn't told you everything about us. Jenna took her hand and smiled. "You must be the forensic anthropologist Wolfe mentioned, and please call me Jenna."

Beside her Kane offered his hand. "Nice to meet you." He glanced around. "Where *is* Wolfe?"

"He took some samples down to the lab. We only have the basic autopsy equipment here. He has everything we need for my side of things and of course the DNA testing set up down the hall."

Astonished, Jenna gaped at her. "He can do DNA testing here now?"

"Oh yes, his equipment is impressive." Jill's lips curled into a pretty smile. "I think he has a fairy godmother—every time he applies for funding, it comes through in record time. Someone in government must be watching over him." She laughed.

Yeah, POTUS can be generous. Jenna heard the door open and Wolfe strode in carrying an iPad. She turned to him. "Ah good. Do you have anything for me yet?"

"Ah… yes and no." Wolfe's gray eyes narrowed. "I see you've met Jill. She has been invaluable and will be staying for a couple of days to help out."

Jenna nodded. "Not a problem but I hope she is staying at the Cattleman's Hotel? I wouldn't put a dog in the Black Rock Falls Motel."

"You don't have to worry, Jenna. I'm staying at Shane's house." Jill glanced over at him. "I've been crashing in his spare room."

"You have no idea how happy Emily is to talk to Jill." Wolfe's stern expression turned into a smile of sorts. "She is much like me at the same age and craves knowledge."

"How is she handling college?" Kane rubbed the black stubble on his chin. "Not planning on creating a body farm in your backyard, is she?"

"Oh my goodness." Jill burst into laughter. "You obviously know his daughter better than you think; she is devouring textbooks about dissection at the moment. I was the same; I played with dead things, bones, and fossils when I was a kid."

Jenna cleared her throat. "It was never dolls for me either. I had a passion for guns." The three people looking at her all dropped their jaws at once and she swallowed the laugh bubbling in her throat. She had a crime to solve. "Can we get down to business? Have you discovered anything we can use to positively identify these people?"

"Yeah, with Jill's help and contacts, we have obtained the dental records for both victims and compared them. They both have the same health insurance and we tracked them from there."

"Yes, I was able to access the database with my password and we've gotten a match. Both victims had X-rays recently, which was a bonus." Jill waved a hand at the shattered remains on the left. "This is Dawson Sanders and his fiancée Paige Allen."

"Once we found a match, I did a search and discovered a newspaper article about them." Wolfe cocked one eyebrow. "He owns a string of hotels and she comes from money. Their engagement party was spread over two pages of the local newspaper."

"He was very young to own a string of hotels." Jenna tapped her bottom lip. "So why come to Black Rock Falls? You would have thought they would have taken a vacation somewhere more luxurious."

"I figure we'll find out soon enough." Kane moved closer to the pathetic remains of Paige Allen. "The skeleton looks almost complete." He turned to look at Sanders' remains. "What happened to their hands?"

"We believe they were carried away by animals." Wolfe's attention shifted to his iPad. "It's still early in our examination of the remains but from the damage we can see on Sanders, we believe the bolt through his head was post mortem."

"Yes." Jill moved around the remains and indicated with one gloved finger. "The lack of bone scatter and teeth marks would indicate, for some reason, the animals left the rest of Sander's body alone. Decomposition leaves traces in the clothing and his appears to be normal, which led us to believe he was soaked in gasoline or oil."

"Yeah you mentioned that before but who would carry a can of gas up a mountain?" Kane flicked Jenna a disbelieving look then turned back to Wolfe. "Have you tested the clothes yet?"

"Not yet."

Jenna caught Wolfe's flash of annoyance. Kane wanted answers yesterday, and what Wolfe and Jill had achieved in a short time had been incredible. She patted Kane on the arm. "I asked for the identities of the victims and they have confirmed that in record time. You know how long it takes to do all the tests."

"We're working with next to nothing here." Wolfe gave her a grateful look and shrugged. "Piecing the skeletons together took hours and we haven't had time to determine the cause of death for Paige Allen." He glanced at Kane. "I suggest you find their camp—it must be within walking distance from where we found them—and look for a gas can in the general area. From the contents of their backpacks they couldn't have traveled for more than an hour from where we found them."

Jenna shook her head. "We are talking about a massive perimeter to search, and bears would have trashed their camp by now. We searched the immediate area in all directions and found nothing. I'm not wasting resources going up there again." She sighed. "I need boots on the ground here. I have a string of local complaints Walters had to place on the back burner while we trekked up the mountain and I need people checking out this couple's movements. Why didn't anyone file a missing persons' report?"

"It does seem strange as they were prominent people in their town." Wolfe leaned nonchalantly against the bench. "Then there is the cellphone. I will look at that as soon as possible. I would be interested to find out who they called in the hours before their deaths. Allen must have been carrying it when she was killed, and there is reception up there—why didn't she call 911?"

"If she did, we'd have a record." Jenna frowned. "This happened on my watch. There is no way a 911 call could slip past us."

"I'll check the logs when we get back to the office." Kane's brow wrinkled into a deep frown as he peered at the woman's remains. "The damage to the spine is a typical incapacitating shot used to keep a person immobilized for questioning." He shot a glance at Wolfe. "The killer wanted her alive, didn't he?"

"As I said, I need some time to do a full report on our findings but, yes, that injury would be enough to paralyze a person. Then there is the belt we found tight around her arms. It doesn't belong to her or her fiancé, they were both wearing belts. It must have belonged to the killer, and before you ask, there are no distinguishing marks on it." Wolfe folded his arms across his substantial chest and sighed. "From what we can see, she suffered and was left for the animals to devour. The male victim was preserved for some reason."

"Which means the woman was tossed aside once the thrill of killing had past. This is typical psychopathic behavior." Kane pushed a hand through his dark hair and his expression turned somber. "But this killer has another twist to his persona. I believe he likes to visit his victims, for whatever reason, and uses the gas to prevent animals from disturbing them. Watching them decompose is an added thrill."

CHAPTER SEVENTEEN

The morning had become one of those days and Jenna had started to believe she was in charge of the Keystone Cops. In fact, if Rowley had waddled by her door in black and white twirling a baton she would not have blinked an eye.

In her absence attending to the cold case, the sheriff's office had fallen into chaos. Fights had broken out all over town, including another ruckus at the Triple Z, and the phones had rung constantly with complaints. The hunting season was in full swing and it brought out a testosterone-fueled competitive spirit from the locals and a few of their guests.

Normally, the rangers, or FWP as the locals called the Fish, Wildlife and Parks enforcement officers, took care of the hunting side of things. They kept everybody honest by running the mandatory checkpoints in and out of hunting areas to check licenses and kills, but some of the excitement had spilled into town now the elk and turkey season had crossed over.

After dispatching her deputies to deal with the complaints, she had taken a well-earned cup of steaming joe into her office and shut the door. She had the task of following up the cold case information collected from Wolfe's primary examination of the remains of Paige and Dawson. The names of both victims came up in the missing persons' records for California. She made a note of the contact number and officer in charge of the case then reached for her phone. The connection rang a few times and a man's voice answered.

"Yeah."

"Detective Stokes?" Jenna glanced at the computer screen. "This is Sheriff Alton from Black Rock Falls, Montana. I have information on two of your missing persons: Paige Allen and Dawson Sanders."

"Just a minute, I'll access the file." Stokes tapped on his keyboard then sighed. *"Okay, what do you have?"*

Jenna cleared her throat. "We found their remains on a trail in Stanton Forest way up the top of the Black Rock Mountain range. My medical examiner believes they have been here for about one year."

"We tried hunting them down in Colorado. Apparently, after their engagement party, they went on a mystery holiday Sanders arranged there. Their families told us they insisted on leaving their cellphones behind and took a burner for emergencies. As we couldn't trace their phones, we had no leads to their whereabouts. What happened to them?"

"I'm afraid we have a homicide." The sightless sockets of the two skulls flitted across Jenna's mind, sending a shiver down her back. "Both were subjected to considerable brutality. I can't give you a full report yet. We have engaged a forensic anthropologist to work with our ME to determine cause of death."

"Do you have a positive ID on the victims?"

"Yes, we have their drivers' licenses and their dental records." Jenna chewed on her bottom lip. "Unfortunately, there is no doubt the victims are Dawson Sanders and Paige Allen."

"I see. Any suspects? Any similar crimes in the area?" He drew in a deep breath. *"Just a minute, Black Rock Falls, yeah I've heard of that place. You caught the Riverside Killer, didn't you?"*

Jenna drummed her fingers on the table. "Yeah and he's in jail for life but he wasn't responsible. The murderer of this couple has a different MO and as the crime happened one year ago, we don't have any evidence to suggest he has killed in Black Rock Falls since.

As he damaged Allen's face, we are considering a crime of passion. What can you tell me about the couple? Is there a jealous lover in the picture?"

"Not that I'm aware of. Give me a few moments to read the file. It's been over a year."

Jenna sipped her coffee and waited.

"Right. The first person to contact us was Bruce Styles. He is Sanders' roommate. After six weeks, the rent was due and Styles hadn't heard from him, which was out of character. Of course, we found zip. It was as if they had vanished into thin air. When Sanders' parents returned from overseas about a week later, they contacted Paige Allen's parents and filed the missing persons' reports together."

Jenna listened with interest. A daughter goes missing for weeks and the parents do nothing? "What about the girl's parents—what was their story?"

"The Allens expected Paige to be gone for one month. They explained the couple had a cellphone ban and wanted to be alone. They thought they had extended their vacation." He sighed. *"I'm not sure how they ended up in Black Rock Falls. Sanders told them they were heading for Colorado."*

"Did they contact any other friends or relatives?"

"We spoke to Sander's workmates and the same for Paige. Like I said, they seemed to vanish. We listed them in the missing persons' database. I put out a BOLO on the vehicle but again nothing came to light. I'll give you the details."

"Yeah, thanks." Jenna took down the make and license plate then leaned back in her chair; it would seem Stokes had done a thorough investigation. "Did either of them have a rap sheet?"

"Nope, clean as the driven snow, the pair of them, and they had no financial worries either." He cleared his throat. *"Now it's a murder investigation, I'll dig deeper into Paige's background and shake down*

her old boyfriends to see what falls out. It looks like we'll have to work together on this one."

"That was the general idea. I'll email you the files we have to date and the full autopsy report when I have a copy." She had a thought. "Ah, before you go. Do you know of any similar crimes in your area? My deputy is a fine profiler and he believes this isn't the first time this man has killed."

"If we knew what state to search in, it would help, but I'll get my team on it and see what we come up with. I suggest you do the same. This is the Hollywood precinct. I'm pushed for time and resources here; we have a heavy caseload as it is without this on top. Problem is with cold cases they tend to get pushed down the line but I'll do my best."

Jenna wanted to bang her head on the table in frustration. Heavens above, she had two of his citizens in her morgue and he had practically yawned his way through the conversation. "Would you at least notify the next of kin?"

"Yeah, that I can arrange. I'll give them your details and they can make the necessary arrangements once the ME has released the remains."

The line went dead.

Jenna stared at the handset in disbelief. "So much for cooperation."

She collected the files she had to date and sent them through to him. The phone rang and Wolfe was on the line. "What do you have for me?"

"It's the cellphone found at the crime scene. I managed to download the contents of Paige Allen's SIM. The last number dialed was 911 in October last year. The call lasted one second, so if anyone answered I doubt they would have worried, especially as 911 calls go through our private cellphones out of office hours."

"It's chilling knowing one of them tried to call for help." Jenna sighed. "Anything else?"

"Apart from the 911 call, no, there are images on the SIM but most of them are corrupted. They are of the general area, the Cattleman's Hotel restaurant, and some mountain views."

A wave of relief spread over her. At last, she had a lead. "So, they could have stayed at the Cattleman's Hotel?"

"It would be worth checking."

Jenna made a few notes. "When will you finish the post?"

"I'll have a full report sent to you later today but there is one thing of interest. In layman's terms, the cuts on Paige Allen's bones are consistent with a hunting knife and a machete." He paused for some moments. *"I'm not ruling out there might have been two killers. The crossbow bolt we found in Dawson Sanders is unusual and out of place. Why did the killer only use it once? It is something we need to investigate further."* Wolfe sucked in a deep breath. *"If that's all, ma'am, I'll get the report underway."*

"Yes, and thank you. Thank Jill for me too."

"I will. Have a good day, ma'am."

"Bye." Jenna disconnected then searched through her contacts for the Cattleman's Hotel.

She was just about to dial when a knock sounded on the door. "Yes, come in."

Rowley stuck his head around the door and appeared ruffled. He sported a large red welt under one eye and his hat was askew. "The ruckus at the Triple Z? It is the same two men as last time. Do you want them in the cells?"

She waved him away. "Yeah, write them up, I'll get to them next." *Why did I take this job?*

CHAPTER EIGHTEEN

Kane finished his lunch at Aunt Betty's Café, picked up a bagel with cream cheese and a takeout coffee for Jenna, then headed back to the office. His morning had been a complete shambles. He hadn't questioned Jenna's insistence to send him out with Bradford this morning, and although he had worked on a variety of ridiculous problems in his time, his patience was running thin.

The morning had consisted of writing tickets for illegal parking and sorting neighborhood squabbles. Right this moment, he would have given a month's pay to be swinging punches at the local ruckus at the Triple Z with Rowley and Webber.

He enjoyed the thrill of profiling and catching killers with Jenna and the team, but he missed the variety of action from his past life. Although the plate in his head, courtesy of a car bomb during his days as a government agent, caused him headaches, it had not slowed him down. The only beneficial adrenaline rush of late came from working out with Jenna every morning, or riding his horse at full gallop, but after seeing active service for so long, life in Black Rock Falls made him yearn for excitement.

He entered Jenna's office and placed the food and coffee on the desk. She had all the windows open and the mingled scents of the pine forest and Jenna's shampoo filled the room. "I've had lunch, what else is on the agenda?"

"One second." Jenna tapped away at her keyboard then lifted her attention to him. She pounced on the takeout bag, inhaled, then smiled. "Oh, *thank* you. Bagels and cream cheese… You *do* read minds, I knew it." She pointed to the takeout. "You are the only person who has ever turned up with food for me when I am famished."

Kane grinned. "Maybe I just like to keep on your good side."

"Keep this up and you'll always be on my good side, Dave." Jenna gave a moan of pleasure and bit into the bagel.

"Too easy." Kane chuckled. It did not take a genius to know she had not eaten since breakfast. When Jenna was on a case she forgot what day it was, let alone allowing herself time for a meal break. "Did Rowley and Webber sort out the fight at the Triple Z?"

"Yeah, it was more of a domestic between Leroy and Abel Finch. Can you handle the interviews? Rowley would have finished his report by now." Jenna sipped her coffee and sighed. "Get Bradford to write the reports from your patrol this morning. Anything interesting happen?"

"Nope and she is already hard at work." He stretched, wishing it was time to head home. "I gather the troublemakers from the Triple Z are in the cells?"

"Yeah, I was going to interview them but I've been snowed under with phone calls and autopsy reports." Jenna leaned back in her chair. "I've spoken to the detective on the Sanders and Allen cold case at Hollywood PD. I'm afraid he has little to offer the murder investigation but we are exchanging case files. He did at least interview the family and close friends at the time they went missing."

"Don't expect too much help." Kane rubbed the back of his neck. "The case will be right at the bottom of his list."

"That's why I'm working the case. I need to chase down any leads here before they vanish. The couple stayed in town at some time before they died, and what happened to their car? It isn't on the DMV list as found or abandoned."

"It could have been sold to a chop shop. They don't ask too many questions about ownership." He rested the palm on the handle of his pistol. "Do you want these idiots from the Triple Z incident charged or released with a warning?"

"I guess it depends on the damages to the bar and if the proprietor wants to press charges." She nibbled at her lunch. "The brothers have nothing of value, and this time they were fighting each other and everyone else joined in. Use your own judgement." She sighed. "I'm heading over to the Cattleman's Hotel with Rowley to see if anyone remembers seeing Sanders and Allen. I hope they'll give us access to their records when I tell them the couple are victims of a homicide."

"They might want to avoid a court order but it's more likely they'll give you specific information about the couple rather than open their books. If they have kept a video it would be useful but it's likely they have overwritten the data by now, and if not we'll need a court order to obtain a copy, privacy laws being what they are." Kane indicated over one shoulder with his thumb. "When I've finished the interviews, do you want me to check out local junkyards and see if anyone has had eyes on Allen's vehicle?"

"Would you?" Jenna popped the last piece of bagel into her mouth and licked a smear of cream cheese from her lips. "If you find anything interesting, call me."

"Roger that."

After contacting the proprietor of the Triple Z and discovering he did not intend to file for damages, Kane interviewed Leroy and Abel Finch. The brothers had argued over a bar tab, and after agreeing to split the amount between them, he let them go with a warning that next time they caused trouble, they would be heading for court.

As he followed them to the front door, he caught sight of Jenna climbing into her vehicle with Rowley riding shotgun. The afternoon sun glistened on her hair and when she turned to glance at him, he gave her a wave. He pushed on his hat and climbed into his rig. They usually worked together, and her insistence for him to go on patrol with Bradford had puzzled him. Maybe he had gotten a little too close to her the previous evening and this was her way of keeping him at a distance. After pulling out into the traffic, he grimaced. He had come close to kissing her goodnight. If this was her reaction, he had better keep his distance. Pity, she was only the second woman in his life he had ever cared for.

The first recycling yard yielded nothing but as he drove into the second he could hear the screaming sound of tearing metal as the crusher compacted cars into neat cubes. Heavy machinery lifted the cubes and dropped them onto a waiting truck that sagged under the weight. Entering through massive gates, he pulled up outside a ramshackle office and glanced around. Rows of vehicles of every description spread out over at least five acres; they ranged from almost pristine to rusty relics from the 1950s.

The air in the office hung heavy with the smell of oil and cigarettes. Stained wooden shelves held car parts, each with a paper tag tied with string. In one corner, a motor looked out of place with its bright chrome pipes gleaming in the dim interior. Kane moved through the office and a scattering of metal shavings and glass fragments ground under his boots. Behind the counter sat a man in his fifties with slicked-back salt-and-pepper hair.

"What can I do for you, Deputy?" He stood then wiped his hands on his filthy coveralls.

Kane stepped closer. "Afternoon, I'm Deputy Kane. I'm searching for a late-model silver Ford Sedan. It went missing over a year ago. Has anything similar come through here?"

"Maybe, maybe not." The man sat down at his computer. "I run this place to the letter of the law. If it came in, I'll have a record."

"That's good to hear."

Long moments passed and then the man printed up a list and handed it to Kane.

"We had two late-model Fords. One was a burned-out wreck brought in from Blackwater, the other from a deceased estate here in town. All the details are listed."

Kane tipped his hat. "Thank you for your help." He headed back to his car.

Once inside he checked the vehicle identification number of the burned-out wreck with Allen's missing vehicle. They matched. He called Jenna. "I've found Allen's car. No plates but the numbers match. It was stripped and burned out in Blackwater then transported here to be crushed."

"That would involve two men: one to drive and one to follow."

Kane stared at the line of rusting vehicles. "It is a possibility but there are ways around it. For instance, the killer could own a tow truck. Take the car to a deserted area, strip it down, and set it on fire. That vehicle wouldn't stick out, they're a dime a dozen here."

"True, but Wolfe still is in two minds about how many killers were involved. Not many hunters carry a rifle and a crossbow." Jenna let out a long sigh. *"Of course, we can't rule out the fact someone else stumbled on the remains and decided to put a bolt through the head either. As Webber believes, the bolts are expensive and not usually left behind, I'll send him out to hunt down the supplier at the local stores."*

Kane scratched his head. "Do you know how many online retailers there are as well? It would be like finding a needle in a haystack."

"I might just find that needle." Jenna cleared her throat. *"The Cattleman's Hotel confirmed the victims stayed there and the dates. Funny thing is, they checked out. I would have thought after a few days in the*

forest they would want a hot shower and a good night's sleep before they headed home. Most hikers do."

"Maybe they were running out of cash."

"That seems unlikely but you have a point. I'm going to be spending the next couple of days digging into the couple's past. The detective I spoke to sent his files. I'll contact their friends. If this is a crime of passion, Paige's BFFs will know about her boyfriends. There is always gossip. I can't let this go, Kane; I'm going to catch the lunatic who murdered Paige Allen and Dawson Sanders."

Kane sighed. "We'll find him." He stared out the window and into the peaks in the distance. "One thing we know for sure, with the reputation this place has gained in the last couple of years, anyone planning on hiking into the mountains unarmed is crazy."

CHAPTER NINETEEN

A cool breeze lifted Bailey Canavar's hair and she turned to embrace it. "Oh, Jim it's amazing here; I can feel the cold wind toning my skin." She giggled and danced along the trail beside him, feeling like a young kid on her first outing. The spectacular views had her spellbound. Jim had picked the perfect place for them to visit. "This part of the forest is beautiful, I'm so glad you convinced me to come with you. I was getting a little bored in the hotel. How did you find this place?"

"After finding the skull, I thought you'd prefer to be far away from any potential ancient burial sites. I promise that will never happen again." Jim's tanned face creased into a broad smile. "I had the maps from the counter at the hotel and wanted to find somewhere secluded. There are tons of old trails people don't use as much here, mainly because they are too far from the highway, but they are perfect for us to get away from people for a while." He caught her in his arms and spun her around. "Thanks for leaving your cellphone behind. I don't want to be disturbed. Mine is at home as well. I'm sure as hell not taking any damn calls from the office on my honeymoon. We can use the burner I purchased for emergencies."

She gave him her best sexy smile, the one that made his eyes smolder, and ran a hand through his sandy hair. "I'm not going to miss my phone for a few days. I think I'll be busy."

A shot rang out and pain struck her side in a glancing blow. "Ouch! Something hit me." She ran her fingers down her side and found a tear in her shirt. "How did that happen?"

"Get down." Jim pushed her to her knees behind a tree. "Are you okay?"

Blood coated her fingers and she sagged in his arms then collapsed to the ground, gaping at him. "What's happening?"

"I don't know." Jim peered around nervously. "I didn't hear a gunshot."

Blood spattered her jeans and oozed from a small tear under her ribs. "Oh my God, I've been hit."

"Stay down. I can't see or hear anyone." Jim examined the wound and his voice dropped. "It's just a nick. You'll be fine. Take a few deep breaths."

As usual, Jim tried to calm her but panic tightened her chest and she looked around terrified another shot would hit her. "Who would shoot at us?"

"Don't be silly. If anyone was shooting at us they wouldn't give up that easy. Look at me, Bailey. You need to calm down." Jim squeezed her arm. "You'll be okay. It's just a scratch. Probably just a stray bullet or something. Some of the hunting rifles can reach five hundred yards."

"Okay. I have a dressing in the first aid kit." She took a few deep breaths. "How did this happen? I thought the hunters were miles away."

"They should be. You fix up the scratch. I'll need to report this accident and get help." He pulled out his cellphone. "No bars. I'll walk up the trail a ways. That huge boulder is probably blocking the signal."

Terrified of being alone, she glanced around. "Okay but hurry. I don't like it here."

"Stay in the trees. I won't be more than a few yards away."

Bailey watched him walk out of sight then took a few seconds to check her side. She shrugged out of her backpack and pulled out the first aid kit then heard the sound of something big moving through the undergrowth. In sheer panic that a bear had smelled blood and was heading her way, she searched the backpack for bear repellent then froze in terror when a man dressed in army fatigues came out of the forest.

The man had his face covered with camouflage face paint, he had a strange contraption covering his mouth, wore sunglasses and a woolen cap pulled low over his ears. She tried to crawl away but the man was on her in seconds and dragged her to her feet. Bailey tried to slap him. "Let go of me."

A backhand from Face Paint sent her reeling and she fell onto her back, head spinning. She tasted blood in her mouth. Confused, she scrambled on hands and knees to get away. Her husband was only a few yards away and he would hear her. "Jim, I need help."

Without a sound, Face Paint lifted her with ease, pushed her to her knees, and dragged back her arms with such force she cried out. As tendons ripped, pain shot through her shoulders. She sobbed as he fastened a zip tie around her wrists and pulled it so tight it burned through her flesh. "Stop it, you're hurting me!" She let out a long scream. "Jim, help me!"

No one came running and Bailey let out a sob of fear. "Why are you doing this?"

Relief flooded over her when she heard footsteps coming down the trail. "That's my husband and the rangers will be on their way."

"Get over here. I wouldn't want you to miss all the fun." Face Paint's voice was strange. A smile flashed white against his gruesome, multicolored, camouflaged skin. He stared at her. "Do as you are told and everything will turn out just fine."

With every muscle trembling, Bailey gaped at him in terror. What was happening? Tears stung her cut lip and she tried to crawl away but Face Paint's boot blocked her way. Her disorientated mind tried to make sense of what she was seeing. *How does Jim know this lunatic?*

She looked up at Face Paint through her tears. "*Please* let me go. I'll give you money. I'll give you *anything* you want."

Face Paint smiled down at her.

"Hello, Bailey. Now, let me think. What *do* I want? Tell me, how fast can you run?"

CHAPTER TWENTY

Thursday

The following morning, Kane ducked a kick to the head, twisted his hips, and swept Jenna's feet from under her. He stepped to the side and aimed a kick at her head. When Jenna's foot brushed his thigh, missing his groin by the width of a hair, he grabbed her ankle and dropped to the mat. He had taken a few direct hits from her this morning but drew the line at permanent damage and pinned her to the floor. She squirmed under him like a crazy woman.

"Hey, Jenna, cool it. What's wrong with you this morning?"

"That's better." She relaxed and smiled at him. "I don't want you to go easy on me. I thought if I hit you a few times, you'd start to get rough."

His attention drifted to a drip of perspiration running down her cheek then he shrugged. "I never go easy on you. Have you forgotten your training? Learning the moves and keeping fit is the key. If you want to punch something, attack the bag."

"Oh, I punch the bag more than you know." She rolled onto her back and gave him a long, considering look then blew her bangs from her face. "You just seem distracted of late."

He flopped onto his back and pushed a hand through his damp hair. "You think?"

"Yeah. You've hardly said a word to me all morning." She rose up on one elbow and squinted her eyes at him. "In fact, you spoke to the horses more than me. That's not like you, Dave. We always discuss things in our downtime. Is your head hurting?"

He mirrored her position and shook his head. "My head is fine. I've had a few things on my mind is all."

"Anything you need to discuss?" She looked at him with an expression of interest.

Oh, he had things to discuss, but the outcome could ruin their work relationship. He shook his head. "Now is not the time." He rolled to his feet and offered his hand.

"I think it is, Dave." She took his hand, and when he pulled her to her feet, her blue eyes locked on his.

His mind whirled. How could he discuss the tension between them the other night? For heaven's sake, he could have easily kissed her. She was his boss and he lived on her property. Dammit, he still loved his late wife, and now he felt as if he was being unfaithful to consider such a thing. *It's not going to happen.* He shook his head. "I just wanted to say how much I value our friendship and I hope going away together won't spoil it. I'm still very much in love with my wife and I'm not ready for anything else just yet."

"Oh, I know that, Dave." She smiled at him. "You're the best friend I've ever had and you won't ever try to steal my boyfriends… not that I plan on having anyone in my life at the moment either."

"Okay." Kane gave her a quizzical stare. "So are we good?"

"Sure we are." She danced away from him, grinning. "Now maybe we can get our lives back to normal." She headed for the door without a backward glance.

It hadn't taken long for Kane to realize that hunting season of one type or another seemed to go on all year in Montana, but late fall attracted visitors from all over the state to Black Rock Falls to hunt elk and deer. They packed the motel to capacity and many people welcomed relatives into their homes. Most times the sheriff's department handled minor disturbances and had nothing to do with the hunting side of things, because the Fish, Wildlife and Parks enforcement officers were diligent.

Local squabbles seemed to be taking up his entire day when he would rather be working on the cold case with Jenna. It was days like these he craved to be involved in a decent investigation. Hopefully Wolfe had come up with some new evidence he could get his teeth into, he walked into Jenna's office. When she issued him with orders to head out again, he gaped at her in astonishment. "You want me to do *what?*"

"Take Bradford and go and sort out a complaint about some puppies." Jenna handed him a sheet of paper. "Here are the details."

He stared at the paperwork in disbelief. It wasn't like Jenna to give him all the grunt work. "Can't Webber or Rowley handle this one?"

"Kane, Webber is an expert on crossbows and I've sent him out to all the stores in town that sell the bolt used on Dawson Sanders." She leaned back in her chair and raised one dark eyebrow. "This case requires a negotiator and Bradford needs the experience. Seeing you in action will be a good training exercise for her."

I've been training her all damn week. "Okay, but—"

"No 'buts,' Kane." She lifted her chin and her mouth formed a stubborn line. "I'm snowed under, and with Wolfe occupied at the morgue, you're the only deputy available. I don't have an option."

He let out a long sigh. "Copy that."

CHAPTER TWENTY-ONE

He merged the footage from all the trail cams and his body cam into one movie and savored the footage of the exquisite death of Bailey. His heart pounded with the memory, so vivid it was, as if he still had the bloody knife in his hand. The scent of her lingered in the T-shirt he held to his nose. The sight of confused blue eyes and her soft dying pleas made him want more; he could not wait. *The snow will be here soon. I need to act now.*

After entering his username, he uploaded a small clip to his site on the dark web and waited to find another client. They never took long to bite. On this encrypted site, the signal pinged across the entire world and was untraceable. Here, hidden from sight, people advertised their extraordinary tastes and desires. A buyer could obtain anything from drugs to people. He leaned back in his seat and yawned.

As if on cue, his messenger pinged. He read the offer and sat back in his seat, shaking his head in amazement. Someone had suggested a dangerous but thrilling idea he had not thought of before. He looked over the details and grinned. "I'll need a very special couple for this one."

CHAPTER TWENTY-TWO

Friday

When the ringtone designated to incoming 911 calls pealed, Jenna ran from the shower. She glanced at the digital readout on her bedside clock and reached for her cellphone. "Sheriff Alton, what is your emergency?"

"We think we found a body up near Bear Peak. It's not full daylight yet, but we're pretty sure it's a body."

Jenna grabbed a pen and notepad. "Okay, can I have your names and contact details?"

"I'm Luke Evans and I'm with Jack Turner." Evans gave their details as residents of Black Rock Falls.

"What is your location? Do you have a GPS?"

"Sure enough." He rattled off the coordinates. *"We caught sight of a ten-point buck heading for a designated hunting area, and followed him along this old trail. We could smell something dead and thought it was an illegal kill, so went to investigate."* He took a long, shuddering breath. *"I contacted the ranger at the checking station. He said to stay here, not to touch anything, and contact you. He can't leave his post but is calling it in."*

"You did the right thing. Is there road access in that area?"

"Sure is, take the back road past the falls. The FWP have a check station signposted, take the road on the left into the forest, it leads to a parking lot. The ranger there will point you in the right direction. You can take the trail from there. I figure it's 'bout a thirty-minute hike."

"Okay, we're on our way. Stay where you are and I'll call you when we get to the parking lot. We'll be coming in on horseback." Jenna disconnected and called Kane. "We have a body up near Bear Peak. We'll take the horses; you get them ready and I'll contact Wolfe and Rowley. The others will be able to manage the office in our absence."

"Roger that, I'll be ready in ten."

A cold wind rustled the pines, buffeting Jenna and lifting the sides of her open jacket as she stepped from Kane's SUV. She glanced around, taking in the number of vehicles in the parking lot and the variety of both men and women lining up to check in with the ranger before proceeding to their designated hunting areas. The excited conversations masked the usual eerie moans and creaks from the dark depths of the forest. She walked to the front of the line and waited for the ranger to finish speaking to a hunter.

"Morning, I have a team with me to investigate the complaint we received this morning." She glanced at the faces of the people eager to get going, not wanting to advertise the fact someone had found a body. "We can manage on our own, and by looking at the people lined up, I figure you'll need all your men here."

"I would appreciate it, ma'am." The ranger offered her a smile. "It is a busy time and we're spread thin over the checking stations."

"I'll keep you informed." She turned away and waved to Wolfe as he arrived with Rowley then strolled into the trailer to help Kane unload the horses.

Duke barked and spun in circles with an exuberance she hadn't seen before. "Have you been giving that dog coffee or something?" She took hold of her mare's bridle and followed Kane's horse down the ramp.

"Nah, he does that when I come home too. It's his happy dance. I figure he is used to seeing these folk and believes we're going hunting."

Kane's eyes narrowed and he indicated with his chin to the other end of the parking lot. "Looks like Blackhawk is here." He glanced at her. "Did you call him?"

"No. Wolfe told me he planned to hire him when necessary, just in case we find anything close to the res. He won't be working with us all the time." She turned and her attention went straight to Blackhawk's stunning Appaloosa. The coat of the spotted horse rippled like silk over its toned, muscular body. "Oh, wow, that is one beautiful horse. He must spend hours grooming it to make it look like that."

"Yeah, he would." Kane's lips quirked up at the corner as he moved to her side and cupped his hands for her to mount. "Food is important too. I make sure both Warrior and Lady have all the supplements they need."

She took the offered leg up and mounted Lady. Noticing the way the sun glistened on Warrior's black coat, Jenna turned and smiled at Kane. "You polish him more than you do your car and that's saying something."

"Morning." Blackhawk touched his hat. "Shane called, said you needed a tracker, so here I am. I know the trail."

Jenna smiled at him. "Great! You can show us the way."

Wolfe rode up to her side with Rowley beside him. "Webber is on his way. He is bringing a packhorse and the rest of my gear. He should be here soon." He frowned. "Did you get any details on the body?"

Jenna sighed. "No, the men didn't get close. They are on scene waiting for us."

A truck with trailer attached approached in a cloud of dust and parked beside Kane's black rig. Before Jenna could say a word, Kane offered her Warrior's reins and strode off to help Webber unload the horses. A few moments later, they all headed into the forest with Blackhawk in the lead.

They had traveled about half an hour when Duke let out a howl like the devil was chasing him. Kane's horse reared and Jenna's Arab danced sideways, not wanting to continue. She calmed the horse but a sense of foreboding crept over her then a blast of wind curled through the trunks and the smell of rotting flesh hit her full in the face. She gagged and glanced over at Kane. "Can't be far now."

"Here, put this on." He handed her a face mask then attached his own.

As Blackhawk entered a hairpin turn, she heard voices and urged her mare forward. Two men in their early twenties ran to meet them; both carried rifles and appeared shaken.

Jenna held up a hand to quiet them. "Take a breath then show us what you found."

"We're not goin' back there, no way." One of the men wiped the back of his hand over his mouth. "It's through there on the left, in the bushes."

Jenna turned in her saddle to look at Rowley. "We'll go and take a look. Escort these men back to the checkpoint and take down their statements. The rangers will have space in their cabin to conduct an interview."

"Yes, ma'am." Rowley tipped his hat.

The team dismounted, and with Blackhawk and Wolfe in the lead, they moved down a short straightaway, peering into the dark recesses of the dense forest. The stench increased with each step, and without warning a flock of crows rose up like bats then settled in the trees. Jenna swallowed hard. It was the way of nature. The wildlife was hard at work doing its job keeping the forest clean but she had the awful feeling the next thing she laid eyes on would make her sick to her stomach.

CHAPTER TWENTY-THREE

Humming joined the noises of the forest and Kane batted away the flies and glanced up at the fifty or more crows perched in the surrounding branches. Something had disturbed them earlier by the way they flocked en masse to the treetops. At his heels, Duke whined then barked a warning. "Keep on the lookout. Duke smells something and it isn't dead flesh."

He scanned the area, searching the shadows for a bear. The smell would bring them to this location; then again, an eagle wouldn't take too kindly to sharing a meal either. Ahead, Blackhawk stopped walking then turned and raised a hand to halt the team.

"Bobcat." Blackhawk lifted his rifle and took aim at one of the trees.

As the echo of the shot receded, the sound of an animal bounding through the undergrowth replaced it. Another shot blasted from Blackhawk's rifle and he turned around, grim-faced.

"She won't be back for a while. Cats are too smart to risk being shot at twice in one day." Blackhawk pointed to the crows. "Those are a different matter. They aren't frightened of us, not when they want to fill their bellies."

"Have you found anything?" Jenna gave him a worried glance and took a few hesitant steps forward.

"Yeah." Wolfe dropped his bag on the ground and it landed with a thump. "Carnage."

Kane moved to Jenna's side and did a slow visual scan of the area. Carnage was an understatement. Blood dripped from bushes, spattered over tree trunks, and body parts with a generous coating of flies and ants littered the surrounding area. It looked like the aftermath of a violent battle. "That can't be one body, surely?"

"Nope, two at least, or what's left of them, and they've been here for a couple of days." Wolfe had suited up and was edging into the twilight of the dense forest with Webber close behind.

Kane shrugged out of his backpack and pulled out his gear; beside him Jenna did the same. "This could be an animal attack."

"Or a crazy with a machete or both. That looks like the way bears tear people apart; cats are more likely to drag them high into trees." She lifted her pale face to him. "I would prefer an animal attack but after seeing what happened to the other couple, we could have another lunatic in Black Rock Falls."

Kane pulled on latex gloves and waited for her. "We sure seem to attract them. It must be the size of the forest. There are so many places to hide in here and attack people. In truth, it's a paradise for killers."

"Seems so of late." She stared up at him and her eyes narrowed. "I'm starting to believe you are a crazies' magnet. It was a quiet little town before you came here."

He snorted. "Trust me, evil was lurking here well before I arrived."

When Wolfe came toward them wearing a blank expression, the hairs on the back of Kane's neck stood to attention. It was bad, real bad, and he glanced at Jenna, noting her professional mask had fallen into place as well. He straightened to hear the initial report.

"What have we got?" Jenna snapped on a pair of gloves. "Is it an animal attack?"

"Animals have had some input but no, this is a homicide." Wolfe swiped away flies landing on his cheeks. "I think we have one male victim, one female. If you stick to the path and follow me, you won't compromise the crime scene."

"Do you think it is the same killer as the cold case?" Jenna waved Kane forward to go before her, and he noticed her shudder of revulsion.

"I'm not sure." Wolfe's voice drifted on the blast of cold wind whistling through the trees. "This murder is different."

Kane lifted his face, hoping the fresh breeze would dissipate some of the stench, but the odor permeated through his mask, making his stomach roll. He followed close on Wolfe's heels. "How so?"

"You'll see when you get eyes on the corpses."

When Wolfe slowed his pace, Kane picked out Webber's ashen face in the gloom. This deep in the forest, the tall pines blocked out most of the sunlight. He moved to Wolfe's side and swallowed the lump in his throat. It was always the eyes of the dead he remembered. Some clouded over in death; others seemed to stare at him, pleading for help as if life remained. A person's mind could be cruel, throwing people into flashbacks or producing nightmares so vivid they were hard to forget; but for him, his brain tortured him with the memory of his wife's eyes. No matter how hard he tried, he could not push Annie's death stare from his memories of her.

A young woman sat against a tree. The killer had secured her hands above her head, holding them in place with a zip tie looped over a crossbow bolt. Naked and eviscerated with the lower part of her body missing, she barely resembled a human. An involuntary shudder of disgust went through him and he fought down the need to vomit.

No amount of experience helped when dealing with a gruesome murder. So much for the notion the tough TV cops portrayed. They acted with unfeeling nonchalance as if nothing turned their guts then discussed the case over the corpses as if they were storefront dummies. *They are always people to me.* Kane moved his attention back to Wolfe. "This is different from the other murders in one aspect. The woman's face hasn't been touched."

When Jenna gripped his arm with a trembling hand, he glanced down at her. "You okay?"

"I'm fine." Jenna peered at the body. "Oh, no. I'm sure I know her." She moved closer to him. "Isn't she the woman who found the skull? Bailey Canavar?"

The image of the vibrant young woman flashed through his mind. "Yeah, that's her." He indicated to a man flat on his back some distance away. An empty hole replaced his face. "I'm not sure if that's her husband; he had sandy hair."

"It could be bloodstained." Jenna edged past him, stepped around pools of congealed blood, and went to Wolfe's side. "I have an ID on the woman."

Wolfe gave her a patient stare then pushed a marker in the ground beside a body part, moved to the male victim, and lifted his head. "No, this man has black hair." He balled his hands on his hips and looked around. "At least three people had to be involved because, if he tied her up, she couldn't have murdered him."

"We'll leave you to record the scene and take a look around." Jenna turned to Blackhawk. "Do you know of any other trails leading from here?"

"I do but if you look up into the trees, the crows are waiting here, not in any other area. If there was another body, they wouldn't be waiting here for us to leave." Blackhawk shrugged. "But we can circle this area."

Kane turned one-eighty degrees. He had noticed something familiar on a tree and did a visual scan of trees lining the trail, then pushed into the undergrowth and circled back to Jenna. Something wasn't sitting right. "Just a minute." He pulled out his cellphone and accessed the FWP website for the hunting locations in the immediate area. He glanced at Blackhawk. "Do you know if this area has ever been a designated hunting zone?"

"Not that I'm aware."

He moved to one of the trees and rubbed his hand over the rough bark. "See this mark? It is very similar to the damage done by fixing a trail cam. I noticed there is another further down and there are some freshly cut branches over there." He pointed to the spot in the forest he had searched. "It could be a hunter's blind."

"Or a naturalist studying wildlife." Blackhawk's dark eyes moved to Jenna. "Some spend months in the forest and they use trail cams. There are many different varieties of creatures here."

"Yeah, that's likely but I think the killer lured them here—somehow." Jenna turned to Kane. "Have you heard of anyone stalking their victims using trail cams? How would they know they are here? We know this is a rarely used path. If I wanted to kill someone, this is the last place I'd set up a trail cam." She turned and followed Blackhawk into the forest.

Kane hung back and moved along the trail, using his flashlight to check the trees. He noticed further recent damage high up on the trunks. The markings resembled those left from a belt on a trail cam and fixed in the branches to avoid human detection. This setup looked military to him. A trail cam ran in silence so its presence would not alarm animals. It was more usual to place them lower and out in the open. They either collected data to a hard drive within the unit or could run a live feed to smartphones. He turned a full three-sixty degrees to take in every angle. His idea had merit but Jenna was right: How would the killer know people might be on this trail and be able to set up the trail cams before they arrived? Stymied, he rubbed his temple then decided to discuss his findings with the team later.

Duke nudged his leg and he patted the dog on the head. "Seek."

When Duke headed back in the direction of the crime scene, he stared after Jenna for a few moments then hurried after his bloodhound. If his trail cam theory was correct and they did not find Jim's body, he'd be a prime suspect. Jim could have lured his wife and perhaps her lover into the forest and killed them. By the damage to the man's face, whoever killed him had unleashed a whole lot of anger.

CHAPTER TWENTY-FOUR

The way Blackhawk moved through the forest impressed Jenna. He ducked and weaved using his height to search hidden-away places. He would often look behind him and check on her; not that she needed to be coddled but she had to admit the whining trees and unusual silence in the dim, dank forest put her nerves on edge. Especially as Kane had wandered off in a different direction without saying a word but he could take care of himself. Although she had respect for Blackhawk's abilities as a tracker, Kane always had her back. She glanced around, keeping her eyes focused in every direction. The dark shadows between the trees could be hiding a killer waiting for his next victims. She rested one hand on the butt of her pistol. If someone came at them, she would be ready.

One thing was apparent: As they moved away from the stink, finding another body became more remote with each step. After about twenty minutes the awful death smell returned and she filled her mouth with peppermints—at least they would prevent the awful smell permeating her mouth. They had come full circle and Blackhawk bent to examine the animal path leading away from the crime scene. She moved to his side. "Have you found something?"

"Maybe." Blackhawk took flags from his backpack and marked a small area of leaves. "That could be a partial footprint. I'll get Shane to take a look at it." He moved into the bushes and stared up at a tree. "He came through this way. There are traces of blood on this pine and it has a mark on it. Something was secured here and retrieved after the murder." He poked another flag into the bush. "See how the branches are broken? He must have been in a hurry."

Jenna examined the leaves and the trunk of the tree and nodded. "Yeah, Kane saw something similar on the trail. He figured the marks came from trail cams. I'm wondering if the killer set this up before his victims arrived." She smiled at him. "Show Wolfe what you found and thanks, I appreciate your help."

Her mind reeled as they edged their way around the crime scene. She went straight to Kane's side and waited with impatience for him to label evidence bags. "We didn't find another body. It would make sense that if these people traveled here together or met on the trail, we would find their bodies together, or within the radius we searched."

"Yeah, which means we need to find the whereabouts of Jim Canavar." Kane's gaze moved over her face. "It will be difficult to identify the male victim. Whoever did this went out of his way to disguise his identity. His teeth are non-existent and both hands are missing. The killer did not want us discovering this man's name." He frowned. "One thing—the clothes we found have foreign labels, perhaps Chinese."

Jenna nodded. "Blackhawk found a footprint and evidence of possible trail cams. I'm convinced Canavar set this up ahead of time."

" Yeah, it looks more like an ambush every second." Kane lifted his chin and his attention moved away from her. "I'll go and take photos of the footprint." He went to where Blackhawk was in deep conversation with Wolfe.

She pulled out her cellphone and called the Cattleman's Hotel. "May I speak to Jim Canavar? This is Sheriff Alton."

"The Canavars checked out, Wednesday right after breakfast."

Jenna sighed. "Okay, did they have anyone with them?"

"No, but I had the bellhop help them out with their bags. He is right here."

Another male voice came on the line. Jenna introduced herself again and explained who she was looking for. "Do you remember their vehicle?"

"Yeah, it was a rental. A white SUV. I asked him how it was going and he said he couldn't get it back to the airport quick enough and get something else. He tipped me a twenty."

Jenna frowned. "What mood was he in, and did you see anyone else with them?"

"He and his wife seemed happy and they drove off alone."

"Okay, thanks." Jenna disconnected then contacted Bradford at the office. "We found Bailey Canavar and a John Doe murdered. I want you to contact the closest airport and find out the details of a car hired by Jim Canavar. Then get out a BOLO. Next, put out a press release. I want folks to be on the lookout for him and the rental car. We have his details on file in the murder book on the cold case, and get a photograph of him from the Kansas DMV. Make sure you tell them to inform the public not to approach him as he is considered dangerous but to call 911, okay?"

"Yes, ma'am." Bradford took a deep breath. *"I haven't put out a BOLO before but I can handle a press release."*

"Then ask Walters to show you." Jenna chewed on her bottom lip. "Oh, and don't mention anything about the homicide in the press release. Her next of kin hasn't been notified yet."

"Yes, ma'am."

Jenna would have to contact the Canavars' local police and notify them of Bailey's murder. "Can you get me the number of the police headquarters in Kansas? I'll wait."

She pulled out her notepad and scribbled the number then disconnected. After taking in the progress of the crime scene, she called Webber over. "What is the status of the ME's investigation?"

"We have recorded the scene and have bagged the victims." Webber's expression appeared drawn. "I believe Wolfe wants to recreate the murders with Kane then we can pack up and leave."

Jenna nodded. "Good work. After this are you still keen to work with Wolfe?"

"Yes, ma'am." Webber brightened.

She noticed Wolfe and Kane on their way back to the crime scene. "I think Wolfe is looking for you."

"Yes, ma'am." Webber headed in Wolfe's direction.

Jenna made herself comfortable on a boulder with Duke sprawled out at her feet and called the Kansas Police Department. After a few moments, waiting for the desk to connect her to the homicide department in the right division, a woman's voice answered.

"Detective Brennan."

Jenna introduced herself and informed her about Bailey Canavar's death and her suspicions about her husband. "I need to get the press involved and let them know there is a threat in the local area; will you be able to contact the next of kin today?"

"Yeah, right away. I seem to recall a case involving a man named Jim Canavar. I wonder if it is the same person. Give me a moment."

In the small clearing, Kane and Wolfe moved around the crime scene in animated conversation. From what she could make out and from the laser pointer Kane was using, they had determined the trajectory of bullets. One thing sprang out at her: From the damage to the victims, shell casings should be littering the ground but they had not found one. The maniac who did this awful crime had cleaned up the area and removed the trail cams. A chill crawled down her spine. This killer was overconfident and arrogant. He had not only removed all traces of himself, he had lured the couple into an area frequented by bobcats and black bears. He expected the wildlife to clean up his mess.

The voice on the phone startled her. "Yes, I'm still here."

"Well, this is interesting. I checked the DMV info you gave me with the case and it is the same man. Canavar's ex-fiancée went missing and we hauled him in for questioning. Bailey gave him an alibi. In her statement, she said Canavar was staying in Blackwater. She called him every night when his ex-fiancée went missing. He had broken up with his fiancée a few months prior. We checked the phone records. He was where he said and the hotel in Blackwater confirmed he was there. He has stayed in Black Rock Falls before as well."

"Really? So, he does know the area. He didn't give me the impression he'd been here before. Did you find the ex-fiancée?"

"Nope, she is still listed as a missing person. Her new boyfriend is missing too."

Jenna's mind reeled with the implications. "That's interesting. How long ago was this?"

"A little over a year."

"What else can you tell me about Jim Canavar?"

"He works in real estate. I read about his marriage to Bailey, it made the social pages here. His father-in-law owns a number of businesses in the local area and has residences all over the world. He hit the payload when he married Bailey: She is loaded, inherited millions from her grandmother, and there was no prenup. I remember the news team discussing it at the time. Bailey made a point of telling everyone who would listen."

Jenna shuddered as the image of Bailey's damaged body percolated through her mind. "That would give him motive to kill her and leave her in the forest for the animals to devour."

"It sure would. I'll do some digging and see if I can find out anything else of interest and get back to you."

Jenna waved the flies away from her face. "Thanks and pass on my contact details to the next of kin."

"Will do." The line went dead.

As she pocketed her cellphone, she could hear something moving through the forest. Every hair on her body stood on end. She stood, drawing her weapon and scanning the forest. Beside her Duke gave a short bark and lunged forward, tail wagging. "Show yourself, this is Sheriff Alton and I'm armed."

Her loud demand had her deputies pounding toward her, guns drawn, and the next moment, Rowley came around the bend.

"It's Rowley, ma'am. Holy cow something sure stinks around here."

Relieved, Jenna holstered her weapon and turned to her deputies. "Now I have your attention, I've spoken to the homicide department in the Canavars' hometown."

She gave them the information on Jim Canavar and waited for their response.

"That gives him a motive but doesn't explain John Doe." Kane snatched his hat from a branch and pushed it on his head. "We don't know how many people are involved. This looks like more of a thrill-kill to me. Jim could have strangled her and left her for the animals. It would be a clean kill, leaving him the chance to turn up in a few days saying they had gotten lost in the forest. The killer who did this would be soaked in blood. This is another case of overkill."

"Yet I can't link it positively to the cold case as there are too many irregularities." Wolfe removed his gloves and rolled them into a ball. "I'm convinced at least three people are involved and one walked out alive. There is a lot of blood spatter. If the killer was injured, he could have left trace evidence. I'll conduct a blood and tissue analysis. With luck, we might have different blood types but I will run a full DNA on each one."

Jenna sighed and looked at Kane. "Do you know the approximate sequence of events?"

"It's a tough one but let's say Jim wasn't involved. If this murder follows the cold case, the killer could have disabled Jim before killing

Bailey. We found his burner phone smashed and the SIM removed." Kane leaned casually against a tree. "Jim could have come around and been in the fight of his life then escaped. He had no means to call for help and could be lying injured or unconscious somewhere."

"Then who removed the evidence and the trail cams?" Webber rubbed his chin, and his attention moved to Wolfe. "It had to be the killer."

"Or one of the killers." Jenna sat back on the boulder, drawing up her knees. "If John Doe is one of the killers, someone else was here to clean up the evidence."

"Or maybe John Doe was hired to kill Bailey." Kane folded his arms over his chest. "I figure we have it all wrong and John Doe set up the kill zone with the trail cams because Jim wanted to watch Bailey die, then he killed the witness."

Jenna shivered. "His ex-fiancée was never found. How many times has he done this before and where is he now?"

CHAPTER TWENTY-FIVE

It was as if the cave was calling to him, but with two recent kills in the forest, he did not dare go too close to his hiding place. Never mind, his trail cam had night-vision optics, and although viewing through a strange light via his cellphone was not as good as being there, he could at least make sure his captives were safe from predators. The portable electrified fence covering the entrance deterred bears and bobcats but rats would often sneak through.

His fingers itched to pull out his cellphone and inspect the men sitting against the wall of his cave. He loved the way the plastic sheeting pressed tight against their faces, and as each day passed their flesh melted like a candle in a flame. After spending the early morning hunting with a group of men he'd met at the Cattleman's Hotel and acting like one of the boys, he craved some alone time. The men's voices called him back to the now and he offered them a wave. "I'll meet you later in the Cattleman's Hotel for a drink."

He joined the line at the checkpoint to inform the rangers he had nothing to declare then headed for the vehicle his last client had so generously purchased for him. Sticking to the letter of the law was important and he kept his hunting license up to date and on his person at all times. He had enjoyed his time in the forest this morning, but killing animals had lost its allure and he had not bagged a kill. Other things had been on his mind. Amongst the pines, with the pungent smells of gunpowder and death, he had relived the previous day's hunt. Adrenaline coursed through his veins and the need to kill again overwhelmed him. It was just as well his friends couldn't see the images inside his head. To them he was a regular guy.

The sound of air brakes heralded the arrival of the local bus bringing hikers and tourists to the forest. Black Rock Falls ran a bus service from town to the first ranger station every three hours during the peak seasons. He dismantled his rifle and placed it in its case then closed the back of his truck. He took in the eager faces of the people alighting the bus ready for an adventure and bit back a grin. If they wandered into his hunting ground, their visit to Black Rock Falls would remain in their memories forever. The wide-open death stare of Bailey flashed into his mind in a rush of exhilaration. He wanted to relive every second soon.

The bus pulled out in a cloud of dust and headed down the mountain road. Moments later a young couple dashed out of the forest waving their arms. They chased after the bus disappearing around a bend in the road. He stared after them. The woman was just his type, small with dark brown hair, longer than he usually preferred, but he could almost feel the silken strands running through his fingers. Her companion would be a challenge for him—strong and muscular—but the risk would be worth it. He climbed behind the wheel and drove out the parking lot.

As he turned the corner, he almost ran over the couple, thumbs out, hitchhiking. He couldn't believe his luck. On the way back to town, he would be able to get up close and personal with them, perhaps discover their plans. He pulled up beside them. "Heading into town?"

"Yeah." The young man in his twenties smiled. "We got a ride up here. We wanted to find out the best trails and start out fresh on Sunday morning then we missed the darn bus."

He pushed open the passenger door. "Jump in. I'm heading into town."

"Great. I'm Colter and this is my girl Lilly." They slid into the front seat.

He didn't offer his name and bit back a groan as the heat of Lilly's thigh soaked through his jeans. "Where are you staying?"

"The Black Rock Falls Motel." Colter smiled. "We had no idea this area would be packed with people. My idea of an idyllic Sunday hiking in the forest has melted like last year's snow."

"There are many old trails to explore; the forest is endless. You just need to know where to find them." He pulled out onto the road and headed for town. "I can give you directions to an old trail away from the hunting areas and I have a bunch of old maps in the glove compartment. I'll give you one. I can guarantee you won't be bothered by tourists."

"Yeah, but we are dependent on hitchhiking or the bus." Colter sighed. "We can't hike all the way from town, it would take all day. We only have Sunday—we have stuff to do tomorrow and we have to be back in Blackwater for work on Monday."

If he could convince them to explore a secluded spot of his choice, he would have all Saturday to set up his trail cams. Excitement surged through him and he forced his voice to remain calm and disinterested. "If I remember, the bus stops at the mouth of a trail to the waterfall around eight on a Sunday. If you get off there, you can hike across the face of the mountain. It drops down to a secluded trail that runs along the edge of the reservation. It's worth the walk to see the rock pool. It will take you an hour or so to get there but you'll be able to hike back in time to catch the afternoon bus back to town."

"Yeah, and the bus home doesn't leave until late. We'll have time for dinner before we head home." Colter grinned. "Thanks, man."

"It sounds perfect." Lilly glanced at him and her long, black lashes dropped to cover cornflower-blue eyes.

He smiled at her, imagining her eyes filled with terror as she ran from him. *Yes, you are perfect—I can't wait.*

CHAPTER TWENTY-SIX

Saturday

It had been an exhausting week but then murder cases took priority over little things like eating and sleeping. Kane dropped into the chair in Jenna's kitchen, grateful for the chance of a hot breakfast. Since the start of the investigation into Bailey Canavar's murder and the mysterious John Doe, Jenna had the sheriff's department working around the clock. He reached for the cup of hot coffee Jenna had set before him and smiled. "Thanks."

"Ham and eggs okay?" Jenna turned back to the stove. "Oh, and will toast do? I didn't have time to make hotcakes this morning."

"I love toast." He eyed her over the rim of his cup. "Are you coming into the office today, seeing as it's your day off?"

"Of course I am. Do you think I'd take personal time in the middle of a murder case?" She loaded up two plates and placed them on the table.

Kane shrugged and stared at his plate for a few seconds then lifted his chin and looked at the dark circles under her eyes. "I wish I could convince you to grab a couple of hours as we are in a lull at the moment. Until we have more information we have nothing to investigate." He forked eggs into his mouth and chewed.

"That lull could change in a second." Jenna's forehead creased into a deep frown.

He ate slowly, watching her expressions change, then put down his fork. She thought of everyone else's welfare but not her own. Kane cleared his throat. "When we have the autopsy report, we may have more information. Someone will report John Doe as missing and if he is not local, we'll be able to look into why he was in Black Rock Falls." He sipped his coffee, enjoying the rich brew spilling over his tongue. "Jim Canavar hasn't been seen and we have had the hunters, hikers, and rangers on the lookout for him in case he is lying injured somewhere in the forest. The problem is, if he is bundled up in camo hunting gear he'll blend in like the hundreds of other men in town for the hunting season."

"Blackhawk took a few trackers out with him as well but after searching until dark yesterday they found no trace of him. Wherever Canavar is, he isn't injured or Blackhawk would have found a blood trail. I think he got clean away or has plenty of cash with him and is holed up somewhere." She gave him a long look and stifled a yawn. "Blackhawk called me just before you arrived, said he would expand the search this morning, but if Canavar used the more popular trails, tracking him would be difficult."

Kane's cellphone vibrated in his pocket and he pulled it out. "I'd better take this, I'm the 911 contact this weekend." He accepted the call and put his phone on speaker. "Deputy Kane, what is your emergency?"

"This is not an emergency. This is Joe from Avis at the airport. You asked me to inform you when Mr. Canavar returned his vehicle?"

"Yeah, when did he arrive?"

"Well, that's the strange thing. We found his car out front. He left it with the keys inside. He has six more days paid up on his rental as well."

Kane flicked a glance at Jenna. "Don't touch the vehicle, leave it where it is, it could have been used in a crime."

"Oh, I'm sorry, Deputy, I didn't know. I had it steam-cleaned inside and washed. It went out about ten minutes ago with another client."

"Were there any personal possessions inside?"

"No."

"Okay, thank you for letting me know." He disconnected and looked at Jenna. "Well, I guess we can check the airport and see if he took a flight."

"I've had the airport on alert since we found him missing." Jenna lifted her cup. "The security there would have picked him up if he tried to board a flight. He must be in the area or he got a ride with an accomplice."

"With an all-points bulletin out on him and state-wide media splashing his picture all over the news, someone will see him." Kane finished his coffee. "I hope."

She sat at the table and refilled their cups. "Right now, we have Canavar as our main suspect, but for all we know, he had a domestic with Bailey and she took off with John Doe. We have no blood evidence, in fact nothing to prove Jim Canavar was even on scene. He could have hitched a ride with anyone leaving the area. We have people coming and going all the time and he could be anywhere between here and Kansas by now. The timing bothers me as well. It's been one year since the cold case murders. Is it a coincidence or the same killer? I figure we need to expand our search for possible suspects."

Kane nodded in agreement. "So do I."

"Do you have a profile on the killer?" Jenna spooned sugar into her cup and stirred. "If we consider the same person is responsible for both the cold case and the two recent victims?"

Kane poured cream into his coffee. "Yeah, as I said before, I figure the male victims were collateral damage. He murdered Dawson without mutilating him. He was likely paralyzed when he was tied him to a tree. Maybe he made him watch while he mutilated Paige.

The killer centers his attention on the female. He wants to inflict as much damage on her as possible."

"I don't call what happened to the John Doe an easy death."

Kane lifted his cup and sipped. "It was, if everything inflicted on him was post mortem and done to conceal his identity. The killer wouldn't have taken much enjoyment out of his murder." He placed his cup on the table and looked at her. "His thrill comes from the suffering he inflicts on his female victims. I'd say we're looking for a male, mid-twenties to late thirties, has a history of unstable relationships with women. I would say from the use of trail cams and the types of weapons, this person is a hunter and likely has an arsenal of weapons. From what I have seen from the injuries, he places his shots for a reason, likely not to kill but to disable. That takes a certain amount of skill, so perhaps ex-army or similar."

"What keeps nagging at me is the fact Bailey Canavar and Paige Allen, the cold case victim, are similar in appearance." Jenna leaned on the table. "They are about the same height and build and have dark hair."

"Yeah and they have blue eyes as well." He shrugged. "I have two possibilities; one hinges on the type of women he is killing. The viciousness of the murder would make me believe he is taking revenge against a woman who jilted him or humiliated him in some way. Perhaps as a young man, one of them told him he was a lousy lover or embarrassed him in front of his friends." He sipped his coffee and sighed. "The majority of people would get over something like that but that type of incident could trigger a psychopath. I would say he is a player, good-looking or charismatic, and used to having women fall at his feet."

"You mean like Ted Bundy?"

A shiver went up Kane's spine. That would be the last type of psychopath he needed running loose in Black Rock Falls. "Yeah, and if it is, we are in big trouble. This type blends into society as a nice guy and some are married with kids. For some unknown reason, they don't kill their close friends even though they might fit the profile of an ideal victim. They are unpredictable because they are prepared to wait for a potential victim but they do escalate if the type of victims they prefer are plentiful. Remember Bundy pretended he had an injured arm to get women to help him load his groceries or whatever then bundled them into his car. The next thing he went ballistic and broke into a college and killed random women."

"Okay, so we can assume the victims would be the same type of person: age, hair, and so on." Jenna rubbed her temples. "Do we have another possibility?"

"Yeah." Kane stretched out his legs and leaned back in his chair. "Or we have a man with financial troubles, a Casanova type who is in the relationship for the cash." He leaned back in his chair. "This would fit Jim for Bailey's murder but not for Paige Allen and Dawson Sanders. My money is on the first type."

"It wouldn't hurt to pull up any cases of violence against women." Jenna leaned back in her chair. "See what you can dig up."

Kane finished his coffee and stood, collected the dishes, and carried them to the bench. "Okay."

"Leave the plates. I'll put them in the dishwasher later." Jenna's cellphone blasted out a heavy metal ringtone and she picked it up. "Sheriff Alton." She held up one finger to him. "Hold for one second, Detective Brennan, Deputy Kane is here, I'll put you on speaker. Okay, go ahead."

"We've had officers at the airport, no sign of Jim Canavar. His credit cards haven't been used since he arrived in Black Rock Falls but he did withdraw a substantial amount of cash before he left. As far as we know nobody has heard from him."

"No sign of him here either." Jenna's dark lashes covered her expression. "Have you interviewed any of his associates?"

"Yeah, I didn't get too much information from his friends but Bailey's were a fountain of information. The consensus is Jim was a player with other women on the side. They warned Bailey he was after her money and she still refused to sign a prenup. She is insured as well, so he gains millions on her death." Brennan tapped on her keyboard. *"I dug a bit deeper and looked into his finances. He received a huge bonus from her father's company the day they married and I found his current booty call. It was quite a surprise. The booty call is one of three women he meets in a bondage club for group sessions. Apparently, Bailey wasn't aware of his fetish; he planned to ease her into the idea after the honeymoon."*

Kane cleared his throat and glanced at Jenna. "Detective Brennan, this is Deputy Kane. Did they mention if he was dominant or submissive?"

"I had the same question for them. He was dominant and they mentioned bondage and whips. That is all I have for now. I'll keep digging."

"Okay." Jenna pushed a strand of dark hair behind one ear and met Kane's gaze. "Thanks for letting us know." She disconnected and sighed. "Now what?"

Kane rubbed his chin, thinking over the implications. That twist did not fit into his profile. "I may be wrong but I think we need to be looking for him closer to home."

CHAPTER TWENTY-SEVEN

The crisp morning battered against the metal plate in Kane's head, bringing the now familiar throb of an oncoming headache. He had hoped that by winter, he might be over the torture endured from the bitter cold, but the cool morning had proved otherwise. After exchanging his cowboy hat for a thick-lined woolen cap complete with sheriff's department badge, he headed for the office.

The ride into town was like moving through a picture postcard. The wide-open landscape and pine forests climbing endlessly up the mountainside displayed every color on an artist's palette. He had to admit fall in Black Rock Falls was uniquely picturesque. His past life living in Washington, DC, had drifted into a memory and he enjoyed a comfortable connection to Black Rock Falls and its townsfolk. He had a warm feeling of belonging.

A familiar waft of honeysuckle perfume drifted on the air as he strode into the office. He gave Maggie a wave as he passed her at the front counter and headed for his desk. He was about to put Rowley to work searching for local cases of violence against women when his cellphone vibrated in his pocket. He slid it out and glanced at the caller ID. "Morning, Shane, what's up?"

"I called Jenna and she is busy chasing down some leads." Wolfe cleared his throat. *"Could you drop by my office this morning? We have completed the autopsies on the latest victims. I'll write up a report of my findings later but it will be extensive and it would be quicker to show you what we've found."*

Kane stared at his computer screen. "Sure, when?"

"Ah... as soon as possible."

"I'll be there in five." He disconnected and headed for Rowley's cubicle.

He noticed Rowley scrolling through Bailey Canavar's Facebook page and smiled. One thing for sure, Rowley could work alone when it came to investigations. He was an asset to the team and thought outside the box. "Find anything useful?"

"Not really, just the usual." Rowley leaned back in his chair. "I was checking out her friends, seeing who she friended recently, then looking at the cold case victims and seeing if any of them match."

Impressed, Kane smiled at him. "Looking for a stalker?"

"It's all I could think of—we haven't had any viable calls coming in about Jim Canavar as you figured his description could fit most of the men in town at this time of the year. It's as if he vanished into thin air."

Kane nodded. "Nothing from his hometown either, we heard from the detective working the case this morning. I'm heading over to the morgue to get the preliminary autopsy reports. Get onto the main database and track down any violence against women reports in the last couple of years. It's a long shot but we need to know if any of these people knew each other." He glanced around the too quiet office. "The sheriff is chasing down some leads but she'll be in soon."

"Yes, sir."

The sight of Wolfe's teenage daughter, Emily, sitting at the front counter surprised him although he was aware her studies in forensic science often brought her to the morgue. She was sitting beside Webber, and they were so engrossed in whatever they were doing, they did not hear him enter the building. After Wolfe had made a point of not wanting Emily involved with Webber, he slapped a hand on the desk. The sound cracked like a whip. "Morning."

Deputy Webber shot to his feet as if launched from a cannon. "Sir?"

"Deputy Kane." Emily gave him a brilliant smile. "Dad is waiting for you. I've been explaining the new filing system to Cole."

Kane gave Webber a long stare then cleared his throat. "So I see."

"Oh, the latest homicide is incredibly interesting." Emily stood and led the way to the morgue. "Dad has been working all hours to get it finished; he even allowed me to assist, along with Cole of course."

The idea that she found dismembered bodies "incredibly interesting" amused him in a macabre way. He couldn't help grinning at her. "I thought you might. You sure are your daddy's daughter." He shortened his step to keep pace beside her as they walked down the hallway. "I don't think you'll have trouble in medical school."

"I'm studying forensic pathology. I could have studied to become a medical doctor but curing people is not what I have in mind. I want to discover what killed them." She sighed and shook her head. "It depends on what state you live in as to what qualifications you require; some coroners are medical doctors but some can be the local undertaker. I'm studying forensic pathology because it's the most useful, in my opinion, and of course the laws pertaining to homicide." She glanced up at him. "Do you think I'm weird?"

Kane swallowed his chuckle and shook his head. "Not at all. You know what you want in life and that is a good thing. Your dad is a genius. He never stops studying one subject or another and you're going to be the same."

"Hmm, he does have a superior intellect. I guess that's why he spent so much time working for—" She stopped speaking mid-sentence and glanced up at Kane; her cheeks pinked and she coughed. "The local hospital."

Dear Lord, Wolfe had told her he once worked for the government and she nearly blurted it out in front of Webber. He said the first lie to come to his mind to cover her lapse in judgment. "Yeah, he told me, and as a computer programmer, I believe?"

"Yes. That's right." Emily gave him a sideways glance then stared straight ahead.

The smell of the morgue drifted toward them with each step along the stark-white passageway. It had its own unique odor of chemicals and death. The air extractors were working overtime but as Emily pushed through the door, the stink hit him full force. Inside it was cold, very cold, like stepping into a refrigerator, and he figured the temperature was low to slow down the decomposition of the bodies. He pulled a face mask from his pocket and jammed it over his nose.

Wolfe lifted his blond head from a microscope as they entered, then straightened.

"Ah, good. I want to get John Doe back on ice. The smell is getting a bit overwhelming even for me in here."

Kane's stomach gave a backflip at the sight of the two gurneys covered with white sheets, and the memory of the scattered half-eaten limbs and Bailey's staring eyes flashed into his memory. He pushed the images into the dark recesses of his mind and moved his attention back to Wolfe. "Could you get a cause of death from the mess we found?"

"As a matter of fact, I discovered quite a few interesting facts." Wolfe pulled back the sheet on the reassembled remains of John Doe. "I'll explain but first, I found three different blood samples. It is very unusual to find three different blood groups in a group of one hundred people, let alone three."

Intrigued by Wolfe's enthusiasm, Kane rubbed his chin. "Okay."

"The majority of people in America are O Rh-positive. The male victim is B Rh-positive and the female O Rh-positive but I found a few drops of A Rh-positive as well, not a lot. It was on Bailey Canavar's hands." Wolfe moved to a pile of bloodstained clothing. "These have labels from Chinese retailers; add to this the majority of people of Asian descent have type B blood, I would have to assume our John Doe is a visitor from China." His eyes twinkled over his mask. "We have to assume our killer is injured and type A blood. This is also a very common Caucasian blood type. Without a sample of Jim Canavar's blood, I would need to obtain a sample of his mother's DNA to check it against, and mitochondrial matches are the most accurate."

Kane folded his arms across his chest. "So this confirms there were three people involved but why would the blood be on Bailey's hands unless she stabbed her assailant?" He stared at the corpse; seeing the bits and pieces lined up and the Y-shaped stitching on the victim's chest made him think of Frankenstein's monster. "So, can we rule John Doe out as Bailey's killer?"

"Not entirely." Wolfe moved to the gurney. "The killer strangled John Doe. The marks on his neck are clear impressions of thumbs digging into the throat as if the killer lifted him up by his neck. In most cases a chokehold like this restricts oxygen to the brain and we would see petechial hemorrhages of the eyes, but due to the extent of the facial damage, I had to look for proof of cause of death elsewhere." He indicated to the marks on the man's throat.

Kane moved closer. "Yeah, that's pretty clear, but that could have happened in a fight— what proof do you have he was choked to death?"

"He has a fractured hyoid bone." Wolfe turned to an X-ray illuminated on a screen. "See here, and here? His larynx is crushed and a laryngeal fracture would restrict air flow to the brain enough to cause asphyxiation."

Questions stormed into Kane's mind and he gathered his thoughts, staring at the pile of body parts that once was a man. "My first question to make all this relevant is who died first?"

"Time of death is the same. I would estimate they died sometime on Wednesday. I believe Bailey died first but I can only go on the blood spatter evidence. Some of Bailey's blood was overlaid by John Doe's." Wolfe opened images on his iPad and showed them to him. "I found her blood under a discarded shirt, and his blood was on the uppermost side of the shirt and on a bush beside the shirt."

"So if he killed Bailey and was attacked by Jim and killed, why would Jim hack him to pieces before heading for the hills?" Kane stared at the corpse, and vivid memories of crimes involving underworld criminals came to mind. "Did you find his hands?"

"Nope and we found no viable prints at the scene either. I hoped to find evidence on the clothes but the killer or killers wore gloves." Wolfe lifted his chin and his eyes narrowed. "John Doe's teeth are missing as well. They should have been at the scene but the lower part of his mandible is completely gone."

Kane shot him a glance. "I've seen this before to remove a person's identity. Useless now with DNA but you would need a relative to check a sample against. If this man is from overseas, we may never identify him." He made a mental note. "I'll contact the FBI and see if they can track down any possible missing Chinese tourists. They would need visas, and if they overstayed they would be red-flagged." He moved his gaze to the other sheet-covered gurney. "What do you have on Bailey?"

"In layman's terms, Bailey died as a result of a fatal stab wound on the left side of the abdomen that perforated the abdominal aorta, causing a hemorrhage." Wolfe only partially uncovered the body, offering Bailey the utmost respect.

Disassociating himself from the vibrant woman he had met, Kane peered at the corpse and then back at Wolfe. "So after the killer finished having his fun, he used a one-strike kill, which makes me believe he has military or self-defense training." He snorted. "It was almost as if he was offering her mercy."

"I don't think so." Emily moved into Kane's periphery. "Whoever did this has no concept of the word. In my opinion, I think he tired of her; maybe she stopped fighting back or gave in too easily." She looked up at Kane and her pale blue eyes searched his face. "I've been studying psychopathic behavior. I know a victim can't reason with them, and if they try, the violence is usually more intense. The killer only gets enjoyment if the victim is suffering."

Out of the mouths of babes. "Sure, that is the case, but there are so many different types of behavior and some forms merge with others. It's not an exact science. We may have two separate killers, or one who hasn't killed for a year. That in itself would be unusual at the level of violence of the cold case. Looking at the damage here, this killer has killed before and likely often."

"Exactly, and here is where the similarities between the cases merge." Wolfe covered Bailey and moved to the other gurney, pulling back the sheet with a flick of his wrist, displaying the skeleton of Paige Allen. "I found both Paige Allen and Dawson Sanders had gunshot wounds to the lumbar spine; both injuries would cause paralysis of the lower extremities. Bailey's injury was identical; both her injury and Paige's could have been inflicted by the same person—they are precisely the same. Not so for Sanders. As you know he received at least three shots in the back: One severed his spinal cord, the other two were kill shots." He raised an eyebrow. "One thing is troubling me. In my opinion, from the angle of entry, both women were running at the time. The ammunition used is small caliber, so to disable rather than kill."

Kane swallowed hard. He had seen the evidence of prolonged torture many times but placing this murder alongside the facial mutilation of Paige Allen's skull did not fit the profile of his killer. "Okay, so we have similarities, but the cold case looks like a crime of passion. The killer ruined Paige's face so why would he change his MO and not touch Bailey's? I can't see the comparison."

"I can." Webber's voice seemed overloud in the small room. "From the marks on the bones of the forearms, Paige suffered deep lacerations consistent with defense wounds. She was paralyzed but fought back hard." He shrugged. "The killer got mad. He couldn't control her so hit her, likely with his pistol."

"The broken jaw is consistent with blunt force trauma." Wolfe nodded. "I agree the butt of a pistol could have been used as the weapon."

"That would account for the discrepancies." Kane recreated the scene in his head. "Then we have Bailey, who often used her looks to get her own way. Rich and beautiful, she would likely try and reason with her killer or buy her way out of trouble." He glanced at Wolfe. "By the time she allowed him to tie her hands above her head, it was too late."

CHAPTER TWENTY-EIGHT

After the morgue, it was good to get outside and into the sunshine. Kane leaned against his rig and inhaled, replacing the disgusting stench in his lungs with the pine-scented breeze drifting from the forest. To his surprise, Emily came out the door and headed toward him. He smiled at her. She was a credit to Wolfe and one of a trio of fair-haired daughters, who all had their father's brains "Getting some fresh air?"

"Well, no." Emily lifted her chin and gave him a direct, no-nonsense look. "My dad would prefer if I didn't offer an opinion during an autopsy briefing so I've come to apologize."

Kane could see by her expression that she disagreed. "I thought you had a valid point but making conclusions without considering all the possibilities is a mistake."

"I used the Hare psychopathy checklist and going on what we know I—"

"Wait! I have a few other things for you to factor in before you make a decision." He looked down at her, so keen to learn but so young. "As we don't have a suspect to run the test against, you have other things to consider; for instance, the influence of drugs. There are certain drugs that change a person's brain chemistry. Some make people exhibit violent behavior. Look at people strung out on ice, for instance. If they exhibit violent behavior, how could you classify them with any degree of accuracy?"

"Now you're angry with me?" She stared at the ground.

Kane barked out a laugh. "I'm not *angry* with you. I admire your tenacity."

"Dad said you are the best profiler he has ever known. I know he is great at his job but I want to see forensic science from all angles. Knowing more about *why* people kill is important to me." She let out a long sigh. "Do you mind if I ask you questions sometimes? I won't be a pest, I promise."

Kane's cellphone vibrated in his pocket. "You can talk to me anytime but right now I have to take a call." He watched her race back inside, blonde ponytail swinging, and lifted his phone to his ear. "Kane."

"This is Rowley. We have a fight outside Fishing, Guns and Ammunition store. The proprietor of the store called it in. There are three men involved. I'll need backup."

Kane slipped behind the wheel of his car. "What's your position?"

"I'm on Main Street heading there now."

"I'm on my way."

On arrival, he recognized the group of men surrounded by a gathering crowd: Leroy and Abel Finch, the brothers who lived in the mountains near Bear Peak, and the man they had tangled with at the Triple Z, Ethan Woods. The larger man, Woods, was handling himself well against both brothers. The smaller men ducked and weaved around him like annoying flies.

Kane pushed his way through the crowd with Rowley at his side. "Break it up." He blocked a blow from one of the brothers and glared at him. "I said, break it up." He had him turned around and cuffed before he knew what had happened then patted him down and took a hunting knife from his belt. He turned to the crowd. "Nothing to see, folks. On your way."

Rowley soon had the other brother restrained and Kane turned his attention on Woods. "Turn around, hands on the wall, and assume the position."

"No way." Woods wiped a smear of blood from the corner of his mouth and glared at him, fists raised.

"You planning on fighting me now?" Kane gave him a long, hard stare. He had to be joking; one punch and Woods would be nursing a broken nose for weeks. "You wouldn't want to do that, Mr. Woods."

The man lunged forward, swinging his fists, and Kane sidestepped, leaving air in his place. The momentum from Woods' punch unbalanced him and he staggered forward. Kane caught him by the collar and swung him around to face the red-brick wall. He flicked a glance at Rowley. "Add attacking an officer of the law and resisting arrest to the charge of causing a public nuisance."

"I'll stand up in court if needs be as a witness, Deputy." A white-haired elderly man stepped forward. "And so will my son, we got everything with our cellphone camera. He'll tell you everything you need to know." He shook his head. "I don't want no ruckus outside my store—its bad for business." He turned and went slowly up the steps and into the store.

A man stepped forward. "I can send you the pictures."

"Thank you, sir. Rowley here will give you my card. Send the file to me with your details."

Kane pushed Woods against the wall and cuffed him, kicked out his legs, then frisked him none too gently. "Is that your rifle?" He indicated to the Winchester 70 Featherweight leaning against the wall.

"Yes, and I want my lawyer." Woods glared at him over one shoulder. "In case you have forgotten, it's James Stone."

Kane ignored Woods and turned to Leroy Finch. "What happened here?"

"We caught him sneakin' around our cabin." Leroy's mouth turned down. "We got ourselves a night-vision camera, thought we had a bear causing a ruckus, but it turns out it was him. Last night he slept in our barn. He ain't got no right to be creepin' around our property at night."

"And you've got no right to be fighting on the sidewalk. You could have injured a bystander. I'm charging you this time." Kane read them their rights then pushed Woods toward Rowley's cruiser. "All of you inside." He collected Woods' rifle. "I'll be following right behind. Any sign of trouble and you can walk in front of the cruiser. Understand?" He shut the door and looked over at Rowley. "As if we don't have enough to deal with."

"Black Rock Falls, perfect one day, crazy as hell the next." Rowley grinned then swung inside his cruiser.

Crazy as hell, now there's an understatement. Kane followed the prisoners and Rowley into the sheriff's department foyer, passed the counter, then stopped at the sight of Jenna emerging from her office. "Chase down anything interesting?"

"No, all dead ends." Jenna glanced at the retreating figures on their way to the cells. "What have we got?"

"Not much." Kane leaned one shoulder against the doorframe of her office. "I do have a video of the arrest and Woods' assault on me, so we have him to rights. Apparently, Woods has been hanging around the Finch brothers' cabin. I'm not sure who started the fight, but this rifle belongs to Woods, so I'll need to add it to his property list."

"I'll lock it in the weapons locker." Jenna's attention moved to the rifle. "Nice." She lifted the weapon from Kane's hand and checked it out. "I hear these are pretty accurate."

Kane followed her inside. "Not bad for a hunter, but not what I'd have in my arsenal; but then, I don't use my Light Fifty to hunt animals."

The delicious smell of hot coffee filled the room. Kane glanced at Jenna's desk, noting the takeout bag, and his stomach gave a slow rumble. He gave her an apologetic smile, his thoughts on the cookies in his desk and the always full coffee pot waiting in the small kitchenette. "I'll go and interview the prisoners—well, the brothers at least. Woods lawyered up. I called Stone already."

"The Finches can wait ten minutes. Rowley won't have finished processing them yet." She waved him to a seat. "I thought you might be busy, so I've brought lunch for you, and while we're eating you can give me a quick rundown on the autopsy report. Wolfe hasn't sent me anything yet but I'm sure he'll have a preliminary report over to me soon."

Kane dropped into a chair and sighed. "Okay and thanks, I'm famished. I haven't had time for a break this morning." He peered inside the bag and the smell of chili filled his nostrils. "You are an angel."

As he ate, he outlined Wolfe's initial findings. He sipped his coffee, waiting for her to digest the information.

"I figure it's the same killer." Jenna pushed to her feet and went to the whiteboard. "He likely lives out of town but in Montana. We need to scan the databanks for any other similar crimes. If he committed this type of murder before, he could be active throughout the state. People come from all over Montana to hunt here and the same would be for most hunting areas statewide. He would keep his licenses up to date, and visit the checkpoints. He slips into society without anyone noticing."

"Not many serial killers choose hunting seasons; there are too many rangers and hunters roaming around." Kane shrugged. "I don't figure this is an opportunistic thrill-kill. The evidence points to him using trail cams to track his victims, but how does he know they will be in that particular area? He has to know to set up the trail cams beforehand."

"Easy." Jenna's eyebrows rose. "He sets them up all over but in some of the more remote areas. Tons of couples prefer the more secluded trails. They want to be alone." She shrugged as if it was a done deal and returned to her seat. "If he can access the trail cams via his cellphone he waits to see a possible target moving into his area then jumps out and kills them." She held up a finger to stop his reply. "Also, it's unusual for people to steal trail cams because they know the owner would have video evidence of the theft. Hunting season is a perfect time to kill people in the forest. It's hunting season here most months of the year and if a man comes out of the forest blood-spattered, no one would bat an eyelid. They dress their kills on-site."

Kane leaned back in his seat and stretched out his legs. "Point taken. The only possible way I could see this idea working is if he lived in the mountains. He could see a couple heading for one of his trails but he'd still need to get there and hike or ride a horse to their position… *unless* he makes his choice out of couples who plan to camp overnight. The trail cams have audio, so he would be able to listen to their plans."

"And if he was close by, he would have time to get there and set up an ambush." Jenna chewed on her fingers then stared frowning at the whiteboard. "Leroy and Abel Finch live in the mountains near Bear Peak and they caught Ethan Woods prowling around their cabin at night. The three of them are volatile. Do any of them fit your profile?"

Kane considered her question. "The brothers are an unknown quantity: One is dominant and that alone would fit the profile of those who kill in pairs. They live in the forest, which could make them a possibility as well." He thought for a moment. "Ethan Woods is a regular visitor and used to be a resident of Black Rock Falls, so he would know the area. He has money to purchase the best equipment so I find it hard to believe he slept in the Finches' barn." He looked at Jenna. "Yeah, he is a possibility as well, especially as he lawyered up the moment I arrived."

"Hmm." Jenna moved around her desk to the whiteboard. "I'll add their names to the suspects list."

Kane rubbed his chin. "I sure would like to take a look at their cellphones and see if they have a trail cam app and any recent footage."

A rapping came on the door and Rowley's face appeared. "The lawyer, Mr. Stone, is here, and here's the arrest files on the Finch brothers." He handed Jenna two folders.

"I'll be there in a moment." Jenna's dislike for Stone was evident. "I should have stayed at home."

CHAPTER TWENTY-NINE

"Ma'am." Rowley's voice came from behind Jenna. "I need a word with you before you speak to Mr. Stone."

Jenna waved Kane toward the waiting lawyer and turned to Rowley. "Sure, what's wrong?"

"It's about his client, Ethan Woods." Rowley's voice had dropped to just above a whisper. "If you recall, I was asked to search for cases concerning violent crimes, especially against women?"

She stared at him, wishing she had a fast forward remote to aim at him. "Yeah, I recall asking Kane to initiate a search."

"Well, Woods was red-flagged on the cases I looked at this morning. He was never charged but had an Order of Protection against him by his ex-wife for domestic violence and it came up in his divorce."

The hairs on the back of her neck stood straight up. "Thanks, that is very useful information. Does Kane know about this?"

"No, he went to the autopsy before I had time to inform him." Rowley shuffled his feet. "We've been kinda busy since then, ma'am."

"So I gather." Jenna sighed. "We'll need the information right away. Will you print up a copy of the file and bring it down to the interview room?"

"Yes, ma'am."

Jenna turned and met James Stone. Dressed in an Italian silk suit, he stuck out like a sore thumb in Back Rock Falls amidst the cowboys and hunters. She offered him a smile although he was the last person she wanted to deal with today. From the hostile look he sent her way, he was a changed man from the one who had pestered her for a date the previous year. "Good morning, Mr. Stone."

"You used to call me James, and I'm sure we can continue to be civil to each other." Stone moved close and she could smell his aftershave. "You make a point of avoiding me every time I come here and you've hardly said two words to me in ages. Am I so abhorrent to you?"

For goodness' sake, she had only had dinner with him a couple of times and that was ages ago. "Not at all. I wasn't looking for a relationship at the time and tried to explain but you refused to take no for an answer."

"So you asked the Neanderthal to intervene."

"I didn't have to." Jenna forced the smile to remain and tried to prevent it turning into a grimace. "It's my deputy's job to watch my back." She changed the subject, wanting to remain on a professional standing with him. "I have your client in the interview room. We would like to speak with him today as he is facing charges of assaulting a law enforcement officer and resisting arrest. I gather from speaking to Deputy Kane, this might include criminal trespassing as well."

"A $500 fine at best." Stone gave her an annoyed look but moved closer, invading her personal space. "Can't you make the call on these minor infringements rather than fill the court with such trivial matters?"

"Assaulting one of my deputies is not trivial, and I'm here to enforce the law, Mr. Stone." Jenna lifted her chin and glared at him but stood her ground. If he thought he could intimidate her, he had sure picked the wrong person. "I let your client walk with a warning last time as the proprietor of the Triple Z agreed not to press charges once Mr. Woods agreed to pay restitution for the damages, but this is out of my hands. We have witnesses. He will be charged."

"Do you want me to escort Mr. Stone to the interview room, ma'am?" Kane appeared behind her without a sound and dropped into his expressionless mode as he looked down at Stone.

He always has my back. Jenna straightened. "Yeah and I'll speak with Mr. Stone's client after I've interviewed the other parties in the case."

Relieved, she turned away from Stone's annoyed look to find the interview room holding one of the Finch brothers. After swiping her card on the reader, she moved into the room. As usual, Rowley had taken the precaution of attaching the prisoner's handcuffs to the ring on the table. She placed the arrest file on the desk and took a seat. An odor of stale sweat crawled across the table toward her and she leaned back in her seat to gain a few inches of fresh air. The man before her sported an unkempt beard and long, shaggy, dirty-blond hair. The two brothers were like bookends and she could not tell them apart. "State your name for the record, please."

"Leroy Finch, ma'am."

Surprised by his courtesy, she opened the folder with his name on the front cover then took out her pen. "You have been read your Miranda rights and have waived the right to an attorney. You are aware I am planning to charge you with creating a public nuisance?"

"Yeah but we didn't start the fight. It was self-defense." Leroy slumped back in his seat and picked at his dirty fingernails. "I noticed Woods comin' out of Guns and Ammo. He's been trespassin' on our property. I know for a fact he has been sleepin' in our barn. I wanted to give him a warnin'. I told him the next time he trespassed on our land, I would shoot him." He gave her a surly expression. "You know darn well I'm within my rights. That man figures because we live in the mountains we're stupid or somethin'."

Jenna understood he was referring to the ancient 'castle law' and the right to use force to protect home or property. "Why did you wait until now to call him out? And if you had a problem, why didn't you inform us?"

"Nothin' says we have to call in the law to deal with protectin' our property." He scraped his chair closer to the table. "You wouldn't have done nothin' anyways."

Jenna made a few notes then lifted her gaze back to him. "The problem is, Mr. Finch, you do have the right to defend your property but the castle law does not apply to outside your property. You can't brawl in the streets."

"There you go again, blamin' me." He bent to his handcuffed hands and rubbed his nose. "I walked up to Woods, told him to keep off our land. He told me to get lost, that I had no proof." He gave her a smile, displaying yellowing teeth. "When I said I had night-vision cameras he went real quiet. Then he offered me five grand to delete the files." He snorted. "I laughed at him and he went ballistic and tried to steal my cellphone. Stupid man, I told him I had copies."

Jenna could almost see his mind working on a scheme. She glared at him. "I hope you weren't planning on blackmailing him?"

"Woods?" Leroy's black eyes searched her face. "Nope and I wouldn't take money from him either. His lawyer would have found a way to have us sent to jail for life. No, I just wanted to see the rich boy squirm."

She needed to see the footage on Woods. The Finches' cabin was no more than a half-hour walk from the Canavar murder scene. "Okay. Is your footage date-stamped?"

"Sure is."

"I'll need to see it, and I want you to write down everything you told me and sign it." She pushed a pad and pen toward him.

"It's on my cellphone and you can make a copy." Leroy smiled. "I'll write that down too."

"Thank you, it will help with your case." She made a few more notes then stood. If his story checked out, she would not be pressing charges. "You'll have to wait until I speak to the others involved. Would you like a drink?"

"I would, thank you, ma'am. Coffee, black."

She walked into the hallway and went to bring Kane up to date. He was leaning against the wall waiting for Stone to finish speaking with his client. "I have written permission to access the footage from the Finches' night-vision cams. If Woods was in the area at the time of the murders, he goes to the top of our list of suspects." She glanced up at him. "We'll have to sweet talk them into giving us access to their barn as well. Woods stayed there overnight."

"If Woods is our killer, it would be a perfect place to wash up and change, maybe dispose of his bloody clothes." Kane's mouth turned down in disgust. "From the crime scene, the killer would have been soaked in blood; problem is, night-vision cameras aren't likely to pick it up. We'll have to hope he left trace evidence behind."

Jenna thought for a moment, adding pieces to the puzzle. "We need to establish a timeline. I'll grab a coffee for Leroy Finch then speak to his brother. I want in on the Woods interview—call me when Stone has finished." She chewed on her bottom lip. "I want you to take the lead and see what information you can extract from Woods."

"Yes, ma'am, but I don't want a conflict of interest over the assaulting an officer charge. It might be better to drop that charge if you want me involved." Kane smiled at her. "I hope Woods is our guy. It would be good to wrap this one up."

"Sure." Jenna chuckled. "I love an optimist but don't forget this is Black Rock Falls."

"Yeah, I know." Kane's brow crinkled. "Beautiful one day, crazy as hell the next."

"Now you're sounding like a Montanan."

*

Jenna's interview with Abel Finch was a duplicate of his brother's account, and as they had separated them since the incident, she needed to hear Woods' version. The footage on the cellphone proved without doubt Woods was on the Finches' property on Tuesday and Wednesday nights. She entered the interview room with a certain amount of unease at the thought of dealing with James Stone again. She could see Kane had given both men a beverage and was reading through the file when she arrived. After sitting beside Kane, she turned to Stone. "This interview will be recorded." She lifted the remote control from a desk drawer and switched on the camera.

After all parties had introduced themselves, she turned to Kane. "Deputy Kane will be conducting the interview."

"That is a conflict of interest." Stone glared at her. "He is the officer my client is accused of striking."

Jenna leaned forward in her chair. "I am fully aware of the charges, Mr. Stone. Deputy Kane has withdrawn the assault charge and will be questioning your client about trespassing."

"Mr. Woods, can you tell me why you found the need to sleep in the Finches' barn on Tuesday and Wednesday nights?" Kane wore a bored expression as he twirled a pen in his fingers.

"I was in the forest, heading for a hunting area, when I got turned around." Woods shrugged nonchalantly. "It was dark. I saw the barn and took shelter."

"I see." Kane scribbled on the file. "So twenty-four hours later, you were still lost?"

"Yes, I walked a complete circle and ended up back at the barn." Woods glanced at Stone, who was glaring at Kane. "I slept there again and left the next morning. I heard voices and found a hunting party and went back to the road with them."

"I gather you don't own a cellphone?" Kane's attention fixed on Woods' face. "If you get lost, there are rangers all over to help you, or you can use the GPS app on the phone."

"My battery needed recharging."

"Why didn't you ask the Finch brothers for assistance or directions back to the trail?" Kane lifted his gaze and one eyebrow rose in question. "After two nights' sleeping rough, it would have been the sensible thing to do."

"They had signs all over, no trespassing." Woods glanced at Jenna. "You understand what these mountain men are like, Sheriff. They shoot first and ask questions later."

"So you admit to entering a signposted property and sleeping in their barn?" Kane's lips quirked up into a half smile.

"What can they do? Sue me?" Woods snorted. "They wouldn't have the money to pay for a lawyer."

"How far did you walk on Wednesday, and in what direction?" Kane leaned forward in his chair and Woods' hands trembled slightly. "Do you remember any landmarks, for instance?"

"I was told there is an old trail that cuts along the bottom of Bear Peak; it is a shortcut to one of the hunting grounds. I took the trail from the road I was told ran into it but it wound around everywhere, split into so many different paths I lost my way." Woods shrugged. "Real men don't ask for directions and I found my way out in the end."

"My client is happy to pay the Finches for accommodation." Stone's smile was like granite. "If they'll drop the trespassing charges."

"We'll speak to them." Kane's stare remained on Woods. "Since you arrived in Black Rock Falls, you have been involved in two fights, and I see you have an Order of Protection against you. You have a history of violence against women as well." His expression was menacing. "You admit to being in the vicinity of Bear Peak on

Wednesday, which happens to coincide with a double murder." He laid the graphic images of Bailey Canavar and John Doe on the table before Woods. "Did you murder this couple?"

"You don't have to answer that question, Ethan." Stone looked straight at Jenna. "My client has nothing further to say, Sheriff."

Thrilled at how ruffled Kane had made both Woods and Stone, Jenna shrugged. "Very well, as we have video evidence of the trespassing, plus your client has admitted to being in the vicinity of two vicious murders and has a history of violence, we will be charging him and remanding him in custody."

"James, get me out of here." Woods' eyes flitted to the images and back to Stone. "I'm not rotting in their stinking cells until I'm cleared in court."

Jenna collected the photographs and slipped them back into the file. "All deals are off the table and we'll be opposing bail."

"You have a few minor infringements and circumstantial evidence at best." Stone barked out a laugh then stood and patted Woods on the shoulder. "Don't worry, we'll play their game for now, but I'll have you out of here before dinner." He picked up his briefcase and glared at Jenna. "Let me out of here. I'll wait in your office for the documents."

Oh, will you now? Jenna stood and used her card to unlock the door. "There are seats out front. My office isn't a waiting room."

She noticed Rowley in the hallway supervising the Finch brothers. "Take Woods down to the cells. Did you get statements from the brothers?"

"Yes, ma'am, and they are the same." Rowley followed her back into the room and collected Woods.

Jenna leaned against the door and smiled at Kane. "I like your style. Do you think he is our killer?"

"On body language when he looked at the images, no, but then killers are adept at hiding their true nature. The way Stone jumped in to stop the questioning then didn't bother to confer with his client would make me believe he is covering for him." Kane rubbed his chin, making a rasping sound. "I believe we can deal with the Finch brothers. If they give us permission to send a forensics team to their barn, we could let them go with a warning. From what we know about Woods, it sure looks like an unprovoked attack on the Finches to me. Woods is a loose cannon and an idiot used to getting his own way." He sighed. "You know as well as I do, Stone is correct—we have circumstantial evidence for Woods' involvement in the murder. We need proof."

Jenna considered his argument then nodded. "Okay, go and cut a deal with the Finches." She pulled open the door. "I figure Woods ticks all the boxes for our murder suspect, and if he gets out of this on a technicality, we'll be releasing a possible killer back into society."

If Jenna's stress level had gotten any higher, her head would explode. She sucked in a few deep breaths, which did nothing at all to calm her fury, and gaped at the document in her hand, rereading it for a third time. Not one hour after she had delivered Woods' charge sheet to James Stone, his client was out on bail. She watched Woods' smug expression as he followed his lawyer out of the building, then after listening to Rowley's rendition of the meeting with the judge, she thrust the paperwork into Kane's hands. "The judge said we can't hold Woods without bail on misdemeanors, and any evidence we have against him may be brought up in a court hearing one week from Monday. Stone vouched for him, insisted he wasn't a flight risk and would be staying at the Cattleman's Hotel until his hearing."

She clenched her jaw and went into her office with the overpowering need to slam the door behind her, maybe three or four times.

Wolfe followed her inside and gave her a concerned look. "There's another problem."

Jenna wanted to tear out her hair and scream like a banshee. "What now?"

"We don't have a sample of Woods' DNA to make a comparison."

CHAPTER THIRTY

Sunday

Tall pines creaked and the forest came to life with the first rays of dawn. Wildlife moved around him, oblivious to his position in the blind. A wild turkey pecked and scratched at the ground within arm's reach, and between the rough tree trunks, the antlers of an eight-point buck moved as the animal grazed not ten feet away. The air was crisp from the overnight shower and the forest still held the scent of rain. He checked his weapons with pride; each carried the comforting smell of gun oil. His arsenal was impressive and he had hidden caches of guns and ammunition along the trail.

He had arrived late at night, spent a few hours dozing, then risen in the early hours of Sunday morning. The preparation had become a ritual. He honed the blades on his knives to be as sharp as a cutthroat razor then cleaned and loaded his guns. After pushing extra clips into the pockets of his camouflage pants, he pulled on black gloves. Made from soft kid leather, they molded to his hands and did not interfere with his trigger finger. The gloves offered him added protection against discovery when he covered them with a latex pair for the kill. He sat in the blind and reviewed the footage from his trail cams. From time to time, he glanced at the countdown.

Not long now, before his prey would arrive. His mind filled with fantasies. How would he kill them this time? So many choices and so many thrills to enjoy over and over again via the trail cam footage.

He wondered if others enjoyed the same sport as him? The idea of sharing his videos enthralled him. He checked the time again. The ultimate game of cat and mouse would begin soon.

Covered from head to foot, not one inch of him was visible, but to give his prey the ultimate in fear, he decided to wear a skull mask. As usual, his mic was fitted with a voice distorter. Anyone who viewed his footage would not recognize him but later, alone in his room, he could relive the kills through his body cam and be able to hear each scream and plea for mercy.

He wondered if the shy Lilly Coppersmith would turn into a wildcat once threatened. She gave the impression of being an introvert, but he had a talent that enabled him to push people to their limits. It was all part of the game, and even a mouse if threatened would bite. Oh yeah, he would bring out her primal instincts, he just had to frighten her enough to put on a good show. He chuckled.

His targets had camped in a secluded area not ten minutes' walk from his current position. After a night of passion, the couple had fallen into a deep sleep and he had snuck into their camp. They had not stirred when he rifled through their backpacks and removed the SIMs from their phones. He could have killed them in their sleep, but why spoil the fun?

Deep in the oldest and densest area of the forest, the trail they had chosen wound in and out with so many hairpin bends and switchbacks it was like a maze. Once threatened, the pair would be running around in circles. With the boyfriend disabled, he figured Lilly would go through the same panic-driven stages as the others before her instinct to survive kicked in—and then the fun would begin.

The disbelief on the women's faces when they realized he was hunting them empowered him. The way they tried to reason with him then ran about wildly in all directions like rabbits excited him. Images of what he planned to do to Lilly filtered into his mind, lifting his heart rate. She would try desperately to escape but would be at his mercy. He would catch her with ease. He craved the smell of her fear and the crimson sight of warm, pumping blood.

Women never stood a chance against him. He longed to see her terror but submission was never an option; he needed her to fight back and make him work for the kill. She could scream, but this far into the forest, not a soul would hear her cries. Then she would realize he had claimed her. She was going to die very slowly. Some fought to the end and made good sport but they all died looking at him.

As the couple emerged from their camp, hitting the trail with a small backpack, he glanced at the countdown screen. They would arrive at his position just in time. He adjusted his body cam and excitement tingled through him. *Let the games begin.*

CHAPTER THIRTY-ONE

As if his brain was attempting to block out the horror playing out before him, all the little things filtered into Colter Barry's mind. It had been the best morning of his life. The early-morning sun had glistened on raindrops, dressing the bushes alongside the track with diamonds. The earthy smell of the forest laced with pine and wildflowers had combined with Lilly's unique scent, spicy and so darn familiar. As she strolled beside him, her dark hair had fluttered in the wind to brush his cheek in a caress. They had walked hand in hand, and he had pointed out the brown eyes of a magnificent buck some moments before it had bounded away, its powerful muscles bunched under a tight glossy coat.

Colter swallowed the sob in his throat, too scared to make a sound. The stranger would find him soon. He could hear him, cursing in his robotic voice and methodically moving along each of the animal tracks leading from the main trail. The image of Lilly, cheeks wet with tears, eyes pleading with him for help as the animal killed her, slammed into his mind and he swallowed a sob of grief. At first, he could not believe what was happening. The man had emerged from the bushes and in a voice straight from hell told him he would have the pleasure of watching Lilly die.

Agony ricocheted through his head from the first punch, and he fought like a man possessed to protect Lilly, but he was no match for the skill of their tormentor. Knifed in the spine and tied to a tree, helpless, he protested as much as the gag would allow, but the more he complained, the crueler the stranger became. His eerie voice lingered in his brain. The animal described each tortuous move as if waiting for permission to continue. It was as if Lilly's screams urged him on, but when they ceased and she fell into unconsciousness, he would pause and look at her.

"Stay awake, Lilly, I don't want you to miss anything," his voice had taunted just before he slapped her awake. "Your boyfriend is annoying me; maybe I'll burn him alive. Wouldn't that be fun?"

The beast had laughed at him then tipped a can of gas over his head. The fuel burned his eyes and fumes engulfed him, but the expected flick of a lighter followed by searing hot flames did not come. So sure he could not escape, the maniac returned to Lilly, and long after the life had left her eyes, the killer continued to use his knife, engrossed in his macabre dissection and oblivious to his presence.

Colter shook in terror, then in a spasm of pain the feeling in his legs returned and he wiggled his toes. Desperate to get away, he picked at the rope holding him to the tree and gasped with relief when the knot broke free.

He could do nothing for Lilly now, and his only chance for survival was to reach the hunters' check station, an hour's walk from his current position. Dizzy and trembling, he crawled into the bushes on numb legs and slid between trees and clumps of undergrowth. Horrified, he noticed the wound in his back had dripped blood, leaving a trail straight to him. The basic survival training a teacher had rammed down his throat at a school camp years ago slipped into his mind. *Find shelter, tend the wound, and get help.* That would be useless if the killer found him in minutes.

Clamping shut his jaw to prevent escaping moans of pain, he dragged a fallen branch over the blood spots, making sure the leaves and pinecones would conceal his tracks. He backed up, dragging the branch in his wake, and headed to the shade of a massive boulder surrounded by bushes. He crawled under the clump of thimbleberry guarding the entrance and rolled beneath the huge rock, disturbing a porcupine. The animal flashed its teeth then climbed over him, tearing his flesh with its sharp claws, and bounded into the undergrowth. *I need help.*

Colter slid the cellphone from his back pocket and stared at the screen in disbelief. He flipped it over and forced his trembling fingers to remove the battery cover then cursed under his breath. Someone had removed the SIM. No help was coming.

It was like living a nightmare; he had zero chance against a man loaded for a bear and intent on burning him alive, but he owed it to Lilly to bring her killer to justice. He listened and peered through the bright-green leaves of the thimbleberry but only heard the chatter of red squirrels. Safe for now, he made no sound, eased out of his backpack, took out one of the four bottles of water and flushed his eyes. He stripped off his jacket and shirt and found the medical kit; using his fingers to locate the injury on his back, he managed to push a thick dressing over the stab wound.

His long, showerproof jacket had protected his pants from the gas, but his T-shirt was soaked down the front and the smell would bring the killer to him. He found the woolen hoodie and thermals Lilly had packed for him and pulled them on. The sight of her blood-soaked body and staring, sightless eyes slammed into him and his teeth chattered. *Lilly. Oh God, Lilly.*

The smell of gas wafted around him, and in a panic, he balled up the gas-soaked clothes, pushed them into a deep crevice, and covered them with forest debris. Exhausted and trembling, he drank the rest of the water, eased into his backpack, and listened. His heart went into overdrive at the unmistakable sound of a man crashing toward him through the forest. Frozen with fear, he pressed against the boulder, pulling his black hoodie around his face, and watched the saplings move and birds fly into the air as the killer rampaged toward him.

Colter cringed as the man dressed in army camouflage gear and wearing a skull mask appeared not ten yards from his hiding place. He had slowed and sniffed the air, moving his head slowly from side to side, but Colter was upwind of him and the smell of gas was long gone. The killer took a few steps in his direction. So close now, Colter could smell the sweat on him, see the rifle over one shoulder and the hunting knife in one hand. When the killer bent down and searched the ground on the other side of the bush, Colter's heart beat so fast, he could feel it pounding against his ribs. His breath made a wheezing sound and he pressed his fist hard against his mouth and tried desperately to control his breathing.

Twigs cracked under the killer's blood-soaked hiking boots. The camouflage pattern did little to cover the blood spatter on his legs. Bile rose in Colter's throat, filling his mouth as a scarlet stream dripped from the knife. *Lilly's blood.*

The leaves of the thimbleberry shook and he could hear the killer's heavy breathing. Terrified, Colter waited for the face of death to part the bushes and find him. Tears pricked his eyes; he had failed to defend the woman he loved and now he would never be able to avenge her.

When the boots crunched away, moving out of his line of vision, he sucked in a shuddering breath and listened. The only sound was the wind blowing through the trees, no birds, nothing else at all. He needed to get away but the killer could be waiting for him out of his line of vision. Unsure what to do, he sat staring at the forest for some time. When the birds returned to the trees, he crawled out of his hiding place and scanned the forest for any sign of movement. Confident he was alone, he grasped a tree and stood slowly. Tingling had replaced the partial numbness in his legs. He glanced around to get his bearings. Downhill in the distance he could make out a firebreak cutting across the forest. He took a few hesitant steps; apart from the pain in his back, his legs worked fine.

Muscles bunched and arms pumping, he ran flat out, weaving in and out of the trees. The branches lashed at his face and his heart was about to burst in his chest when he heard a shot way in the distance. He darted to one side. Too late. Pain slammed through his head and he faltered. As if in slow motion, a part of one ear overtook him on a crimson tide. Blood, hot and sticky, poured down his neck but he kept running.

Ahead, two men emerged from the forest carrying rifles. Both stopped and stared at him then came running toward him. The men's faces blurred, and in fear for his life, he turned to run away. Footsteps thundered toward him and he staggered then tumbled face first into darkness.

CHAPTER THIRTY-TWO

Kane tossed wet clothes into the dryer and headed to the kitchen to pour himself a well-earned cup of coffee. Glad of a few hours' respite from the murder investigation, he'd been up since dawn, fixing up the stables and doing his chores. After so long in the military, he found himself cleaning at midnight to keep his cottage up to his high standard. It also gave him some quiet time to mull over the investigation. Weary from the continuous long hours, he wondered if the increased crime rate had become the new normal for Black Rock Falls. Although, he could not really complain—yeah, they had investigated four murders this year, but in Washington they often had reports of four of five violent crimes daily.

Duke nudged his leg, reminding him to refill his bowl. He patted the bloodhound on the head and scooped biscuits into his bowl. "I'll buy you meat soon but right now you eat what the vet recommends."

He straightened at the sound of Jenna's SUV heading for his cottage. It was Sunday but she had dropped into the office to check on a few things. One thing for sure, Jenna put her job first and her personal life at the bottom of the list. He took two cups from the shelf and poured the coffee then added cream and sugar to both. His door opened and Jenna peeked inside. He held up a cup. "Coffee?"

"Lunch?" Jenna waved an Aunt Betty's Café takeout sack in the air. "Wow, your house is sparkling." She moved to his side and sniffed then made a humming sound.

"When do *you* get time to do all of this?" She tossed her jacket onto a chair then sat at the kitchen table and took the coffee with a long sigh.

He sat down opposite and took in her casual appearance. She looked good in a T-shirt and jeans with her hair mussed up from the wind. "Have you eaten?"

"Nope." She sipped her coffee and sighed. "It was a waste of time going into the office. There is nothing new to report. Rowley is handling the 911 line. We've had no positive sightings of Canavar, and although we know he had supplies with him, he could have stayed at the Black Rock Falls Motel. With no evidence to prove Canavar was at the murder scene, I can't obtain a search warrant. No one has reported an Asian man missing either." She shrugged. "Whoever he was, he didn't stay in Black Rock Falls or Blackwater and he must have had wings because I have no idea how he arrived here in the first place."

Kane opened the bag and took out the pile of wrapped sandwiches and cakes then placed them on the table. "The bus drivers don't recall him but they have a ton of passengers. I checked the hunting licenses and none were issued to anyone matching his description either." He bit into a turkey on rye and chewed slowly, enjoying the unique flavor of Aunt Betty's special BBQ sauce.

"I've spoken to the guy on the counter at the Cattleman's Hotel as well." Jenna gave him an exasperated look. "He told me Woods spent most of his time in his room but he did have dinner with Mayor Petersham and his wife." Her expression turned to one of concern. "Wolfe and Webber are at the Finches' cabin. I hate dragging Wolfe away from his girls all weekend but he insisted it was his case and he wanted to check out the barn before any trace evidence deteriorated."

"He'll need time off on Monday. His youngest, Anna, is in a school play." Kane leaned back in his chair as Jenna looked at him with interest. "Without their mom, she needs him to be there."

"Maybe she needs us all to be there." Jenna lifted her chin and sorrow filled her eyes. "Wolfe as well. He treats you like a brother and you spend hardly any time with him."

"I do when we're not busy. I usually end up shooting hoops with his middle daughter, Julie." He shrugged. "As sheriff, maybe you should throw a barbecue once a month and invite the team?"

"That's something to consider." Jenna took a bite of a bagel with cream cheese.

Kane smiled at her. "Getting back to Woods. We can't rely on Wolfe finding anything. The killer is smart and knows how to cover his tracks. I figure we need to dig into Woods' past and see what he has been doing and where he goes. If we can link his movements to any similar unsolved murders in the state, we might be able to hold him on suspicion."

"With Stone representing him, we'll need something substantial."

"Yeah, I—"

Jenna's ringtone interrupted his reply.

"Sheriff Alton. What? Hold a minute while I put you on speaker, Deputy Kane is with me." She gave Kane a look of disbelief. "Go ahead."

"This is Ranger Harris, we have what we thought was a gunshot victim up here on check station five."

"Is the victim alive?" Jenna chewed on her bottom lip.

"Yeah, he is raving some. Said a man killed his girlfriend up near Bear Peak. Two hunters found him and called it in. They said they heard a single rifle shot. We called the paramedics and he is on his way to the hospital. One of my men will stay with him until you get there."

"Thank you. Did you get the vic's name?" Jenna motioned for Kane to pass her a notepad and pen. "And I need the details of the men who found him."

Harris gave the information and Jenna gave Kane a worried look. "Was Colter Barry coherent enough to give a position where the alleged murder took place?"

"No, ma'am, but it must be some ways west of the firebreak. The hunters were crossing through an old hiking area to report here. I have two men and a dog I can spare to go back up there with them and get eyes on the area. The birds will be circling by now if there is anything dead in the forest. I figure it will take about an hour or so to find it."

"Yeah, thanks, and if you find a body, don't disturb the scene. Call Shane Wolfe, the ME, right away. He is close by at the Finches' cabin, west of Bear Peak, this afternoon. If you give him the coordinates, he will meet you there with his assistant, Webber. They'll be on horseback." She relayed his details. "I'll head to the hospital and see what Mr. Barry has to say."

"Roger that. I'll be sure to keep you informed, ma'am." The line went dead.

Tiredness drained from Kane as an adrenaline rush took over. He emptied his coffee cup and stood. "I'll go and get changed."

"No time, just grab your weapon and cred pack. I'll help you get the horses loaded." Jenna sighed and shrugged into her jacket. "So much for a lazy Sunday afternoon."

CHAPTER THIRTY-THREE

Anger trembled through his fingers as he dismantled the last trail cam and pushed it into his rucksack. If his scope had not picked up the two men walking out of the forest, he would have gone in to make sure he made the kill, and they would have discovered him soaked in blood. Dammit, he would have enjoyed playing with Colter Barry.

From the crimson spray, his target had taken a headshot, and the likelihood of him surviving would be remote, but soon the rangers would be out searching the area. It would take the two men at least an hour to get help, carrying a wounded man. He figured he had plenty of time to do the cleanup and get to his designated check station before going home.

He retraced his steps, making sure he kicked dirt over any boot marks. Satisfied, he strolled back to take one last look at Lilly. After activating his body cam, he walked around her, bending close to get the shots he desired. When his prey went quiet and their eyes fixed on him, seeing nothing, his hunger to hear them scream was sated, but like taking the last lick of an ice cream, he wanted more. Careful to avoid the pool of congealing blood around her, he bent to kiss her mouth. It felt strangely exciting through the cotton mask, slack and cold against his lips. In a rush of euphoria, he decided the next guest he would take to his cave would be a woman.

He would visit her often.

Half an hour later, he reached his cave and deactivated the electric fence across the entrance. Pulling out his flashlight, he slipped inside and switched on the lamp hanging on one wall. Here he could wash up, change his clothes, and pick up his spare hunting rifle before reporting to the rangers and leaving the hunting area. He checked the power gauge on the solar battery and smiled. It never let him down. He turned in a slow half circle and removed his mask then scanned the line of plastic-wrapped corpses. Black, empty eye sockets watched his every move as they grinned at him. He chuckled at their welcome. "Hello, boys, did you miss me?"

CHAPTER THIRTY-FOUR

Rain pelted down in a storm that seemed to come from nowhere and Jenna was glad to have had the forethought to grab their rain ponchos before leaving. The swish of the windshield wiper blades sounded melodic and almost soothing. Jenna leaned back in her seat, glad Kane had offered to drive them into town. She glanced over at him, noticing the way the nerve in his cheek ticked when he was thinking. "If this is another murder, our killer is escalating."

"Maybe." He glanced at her before returning his attention to the road. "It could be a copycat. We had little choice but to give the information about Bailey Canavar's murder to the media. It was the only chance to discover the whereabouts of her husband and the identity of John Doe."

"I only gave them basic information, no details." Jenna chewed on her bottom lip. "I guess we'll know more after speaking to Colter Barry."

"Problem is, when people go through this type of trauma, some of them block things out." Kane pulled into the hospital parking lot and drove into their reserved slot. "It's not intentional. I think our brains shut off the memory because we can't cope." He glanced at her. "If we believe the killer waited twelve months between murders, why would he suddenly start a killing spree now?" He scratched his cheek. "Unless something or someone triggered him."

Jenna snorted. "You're assuming he hasn't been killing all over the state. I've found similar unsolved cases and heaps of missing people going back four or five years."

"Yeah but if this injured guy is lucid and someone *did* murder his girlfriend… If she is the same type as the other two victims, then we have another serial killer in Black Rock Falls."

The strong, distinctive smell of hospitals wafted over Jenna as she waited in the hall outside the ER of Black Rock Falls' hospital. After making inquiries at the nurses' counter about Colter Barry and discovering zero information, she waited for a doctor to step out from the ER and marched straight up to him, flashing her badge. "I'm Sheriff Alton, and this is my deputy, David Kane. It is imperative we speak with Colter Barry, a gunshot victim brought in by the rangers earlier. It's concerning the apparent attack on his girlfriend."

"I'll take you through." The doctor slid his card through the scanner and opened the door for her. "He is in the room on the right, my colleague is with him now and there is a ranger guarding him; is he the man responsible?"

"We don't have any details; this is why we need to speak with him." Jenna moved inside with Kane close behind. After scanning the room, she found a ranger standing guard outside a bed surrounded by white drapes. She turned to the doctor. "Thanks, while I'm waiting for the doctor, I'll speak to the ranger."

The ranger looked relieved to see her and stepped forward to meet them. *At least he recognizes me.* She led him out into the hallway. "What have we got?"

"Colter Barry, twenty-six, out of Blackwater. He has a gunshot wound to the head and a knife wound in the back. Looks like someone gave him a beating and he is rambling about murder and blood. He keeps saying, 'Lilly has been murdered.'" The ranger straightened. "We have a search party in the area with two wardens and at least a dozen volunteers. The doc is with him now; he said something about doing an MRI."

Jenna pulled out her notepad and pen. "Thank you for waiting for us. We can take it from here."

"Not a problem, ma'am. We had worries if the same man who killed the other couple is responsible, Mr. Barry might be in danger, getting away and all." The ranger's eyes held deep sorrow. "Seems our beautiful forest is being used as a killing ground of late. I don't envy your job of apprehending this man." He gave Kane a nod and headed down the hallway.

Jenna stared after him with admiration then turned to Kane. "I'm starting to believe the park rangers are a different breed to us."

"They have to obtain a bachelor's degree before they start training. So yeah, they are very committed to their work." Kane shrugged. " I figure we are lucky they are so willing to help us when necessary."

She tugged at the curtain around Colter Barry's bed. "Doctor, this is the sheriff. May I have a word with Mr. Barry?"

A balding man in his fifties wearing surgery scrubs and a stethoscope hanging around his neck peered through the gap. "Yes, Mr. Barry has been anxious to speak with you, although due to his injuries, he has been lapsing into unconsciousness and I'm not confident whether his recollections are fact or fantasy." He stood to one side to allow them to pass. "I have scheduled an MRI. He has significant head injuries and suffered paralysis for some time after his attacker stuck him with a knife in the lumbar region. I would ask that you keep your questioning to a minimum. I'll wait outside."

Jenna took note of the doctor's name on his ID. "Thank you, Dr. Ross."

She scanned the battered face of the man lying flat on the bed, his bloodshot eyes swollen to slits and blond hair matted with blood.

She moved to the bedside and remained standing. Kane stood beside her, his expression serious, notebook in one hand and pen poised.

Jenna touched Colter's hand. "Mr. Barry, I'm Sheriff Jenna Alton and this is Deputy Kane. Can you explain what happened to you?"

The story, broken with sobs and tears, made her skin crawl. She asked him many times if he wanted to continue and he insisted. He appeared to be lucid and not raving, as the ranger had suggested. "Okay, now I need you to try and give me as much information as you can about the man who did this to you and Lilly."

Colter closed his eyes as if drifting off then looked up at her. His mouth turned down in disgust. "He was covered from head to foot in the camouflage gear the army wears and had one of those skull bandana things the bikers wear around his face. His head was covered with a woolen hat much like yours. He was white; I could see the strip of skin above his eyes, between his hat and sunglasses." Barry looked at Kane. "He wasn't as big as you, maybe five or six inches shorter and not as heavy but he was in good shape." He dragged in a ragged breath. "He threw me around as if I weighed nothing. I couldn't do a thing to help Lilly."

"I'm sure you did everything you could, Colter." Jenna squeezed his arm. "What about his voice, did he have an accent?"

"His voice was weird, like distorted or something." Colter made a strange gurgling sound in his throat then coughed and moaned. "Oh, God, I can't get him out of my head."

"Take a minute and look at him." Kane leaned closer to the bed. "He can't hurt you now and we need every scrap of information to catch this animal."

"Okay, okay." Colter seemed to fight a demon and his breath came in pants. "He had an earbud and one of those cop things on his chest."

Jenna glanced at Kane. "A com pack?"

"Yeah, and the other thing was a body cam." Colter seemed to get braver. "He kept asking questions like, 'What do you want me to do to her next?' but I was gagged, he knew I couldn't speak."

Jenna squeezed his arm gently. "Okay, we have everything we need for now. We'll be back to speak to you again. I'm having you moved upstairs into the restricted ward for your own safety and I'll have a deputy on duty twenty-four hours a day. I'll notify your parents; they'll be able to visit you there."

"Just find Lilly, she is all alone out there."

"We'll find her." Kane's expression was set in stone. "We have a search party there now."

Feeling nauseous, Jenna turned to go and looked up at Kane. "Get someone out here ASAP."

"Roger that." Kane pulled out his cellphone and moved into the hallway.

Jenna walked up to the doctor waiting outside. "I'll arrange to have a deputy here soon. Can you call security and have someone guarding him until he arrives?" She lifted her chin. "I want him up in the secure ward as well. He is our only witness and the killer might return to finish him off."

"Not a problem, I'll call someone now and we'll take him there directly from the MRI." The doctor headed toward the nurses' station.

Jenna waited for Kane to disconnect then moved to his side. "We'll wait until a security guard arrives." Her cellphone vibrated in her pocket and she pulled it out and stared at the caller ID. "It's Wolfe." She accepted the call. "Hi, Shane, did you find anything in the barn?"

"We have taken samples but I'll need time to analyze them before I can give you anything conclusive. I've just had a call from one of the park rangers about a possible body near here. We are riding over to join the search party now. It's been raining pretty hard and we'll have one hell of a time collecting evidence."

"I'm at the hospital with Kane. We have interviewed the boyfriend of the victim. There are similarities between his story and the previous murder. The killer poured gas over him and stabbed the female victim. The missing woman is Lilly Coppersmith, twenty, five-six, dark hair, blue eyes. We're waiting for a security guard to watch him until one of our deputies can take over then we'll be heading your way."

"I'll send you the coordinates of a firebreak that runs parallel to the mountain. It's some ways in from the road and you'll need to travel up toward Bear Peak from there but I'm told it's faster than taking the regular trail. It would have made life a lot easier if we had known the firebreak existed for the other murder, but it's not on any of the maps yet—it was cut through the forest the end of summer."

Jenna breathed a sigh of relief as two security guards marched into the corridor. "Security is here now. We're on our way."

"Roger that."

CHAPTER THIRTY-FIVE

Jenna caught sight of the crows circling before Wolfe called her on her cellphone to update the coordinates. They had found Lilly Coppersmith's body, and from Wolfe's preliminary examination alone, he had concluded they were dealing with the same sadistic killer. She relayed the information to Kane and took the chance to inhale the mountain air, fresh and fragrant after the rain. As they left the firebreak and moved down a narrow trail, it was like traveling through fairyland. Each hanging branch or delicate spider's web glistened with raindrops and the abundant wildlife was scampering around as if excited the rain had ceased.

She absorbed the beauty of the mountain as a shield against the horror she would encounter at the crime scene. After the last grisly murder, she assumed the killer would have found more ways to entertain himself with his latest victim. He must have been absorbed to allow Colter Barry to crawl away undetected. As they rounded the bend, she pointed to an orange flag in the distance. "That's Wolfe's marker and I can hear horses."

"If this murder comes close to what Colter Barry described, it's going to be brutal." Kane's concerned gaze examined her face. "If you feel a flashback coming on, take a step back and catch your breath. Don't forget you have a great team to lean on if necessary."

Her last flashback, a leftover from being a victim of a kidnapping, had occurred some time ago but sometimes she found them lurking unexpectedly and she hated having a weakness that interfered with her job. She forced her lips into a smile. "Thanks but I'll be fine. Nothing happened last time and I'm confident I can handle murder cases. The flashbacks were a temporary glitch, nothing more."

"I never had any doubt." Kane's smile was genuine.

The others had hitched their horses to the trees along the trail and she could hear Wolfe's deep voice barking orders. "Okay, we'll leave the horses here and go in on foot."

They took an overgrown path through the forest and she noted the way Kane stopped to check the trees along the way. She waited for him to catch up. "Find anything?"

"Yeah, the same marks on the tree trunks as before. Trail cams, I would guess, and back there I found the remains of a hunter's blind. It looks fresh, and this is not a designated area for hunting, but we can't discount the people who use trail cams and blinds for birdwatching and the like."

Jenna caught the distinct metallic smell of blood on the breeze and her skin prickled. "Maybe, but Colter Barry mentioned the killer used a body cam. He is filming his kills."

"They all have trophies of one kind or another." Kane's attention moved past her and he shook his head in disgust. "It looks like our killer is escalating way faster than I imagined." Kane pulled two face masks out of his pocket and handed her one.

In trepidation, Jenna turned toward the small clearing set to one side of the trail. She gasped at the horrific sight before her then pushed on her face mask to filter out the smell of death. The sound of Wolfe's voice came through the buzzing in her head. She dragged her attention away from the gruesome remains of a once pretty young woman and looked at him. "What can you tell me?"

"The victim is Lilly Coppersmith. I found ID in her pocket and she bears a striking resemblance to the last two victims. The time of death is consistent with Mr. Barry's story. I don't have a cause of death with so many injuries to consider. I'll determine that after the autopsy." Wolfe's pale gray eyes moved over her face as if gauging her reaction. "This is not the same as either of our other murders and yet there are similarities. I gather the only gunshot wound on Mr. Barry occurred during his escape?"

"Yeah, he has a deep knife wound to the lower spine and has facial injuries consistent with suffering a beating." Jenna cleared her throat. "She looks pretty messed up too."

"He didn't shoot her. I think the killer was playing with her." Wolfe led her closer to the body. "I'll know more after the autopsy, but the wounds on her arms and legs are not defensive wounds." He waved Webber to their side. "Show the sheriff the images we took of Paige Allen's bones then the difference in Bailey Canavar's."

"See on Paige's arms the wounds are randomly placed?" Webber pointed at the deep lacerations in the bones. "They are all over, in different directions and of various depths."

Jenna peered at the close-up images. "Yeah, the wounds on Paige's forearms are placed as if she was holding them up to protect her face."

"Now look at Lilly's arms and legs." Wolfe crouched down beside the body, avoiding the pool of blood. "Look here and here. These are the same as Bailey Canavar's wounds."

Jenna swallowed the rising bile in her throat and bent closer. The deep cuts seemed to be the same distance apart in a straight line. She glanced up at Wolfe. "That looks methodical."

"And difficult to achieve if she was struggling." Kane leaned over her shoulder. "He restrained her but from the bruises, he held her still then cut her. Those are finger marks on her wrists." He shook his head. "This happened just as Colter Barry explained."

"Yeah." Wolfe shook his head. "And we know it's not the first time he's done this. He knows how to keep a person alive and still inflict the maximum amount of pain."

"Do you think he raped her?" Webber's Adam's apple moved up and down. "Did Mr. Barry mention that?"

"Nope." Kane's brow furrowed as he glanced at Wolfe. "Can you tell?"

"Not until after the autopsy. There is no evidence as such but we did find an empty condom packet, so it's likely." Wolfe cleared his throat.

Jenna swallowed hard and tried to get her mind around the grisly details. "What are we up against?"

"The killer has unusual traits." Kane shook his head slowly. "He leaves some of the bodies for the animals and others to rot. I wonder if he likes to visit them."

"Is that why he used the gas to protect his victims from the wildlife? So he could come back and look at them?" Webber glanced at Kane, his eyes filled with disgust. "Oh, that is gross."

"It is unusual behavior." Kane scratched his head. "I wonder if he has kept trophies?"

Jenna stood, glad to be away from the staring eyes of Lilly Coppersmith, and turned to Kane. "Dear Lord, you don't think this creep has bits of his victims in his fridge, do you?"

"Anything is possible." Kane cleared his throat. "Anyone who does this to a person is not what I'd class as 'normal.'"

CHAPTER THIRTY-SIX

Monday, week two

Monday morning arrived with a fresh chill in the air and the earthy smell of overnight rain. Kane had his chores finished before daylight, and after their early-morning workout, he met Jenna for breakfast. He had spent his time in the stables mulling over the case and running different profiles through his mind in an attempt to make a fit for the killer. He waited for Jenna to finish eating before he mentioned his concerns. "This killer is different in so many ways, he is difficult to profile."

"I know what you mean." Jenna pulled a face of disgust. "From what I'm seeing at the crime scenes, he is a cross between Jeffrey Dahmer and Hannibal Lecter."

Kane rubbed the back of his neck. "He is displaying traits of the more famous serial killers, which makes me wonder if he fixates on violent psychopaths. Maybe this erratic behavior is role-playing or he wants to make his mark in history. Men have killed for notoriety."

"But why choose the same type of woman?" Jenna sipped her coffee and gave an appreciative sigh.

Kane refilled his cup and added cream and sugar. "If he is fixating on killers, he would know about hybristophilia."

"What?" Jenna chuckled. "That sounds like a cleaning utensil."

"A hybristophiliac is a woman who gets off on having a relationship with a murderer." He met her gaze. "It's often called the Bonnie and Clyde syndrome. I know it sounds a bit farfetched but it could be part of his motive."

"How so?"

"I have two possible causes for this type of psychopathy. From the damage inflicted to the women in particular, we know the killer is consumed by his own importance and likes to be in control." Kane sipped his beverage, enjoying the full-bodied flavor of his favorite brand of coffee. "I figure this goes way back to when he was a kid. If someone he loved—his mother, grandmother, or a girl he liked—belittled him, in front of his friends for instance, the resentment could simmer for years before it's triggered." He glanced at her. "That would be the most likely scenario but an unstable personality could be disturbed if his mother or grandmother died and left him alone or, worse, in an abusive situation. In both cases, he had no way to control the circumstances, but when he murders he has control over life and death. The type of woman he murders all have dark hair and blue eyes. This type is significant to him and he needs to prove to himself he has control over them." He frowned as the images of the brutalized women flashed through his mind. "The torture is important as well. He wants them to beg for their lives because in his sick mind, he is recreating the impossible situation he faced in the past." He sighed. "But by taking control and killing them, he is balancing the scale."

"So how does this tie into being fixated on other serial killers?" Jenna raised one black eyebrow in question.

Kane leaned back in his chair, making it creak. "The variety and method of his kills makes it obvious he is aware of other psychopaths."

"So how do you tie the Bonnie and Clyde syndrome into his motive as well?"

Kane ran the tip of his finger around the rim of his coffee cup. "This is a man with a huge ego. I wouldn't be surprised if he figures by becoming a notorious murderer, women will flock to him in prison and he will have power over them." He frowned at her. "There are women who are attracted to criminals. The most horrific serial killers receive sexually explicit letters from thousands of women; hell, some of them even marry them in jail."

"Then why is he concentrating on couples?"

"This is a narcissistic trait. He disabled the men then tortured the women in front of them to prove the men inadequate because they failed to stop him. It is a typical 'look at me, I'm better than you' situation. He wants to prove his dominance over women but needs a witness to satisfy his ego. So we can add 'likes an audience' to his behavior traits." Kane met her inquisitive gaze. "We know from Colter Barry's statement that the killer incapacitated him and made him watch. That would tie in with the reason the killer poured gas over the male victims, to prevent animals devouring them. In the killer's sick mind, he left the guy to watch the animals eat the woman he loved." He rubbed his chin. "The problem is I can't work out what he is planning next, why he is escalating now. It's as if he's taken on the personas of a number of famous murderers and mixed them together. There is no rhyme or reason to his actions. He doesn't display his victims, or take physical trophies unless he has a refrigerator at home filled with body parts. The fatal injury is different in each case and he uses different weapons."

"We *do* have similarities." Jenna narrowed her gaze. "Always couples, dark-haired women, and hikers who prefer the old trails." She stared into space for some moments. "He has displayed knowledge of disabling people by injuring the spine and has used the same practice each time. I would say he is an excellent shot, but so are hundreds of men around here; both these abilities could be linked to the military, then add the camouflage gear. We assume he uses trail cams, which is pretty individual to him, and if he needs trophies, what better than a video of the kill?"

Kane smiled at her. "You have a point, and Canavar and Woods fit the profile and description given by Colter Barry. Woods has priors and Canavar's ex-girlfriend is missing. They were both in the vicinity at the time of Bailey's murder. It would be hard to split them when it comes to circumstantial evidence."

"There is little doubt the same killer murdered at least Bailey Canavar and Lilly Coppersmith." Jenna got to her feet and leaned back on the kitchen counter. "At the moment neither tie in with Lilly Coppersmith's death."

"Then we need to chase down some more clues." Kane stood and stared at her. "The problem with assuming Canavar was involved in Lilly Coppersmith's murder is that no one has seen him since the day of Bailey's and John Doe's murders."

"I figure we had it right about him before. He'll be living rough, and dressed in camouflage he would blend into the forest and no one would give him a second glance." Jenna collected the breakfast dishes and rinsed them in the sink before loading the dishwasher. "We need to check out where Woods was yesterday."

Kane nodded in agreement. "We sure do."

CHAPTER THIRTY-SEVEN

The wind had picked up again, and as Jenna climbed from her vehicle, icy fingers buffeted her, lifting the edges of her jacket. She glanced skyward expecting to see rainclouds, but a clear blue sky stretched out for miles in all directions. People moved along the sidewalk without thick clothing, seemingly oblivious to the first hint of winter. The rosy cheeks and runny nose on a toddler grinning at her from over his mother's shoulder reminded her to get to the doctor's for a flu shot. She sidestepped a group of kids, heads down peering at their cellphones as they waited at the bus stop, and headed for the front door of the sheriff's department. The streets of Black Rock Falls had been unusually busy for this time of morning, then she remembered it was Monday and local charities set up in the community hall selling everything from preserves to antiques.

Her stomach knotted with worry over the people living in her town and the hordes of visitors arriving daily to enjoy the scenery or hunt in the forest. It was hard to believe violence had visited this beautiful town again. It seemed as if danger lurked on every corner and she could do nothing to stop it. How many more would die on her watch? She swallowed the lump in her throat. Isolated with vast forests and plains, Black Rock Falls hid many secrets, and now it seemed serial killers had picked it as their hunting ground of choice.

She took one last look at the majestic mountains, shook her head, and strolled into the building. As usual, Rowley was at the counter chatting to Maggie. "Morning. Anything to report?"

"There have been a few local unsubstantiated sightings of Jim Canavar, and two in Butte, but that's about all. The Butte office will get back to us once they have spoken to the people who called them in." Rowley pushed a hand through his unruly hair. "I've been reading the murder book on the Lilly Coppersmith case and your interview with Mr. Barry. I think I might have something to add."

Jenna removed her thick jacket and headed for her office. "Grab Kane and come to my office."

"Yes, ma'am."

After updating the whiteboard in her office, Jenna sat down and checked the duty roster for the week. Most of her deputies had pulled double shifts since the murders. She would prefer to take Kane with her to the Coppersmith autopsy but wanted to keep everyone in the loop. Bradford would arrive by eleven but would be too late to relieve Rowley, and Walters did not arrive until after lunch. She glanced up as Kane and Rowley ambled into the room. "Take a seat. What have you found?"

"Not found as such." Rowley placed one of the cups of coffee in his hand before her then sat down, cup in hand. "It's just Mr. Barry mentioned the killer was wearing camouflage gear and a com pack. I've heard of a crazy old Vietnam vet and his son who live up that way, Brayden and Joseph Blythe. They dress like that and use a com pack to keep in touch with each other. Their land is well signposted and they are unpredictable. Rumor has it they live on squirrels but they have a few goats as well."

"Are they out of Bear Peak?" Kane placed his steaming brew on the desk and dropped into a seat.

"Yeah, some ways from the Finches' cabin, I figure their place is about ten minutes' walk down the mountain from the firebreak." Rowley glanced up at Jenna with an expectant look on his face. "I could show you."

Jenna glanced over at Kane, who shrugged almost unperceivably. "We have to attend the Coppersmith autopsy in a few minutes but we'll head up there after lunch." She made a few notes in her daybook then glanced at him again. "While we're away, check up on the whereabouts of Mr. Woods. I want to know where he was at the time of Lilly Coppersmith's murder. Bradford and Walters will both be on duty by then and you can show us where to find the Blythe property."

"Yes, ma'am."

She glanced at her deputies. "I'll release another media statement warning people we have an armed and dangerous man in the forest. I'll give a brief description and ask them to call in on the crime information hotline if they see anyone acting suspiciously." She pushed both hands through her hair. "I'm not banking on getting much response when ninety percent of the men in town carry weapons in the forest and wear camo."

"It would save time if you attended to the autopsy and I collected the horses." Kane's eyebrows rose. "We can easily pick up Rowley's mount on the way." He pushed to his feet and swung the cup from the handle.

Jenna's day was getting more complicated by the second but Kane did have a point. "Sure, that works for me. I'll grab some lunch and we can eat along the way to Bear Peak." She looked up at Kane. "Bring Duke along, he'll enjoy the run."

"Yes, ma'am." Kane smiled at her in a flash of white teeth then headed for the door.

CHAPTER THIRTY-EIGHT

He gaped at the breaking news story splashed across his TV screen in disbelief. The sheriff was giving a stern warning about hiking with a killer on the loose. Photographs of the faces of his latest kills were out there for all to see. This had never happened before, but then no one had found one alive until now. *I must be losing my edge.*

He listened in morbid fascination as the newscaster gave details of Colter Barry's scrape with death. The whimpering piece of shit was alive. Dammit, he had shot him in the head, near sliced his spine through, and he had *lived*. He picked a glass of bourbon from the table and hurled it against the wall. The pungent liquid spilled down the flock wallpaper and spread over the beige wool carpet in an ugly brown stain. Glass fragments mixed with the ice from the glass and glistened in the stream of light from the window, triggering a memory of sunbeams on crimson blood. He touched his lips, still cool from the drink, and could feel Lilly's mouth again, cold against his flesh.

He had enjoyed killing her.

He wished he could kill her again.

The voice from the TV dragged his attention to the screen, and anger bubbled back to the surface. He stood and paced the room listening to advice to avoid the less popular mountain trails until the sheriff had investigated Colter Barry's claims. *How dare she get involved?*

An interview followed with the two men who had found Colter Barry disorientated and raving like a lunatic. One of the men figured a stray bullet could have shot Barry as he was moving close to a regulated hunting area. He stopped pacing and stared at the screen, waiting for the newscaster's comment.

"Well, folks, if you're going hiking, take care; after all, it is hunting season."

He took a bottle of bourbon from the bar and made himself a drink then slipped a video card into his player. As the image of Lilly running away from him in terror flashed onto the screen, his heart raced in anticipation. "Run, run as fast as you can because I know how this movie ends and I can't wait."

CHAPTER THIRTY-NINE

Jenna took three deep breaths and pulled on a face mask, then scanned her ID card and stepped inside the morgue. Her self-confidence in dealing with the deaths of victims had increased tenfold since Wolfe's arrival in Black Rock Falls. The old message that used to play through her head, *The dead can't hurt you*, often came to mind at a horrific crime scene, but Wolfe's calming and reassuring words steeled her resolve during the more grueling autopsies.

His insistence to treat each corpse with dignity, as in life, with a name and a story to tell, was what separated him from the other coroners she had dealt with in her time in law enforcement. Before Wolfe came into her life, she would force her humanity into the background in an effort to deal with horrific crimes. Now she viewed things very differently. Each victim had a story to tell and she needed to be at the autopsy to listen to what Lilly Coppersmith had to say about the man who had taken her life, and prevent him killing again.

She took in the scene before her. Wolfe in mask and gloves with Cole Webber discussing samples taken from the crime scene. "Morning."

"Great, you're early." Wolfe pulled down his mask and smiled at her. "I'm working at warp speed today. Anna is in a school play and I need to be there after she finishes school to help out."

Jenna nodded. "Yes, Kane mentioned her play. We thought we might come along tonight and watch her, if that's okay?"

"It would make her day." Wolfe indicated to Webber to remove Lilly Coppersmith's body from a drawer in the morgue refrigerator.

His attention moved back to Jenna. "As with our other victims, I have used Cole as the law enforcement witness to conduct the autopsy. It means you have the results faster and gives me ample time to explain the different procedures to him. I know some of this is a little grueling for most people. I hope this practice is still okay with you?"

A wave of relief spread over her. She understood the need to be present, but this way, he was able to give her his findings and explain by showing her the evidence. "Yes, having Webber working with you is a bonus for both of us." She glanced at Webber. "How do you like the work so far?"

"It's very interesting and I'm enjoying the theory side as well." Webber pushed the gurney under a huge theatre light. "I had no idea being a coroner's assistant was so involved but I like doing this job."

"I'm glad you're happy." Jenna glanced at Wolfe. "We've had a development in the case. Apart from our two suspects, Canavar and Woods, Rowley mentioned a Vietnam vet who is a bit crazy out of Bear Peak. A soon as I've finished here, we're heading up to interview him."

"Wear your Kevlar vests, just in case." Wolfe pulled back the sheet on Lilly Coppersmith's deathly white body. "Okay, we have a female, Caucasian, identified as Lilly Coppersmith out of Blackwater, Montana. Twenty years old, five feet four inches tall. She was in good physical health at the time of death." He lifted Lilly's hands one by one. "We found no trace evidence under her nails or any indication at all she fought her killer."

Jenna replayed Colter Barry's interview in her mind. "She didn't fight back in order to save her boyfriend from being burned alive."

"There are ligature marks on both wrists, the first consistent with the killer tying her arms behind her back for a period of time." Wolfe's pale gray gaze moved to her face and he frowned. "From the bruising on her upper thighs and genital area, she was alive when he raped her. The hypostasis in the lower arms or discoloration of the skin would indicate the killer placed her in the position we found her, sitting with her arms extended above her head, before he inflicted the wounds to her arms and legs."

Jenna moved closer and peered at Lilly's face. "What do you make of the bruises on her face?"

"The lacerations on her legs and arms would have caused pain and blood loss." Wolfe glanced at Webber. "Cole has a theory about the marks."

"Yeah, they aren't as brutal as the first murder. I figure he was slapping her around to keep her conscious." Webber pointed to a distinct outline of fingermarks on one cheek. "That's a slap not a punch."

"So, what's the cause of death?" Jenna turned her attention back to Wolfe. "Blood loss?"

"Nope." Wolfe indicated to a small wound just below the ribs on the left side. "This is why I believe the killer has military training of some kind. That is the same sharp force injury used on Bailey Canavar. It is a lethal and effective blow often used in mortal combat. I would say, due to blood loss, she was lapsing into unconsciousness, and inflicting pain was no longer giving her killer pleasure."

"Anything else I should know?" Jenna sucked in a deep breath then regretted it, tasting the awful smell of the morgue on her tongue. "So far everything matches Mr. Barry's story about the murder."

"We'll have the results from the samples in a day or so but I doubt they will give us any more information about the killer. It's pointless revisiting the crime scene; heavy rain will have destroyed any further blood evidence or footprints." Wolfe sighed. "As we found no trace evidence from a third person on Lilly's body, it endorses Mr. Barry's recollection that the killer was covered from head to foot. In my opinion from the evidence I've found, he is telling the truth." He shook his head and covered the body with reverence then lifted his gaze to Jenna. "Be careful in the forest. This killer is dangerous; he could be influenced by drugs and is frightened of nothing."

CHAPTER FORTY

Kane rode beside Jenna, allowing Rowley to take the lead. During the time Jenna had attended the autopsy, he had dug into Brayden and Joseph Blythe's lives. After discovering both had priors for assault, he discussed the pair with old Deputy Walters. It was common knowledge around these parts that the Blythes took shots at anyone venturing unannounced on their land. He did not intend to walk into a potentially dangerous situation and had added their phone number to his contacts.

They had left the firebreak and headed down the mountain along an overgrown trail winding its way through the forest. As the pathway narrowed, he fell back, allowing Jenna to ride in the middle. He kept his mind alert, scanning the forest for any movement or glimpses of color.

His attention went to every tree they rode past, checking for any sign of a trail cam. Right now, he trusted no one. As far as he was concerned, they had entered the lion's den. Jenna was a close example of the type the killer enjoyed torturing and could be watching them.

Anyone could conceal themselves within the shadowy depths of the forest. With the wind creaking the branches overhead, and the wealth of wildlife on the move disguising any possible footfalls, a man in camouflage would be invisible. Hell, he had hidden himself in a forest many times during his deployment and had taken down the enemy without breaking a sweat.

The killer had chosen a perfect background for his crimes, and the size of the forest alone gave him a huge advantage; he could be anywhere in an area of over a million acres. Wearing Kevlar jackets would give them a slight advantage, but with three of them, the killer might go for a headshot.

He moved his horse up closer to Jenna as they maneuvered through a tight switchback. "Hey, Jenna. Don't get too far ahead of me."

She slowed and turned in her saddle, a concerned look on her face. "You okay?"

"Yeah, and if that crazy is in the area, I want to be close by." He looked ahead, seeing only the tip of Duke's tail moving through the long grass. "Even Duke is invisible up here."

"I'll be damned if I'm going to allow a serial killer to spoil the forest for me." She dropped her reins and spread her arms wide. "This place is magnificent, and when I'm out here with you, I feel safe not scared. When this nightmare is over, we have to spend a weekend up here and regenerate." She tipped her head toward Rowley moving away in the distance. "He would make a good agent. His head has been turning in all directions. He is getting like you and watching every movement."

He smiled at her. "You trained him well."

Ahead Rowley had stopped and turned around, regarding them with interest. Kane waved at him. "How much further?"

"The border of their land is just over there." Rowley pointed into the distance. "I can see the signs."

"Okay, hold up, I'll give them a call." Kane slipped the cellphone from his pocket and called the number. "Mr. Blythe, this is Deputy Kane. The sheriff needs to speak with you about a man seen trespassing in this area at night. Can we come up to the house?"

"I guess, but I don't know nothin' 'bout no trespassers."

"Thanks, we'll be there directly." Kane disconnected and nodded at Jenna. "We're good to go."

He urged his horse forward and followed Rowley to an overgrown driveway; no gate but "No trespassing" signs written haphazardly in red across rough boards littered the area. The paint on the hand-drawn letters had dripped down the boards like blood, giving each one a macabre tone as if to add to the warning. The smell of rotting flesh wafted toward them, and he shot a glance at Jenna. "That doesn't smell good."

"Be on alert, we don't know what to expect." Jenna's eyes flashed a warning as she uncovered her sidearm and rested her palm on the handle of her pistol.

When Duke gave his characteristic whine, telling Kane to beware, the hairs on the back of his neck stood to attention. He turned to Rowley. "Fall back and stay in the cover of the trees; they don't know you are with us and we might need you to watch our backs. Have your rifle at the ready."

"Sure thing." Rowley moved his horse into the shadows of the pines.

"Oh!" Jenna pulled up beside him, her mouth turned down in obvious disgust. "Are they skins?"

Kane stared at the dilapidated cabin with a rickety old porch. Various skins, squirrel and maybe rat, dangled from the front porch, crawling with flies. "Yeah, I figure they use them for blankets. Walters mentioned they rarely go into town unless it's to buy ammunition. He also said they have an arsenal of weapons and Brayden might be an old man but he is a tough SOB."

"They eat rats?" Jenna's face blanched. "That's disgusting."

Kane wrinkled his nose. "I'd say the men inside the cabin won't smell too good either. How do you want to handle this, ma'am?"

"I'll do the talking." She lifted her chin and gave him a determined stare. "You keep your hand on your weapon. We could be stirring up a bee's nest."

The front door of the cabin creaked open a crack and the long barrel of a rifle slid through the opening.

Jenna's voice rang out, loud and clear. "Brayden Blythe, this is Sheriff Alton. Lower your weapon. I'm not here to arrest you. I just need to ask you some questions."

"I have the right to bear arms to protect my property." Blythe's gray head stuck out. "Throw your weapons on the ground and I'll talk."

"That is not going to happen, Mr. Blythe." Jenna moved her horse forward in a show of courage. "Or do you have reason to hide behind that door? We've had a number of murders in this neck of the forest and video confirmation of a prowler in the area. If you refuse to cooperate, I can only assume you had something to do with the murders."

"I didn't kill nobody." A slight man in his seventies, white hair flowing to his shoulders and wearing a tattered army jacket over filthy camouflage pants, edged his way out the door. "Say your piece then get the hell off my land."

"Is your son at home?" Jenna's attention had not wavered. She sat straight-backed and with her chin set in a stubborn angle. "I would like to speak with both of you."

"I'm here." Joseph Blythe stepped onto the porch, a broken shotgun over one arm. He wore jeans and a squirrel-skin vest over a plaid shirt. "We don't know nothin' 'bout no murders."

"Have you seen anyone in the area or suspected someone has been sleeping in your barn over the last week or so?" Jenna's mare danced on the spot, eyes rolling at the smell of death. "The Finches have footage of a man hanging around their barn at night."

The Blythes turned away and spoke to each other in hushed tones, ignoring Jenna's question. Kane moved to her side. His mount seemed to calm the mare and she settled. He leaned toward Jenna. "What are they up to?"

"I hope they're not planning on murdering us to eat for dinner." Jenna's mouth quirked up in the corners. "Although, you'd likely be tougher than squirrel."

"Thanks." Kane shook his head and dropped his voice to just above a whisper. "Don't worry. I could take them down before they took aim."

"I'm banking my life on it." Jenna's gaze drifted over him for a split second before returning to the Blythes.

Kane took in the size of both men: The older man would not fit the description of being strong and mobile but the son was a muscular man in his late thirties or early forties. Colter Barry had not mentioned seeing two men at the scene of the crime and he would imagine these men did just about everything together. "Joseph fits the description Barry gave us, but it's his father who has the reputation of being crazy."

"Well, Mr. Blythe?" Jenna's expression had turned into exasperation. "If you have something to tell us, spit it out; we have other people to visit this afternoon."

"Nope, we haven't seen anyone." Brayden Blythe moved out onto the porch, his attention focused on Duke. "But I'll trade you for the dog."

Kane jumped in before Jenna had time to react, hoping he might get a chance to see inside the house. "What are you offering? Weapons?"

"You wouldn't." Jenna's horrified expression surprised him. "No way."

"Trust me." Kane swung down from his horse and led his mount toward Joseph. "I'm always looking for a new weapon. Would you mind holding my horse? He is a bit skittish around the sheriff's mare."

"Yeah, Joe will take care of your horse. We have weapons and stuff. Come inside and I'll show you."

Kane moved through the door and ducked his head. The low ceilings closed around him in a claustrophobic nightmare. Inside, the rank stench of rotting flesh overlaid with unwashed male and garbage burned his nostrils. With every one of his senses on high alert, he peered into the dim room, waiting a few seconds for his eyes to adjust to the light before following the old man. He scanned the area for a booby trap, keeping one ear open for Joseph to creep up behind him.

Avoiding the desire to reach for his flashlight, he batted away flypaper hanging all through the house like Christmas decorations and moved through piles of skins, stacked up and tied with string. Old barrels filled with parts of antlers were against one wall and a row of jars containing teeth sat on a bookcase. The only sign of comfort came in the form of two old sofas beside the hearth. Shoot, he'd been inside tanks that offered more comfort. Filthy cushions on the seats sank low to the floor before a coffee table piled high with dirty dishes. Cockroaches scattered, making a rushing sound, moving from one garbage-inspired décor theme to another. The clutter continued through into the kitchen. For an ex-military man, Brayden Blythe sure was messy.

The kitchen at least had windows, where light tried to force its way through the grime. Kane's attention went to a line of pegs beside the back door. Three backpacks in a range of colors and styles hung in a neat row, and beneath them boots of various sizes. "You married? Any other kids?"

"Nope." Blythe indicated with one dirty finger to the backpacks. "They're mine, found abandoned in the forest. I didn't steal nothin'. I hoped someone would offer a reward or somethin' and I posted a found notice in the general store window, all legal like."

Kane noticed the man's belligerent expression. "Can you tell me exactly where you found them and when?"

"Nope, last one was over a year ago." Blythe smiled a yellow grin. "Could have been on one of fifty or so trails, and my memory ain't so good these days."

Kane kept his back to the counter, eyeing the impressive rows of weapons taking up one entire wall. Below they had stacked boxes of ammunition off the floor on a pile of cinder blocks. "You went through them, right?"

"Yeah, didn't find much—clothes most times and food, no IDs." Blythe screwed up his face. "We didn't touch nothin'. People get lost up here or the bears or cats get them. I didn't steal nothin'."

Kane shrugged. "I didn't say you did." He moved closer to the backpacks and examined them. As far as he could determine, the bags had no blood spatter and he had no evidence for a search warrant to seize them as evidence. Although, if Blythe gave them to him willingly and signed a statement, any evidence they found would be admissible. He waved a hand toward the bags. "Although they interest me, what do you want for them?"

"The bloodhound?" Blythe looked hopeful then shook his head. "Nope, I'd have to sweeten the deal. Your dog would be worth a deal of money."

"Well, you don't have anything I'm looking for in weapons, if that is all you have?" Kane kept one hand resting on the butt of his pistol as Blythe still had a firm grip on his rifle.

"That's all." Blythe chewed on his bottom lip. "Shame, I really like your dog."

"Have you seen or heard anything unusual over the last week or so?" Kane watched his reaction but the old man's attention span seemed to drift in and out.

"There is always somethin' going on in the forest." Blythe gave Kane a long, considering look. "I seen things out there. Heard whispers and screams that ain't no cat. Found a thigh bone all chewed up one day. Joe, he brings home the bags when he is out huntin' squirrel." He lowered his voice. "He seen Charlie out there hiding in the woods, waiting to ambush him. He's a smart kid—he doubled back and we locked up the place and kept watch all night. Heard shots and screams, the bastard took down one of ours. He's out there waitin'. You need to watch your back."

Kane nodded. The old man was reliving his time in the Vietnam War. "Charlie" was derived from the radio code, Victor Charlie or VC for the Viet Cong enemy soldiers. Perhaps Joseph had seen the Asian man before he was brutally murdered. Or was Joseph the killer? He needed to get back to Jenna so he pulled two fifty-dollar bills from his wallet. "I'll give you a hundred bucks for the backpacks and the shoes. I'll need you to sign a statement saying you handed over the bags willingly and without duress. Take it or leave it. The dog stays with me."

"Done." The man spat on his hand and held it out with a grin.

Kane looked at the rotting yellow teeth and slapped the bills into the man's hand, avoiding the spittle. "Thanks. I'll write up a statement in my notebook for you to sign."

"Sure, when we're done, send Joe in and we'll throw them in a sack and bring them outside." He opened the door to a huge refrigerator and pulled out a beer. "Beer?"

Kane made sure to take note of the contents of the fridge, relieved no body parts sat on the shelves. "Ah, no thanks, I'm on duty."

Business done, Kane went to the back door and flung it open, glad of the fresh air. "I'll go out this way. I need the exercise." He escaped from the cabin and took a good look around the ramshackle buildings.

Apart from the goats and a few chickens, nothing seemed out of place, and the disgusting smell seemed to be coming from the house. He wandered around to the front of the cabin and noticed Jenna's pinched expression. After nodding to her, he walked to Joseph. "Your father wants help carrying out the rucksacks and boots. Nice place. Does it have a root cellar?"

"Nope, it sits on bedrock." Joseph turned to go.

"Where did you find the backpacks? And your father mentioned a thigh bone. Human, was it?"

"We found them bags all over. I found the bone some years ago and I'm no doctor, it could have belonged to an elk. He would have told you about Charlie." Joseph gave him a curious glare. "I wasn't imagining seeing Charlie up the mountain last week. Two of them in camo, one turned and looked at me, so I hightailed it back here, zigzaggin' all the way. The old man might be crazy but I seen them with my own two eyes."

Kane took in his concerned expression. He saw genuine fear in his eyes. "Are you sure there were two men? Not just hunters moving through the area? The majority of them wear camouflage—why are these men different?"

"Nope, it was Charlie. I saw one of their faces clear as I'm seein' you now. He was Asian."

When Joseph walked into the house, Kane glanced up at Jenna. "You good?"

"Yeah, he was a fountain of non-information." She gave a sarcastic snort. "Find anything interesting?"

"Oh, yeah." He gave Jenna the details. "The backpacks are crucial evidence, especially if we can identify the owners. If the killer has been active in this area for some time, he has covered his tracks well. Choosing a time before bears go into hibernation and eating everything available would be the perfect time to leave bodies for the wildlife to scatter. So far, his victims have been visitors, mostly on hiking holidays, who move around. Some could be foreign backpackers, and when they go missing they might not come up on our radar, or we haven't found a body, so we dismiss the report."

"Then we start finding bodies because the sudden increase in tourism and hunting has made it more likely for someone to stumble over the remains." Jenna wrinkled her nose. "I hate to say it but you stink."

"I hope it washes off and doesn't follow me around." He bent to pat Duke, and the bloodhound sniffed him then sneezed but remained close by. "Now there's devotion." He swung up into his saddle. "He doesn't care."

"Just stay downwind." Jenna lowered her voice. "Do you think Joseph is involved?"

Kane gathered up his reins. "I'm not certain. He is smaller than the man who attacked Barry, but with army boots and a hat, he would look taller. They have an arsenal in the house but one thing was missing—a crossbow, and I doubt they have the cash to buy the type of bolts used in the homicides."

"One thing is for sure." Jenna pushed a lock of black hair from her face and tucked it inside her woolen cap. "We have localized the killing field. If what the Blythes said is true, this maniac is running riot the entire length of Bear Peak."

CHAPTER FORTY-ONE

Tuesday, week two

"I'm fine, stop fussing." Kane pushed the wrapped package of frozen peas against his temple and closed his eyes against the throbbing pain.

"I'm so sorry." Jenna's voice sounded very loud. "I'll pour you another coffee."

Kane opened one eye and blinked at her. "It wasn't your fault. Duke distracted me by barking just as you aimed the kick at my head. I turned into the blow, so it's my bad." He sighed. "I'd love another coffee but I need to take my meds. They help me keep my balance if the pain gets bad."

"I'll go get them." Jenna pushed the cup toward him then examined his face closely. "Your eyes crossed when I hit you. Is that significant?"

His sight had been blurry since she'd kicked him in the temple, but he squeezed her arm to reassure her. "No, I don't think so. The meds are in the bathroom over the sink." He fished his keys out of his pocket and handed them to her. "Thanks."

The moment she stepped out the front door, Kane's cellphone vibrated in his pocket. *This is all I need.* He squinted at the caller ID and, seeing it was Wolfe, accepted the call. "What has you up so early? Great play last night. Your daughter has talent and we really enjoyed watching her."

"Thanks, Anna was over the moon when she heard you and Jenna were there. I really appreciate the support; well, we all do. It means a lot." Wolfe cleared his throat. *"I called Jenna but she didn't pick up."*

Kane glanced out the kitchen door. "She'll be back soon. Can I help?"

"The reason I called is that Rowley got a call from the FBI's Cyber Division and gave them my number as I understand the technical side of things. They intercepted a fragment of a transmission on the dark web involving human hunting."

Kane put down the frozen peas and went for his coffee. "Why contact us?"

"They are contacting a number of law enforcement agencies across a wide area. They had a botanist examine the trees and shrubs in the footage and believe it is an alpine region. Any of Montana's mountain ranges through to Colorado. From the description they gave me, the location could easily be Stanton Forest. After the current murders, it was a head's up."

Kane frowned and instantly regretted it then pressed the frozen peas against his temple. "Yeah, from what Barry Colter said, the killer was acting as if he was hunting them, and we know he used a body cam. Do you figure he could be uploading images to the dark web? The technology is available to just about anyone now."

"From what I understand he could be streaming video from the murder scene. We could be looking at a killer who is running a member's only club online or something similar with a paying audience. You'd be surprised what is available on the dark web."

"You mean a pay-per-view murder? Holy cow, I've heard everything now." Kane allowed the information to permeate into his brain. "I need to think on this one. If this is our killer, we have a new breed of psychopath in the area."

"If anyone can profile him, you can." Wolfe sighed. *"Whoever he is, he is brutal, and from Barry Colter's statement, he gets a great deal of pleasure out of making his victims suffer."*

After taking a few sips of his coffee, Kane pushed through the ache radiating from the metal plate in his head and tried to think straight. "You have the equipment to hack into the dark web. Do you think you can track the people involved and see if the trail leads back here?"

"Not one chance in hell. They bounce the signal around the world. It would be impossible to locate them, but from the information the FBI gave me, I might be able to locate the site or a ghost copy of the page the organizer used. If I can find that, the FBI can take it from there. I'll work from home as my equipment is not what you might call 'standard issue' and leave Webber in charge of the ME's office for the day. He will process the backpacks you collected from the Blythes' cabin and email a list of anything useful he finds. I'm not expecting the test results to arrive from the samples we took at the crime scenes for a day or so."

Kane sighed. "Okay, let me know if you run down some leads."

"Sure, and thanks again for coming to the play. You made my little girl very happy."

"That's what family is for." Kane smiled as the line went dead.

"Whose family?" Jenna walked into the kitchen and stared at him with incredulity stamped all over her face. "Jesus, Kane, you didn't break cover, did you?" She handed him the bottle of medication.

"Nah." Kane opened the bottle, tipped out two pills, then swallowed them with coffee. "That was Wolfe thanking us for going to the play." He leaned back in the kitchen chair and stared at her, willing his eyes to focus. "He had a call from the FBI."

After explaining, he tossed the peas into the freezer. "He'll let us know if he finds anything and Webber will email copies of any info he finds in the backpacks we picked up from the Blythes' cabin. He will be going over them looking for trace evidence of foul play as well."

"It sounds like Wolfe has everything under control his end, but I guess it will be just me, Bradford, and Rowley today." She pushed to her feet. "Although, I don't like leaving you alone with a head injury." Her cool hand rested on his forehead. "Maybe I should stay home. I can run things from here."

Kane snorted. "Once the pills kick in, the dizziness will subside and I'll be good to go." He smiled at her. "I've had bigger hits playing football. It's not as if you knocked me out. This plate in my head obviously makes me more vulnerable than I realized."

"I don't think so. It was like hitting a brick wall; my heel is still sore and you didn't move one inch." Jenna wiggled her foot. "I went full force and thought you would duck out of the way as usual." She sighed. "I should be able to take you down by now."

"Not necessarily." Kane sighed with relief as she came back into focus. "But you would be able to take down the majority of men my size." He finished his beverage and looked up at her. "From the information Wolfe gave me, if this killer is using Bear Peak as his personal killing fields and streaming it to an audience online, we are dealing with a very complicated type of psychopathic behavior. Most are in a world of their own making. They act out a scene in their minds, or kill in a certain way to satisfy a need." He twirled the medication bottle on the table and stared at it for some moments. "If this man is killing to entertain others as well as feeding his own need, we have a killer wearing a coat of many colors, unpredictable and deadly."

CHAPTER FORTY-TWO

Later that morning, Jenna called the deputies into her office and brought them up to date. She had been keeping a close eye on Kane. After she had kicked him in the temple, he had stood there and stared at her with his gaze slightly off center for some moments before reacting. It had frightened her more than she would ever admit. With a plate in his head, she was aware, he suffered headaches in winter and was not sure if his silent agony was a tough guy thing or he had the ability to ignore pain from his years of military training. His face was still pale when he took a seat in front of her desk. He had insisted on coming into the office but had at least taken the ride she had offered.

She waved at the copious amounts of notes she had added to the whiteboard. "Our suspect is Caucasian, between five ten and six feet tall, muscular build, strong. He disguised his voice, so we don't have an accent."

"I could step outside and haul in six men off the sidewalk who match that description." Bradford wrinkled her nose. "My bet is the killer is Jim Canavar. He seems the most likely to be doing this, going on his history."

Jenna welcomed discussion. She stood and went to the whiteboard. "Yes, he is on the suspect list. The husband is always a person of interest, and as his last girlfriend went missing and he seems to have vanished, he goes to the top of my list."

"Don't forget he is a player." Rowley straightened in his chair. "Bailey's friends didn't hide the fact he likes to play the field."

"Jim and Bailey seemed pretty devoted to each other." Kane crossed his long legs at the ankles and looked at Jenna. "Although, I'm surprised he took Bailey back up the mountain after she found the skull. She seemed a little freaked out to me. Her money would be a motive for killing her—if he had planned to have her vanish like his girlfriend. Something could have gone wrong and animals did not have time to scatter his victims' remains. It would be just dumb luck for someone to trip over the bodies in an area the size of Stanton Forest." He lifted his chin. "I gather from the gossip he was involved with Bailey in the weeks before his ex-girlfriend went missing, which makes me wonder if the girlfriend was a trial run."

"What if he killed the first couple as well?" Rowley's eyebrows rose in question. "He could have taken his wife to the murder scene just to see how well the wildlife had scattered the remains."

"That is a possibility. It might be an idea to look at his phone records and see where he was at the time." Kane rubbed the darkening bruise on his temple. "They might not show us much if he makes a habit of ditching his cellphone and taking his women off the grid to kill them."

Jenna nodded in agreement. "Yeah, but we'll need to do a search of his movements going back a year. Rowley, call Detective Stokes at the Hollywood precinct and tell him what we need. They might be able to chase down some leads."

"I'm sure he is the killer. I read his file and he is a typical sleaze ball." Bradford gave Jenna an exasperated look. "I figure the Asian guy was his accomplice, but he killed him and used his vehicle to make his getaway."

Deciding to explain rather than challenge Bradford's assertions, Jenna folded her arms and leaned against the wall. "That could be true, and as we haven't any clues to John Doe's identity, I'm not ruling out he was involved in some way."

"I disagree." Kane shrugged. "We have no evidence to suggest John Doe was involved. The blood spatter evidence suggests he died after Bailey. He could have tried to assist her and the killer murdered him as well."

"We've had an all-points bulletin out on Canavar since his wife's body was discovered and his face has been splashed all over the news." Jenna stared at the faces of her deputies. "Not one of the leads panned out even with the substantial reward Bailey's parents have offered. He hasn't accessed any of his bank accounts, so if he is still in the forest he is living off the grid."

"Okay, but if it is him, why keep killing?" Rowley looked bemused. "If money is a motive, as you believe, he wouldn't gain one cent for killing Lilly Coppersmith."

"Most psychopaths—and we know this killer is one from what we have seen of his behavior— are very smart. Money would be a very small part of his true motive; those dark, disturbing thoughts would be buried deep in his psyche but the allure of money is tempting as well." Kane sipped the cup of coffee he was cradling in his hands. "If Canavar is involved in live-streaming murders to the dark web, it would be very lucrative, so don't count him out just yet."

Jenna cleared her throat to get everyone's attention. "The next person of interest is Ethan Woods. Although he seems to keep slipping through our net with the help of his lawyer, I still have him firmly in my sights." She turned to the board. "He fits the general description and we can place him at Bear Peak at the time of Bailey Canavar's and John Doe's murders."

"It is likely he was in the forest when Lilly Coppersmith was murdered as well." Rowley flicked through his notes. "I went to the Cattleman's Hotel last night for a meal and ran into a group of men I know who hunt in that area. As luck would have it, Woods was sitting at the bar with James Stone. I asked them if they knew

Woods, and all of them mentioned seeing him at the checking station up that way the day before Lilly's murder." His mouth curled into a smile. "They said he looked like he planned to stay a while from the gear he was carrying."

Jenna glared at him. "And you are telling me this now?" She dashed a few notes onto the whiteboard. "You should have informed me about this evidence immediately."

"I added it to his file, and the names of the people I spoke to last night." Rowley shut his notebook with a snap. "I knew we'd be discussing the cases first up this morning. I didn't consider it to be urgent."

Jenna turned back to the whiteboard. "Okay, the only other persons of interest are Joseph Blythe and his father, Brayden." She glanced at Kane. "During Kane's interview with Brayden Blythe, I tried to make conversation with Joseph. He acted suspiciously and refused to look me in the eye. I noticed blood caked under his fingernails, and when I questioned him, he informed me he had been skinning squirrels, which may well be true."

"Let's look at the evidence. They live in the area of all three murders and have priors. Both men wear army camouflage gear and have an arsenal of weapons. Either one could be the killer." Kane placed his coffee cup on her desk. "Although I didn't see a crossbow with their weapons, they did have a number of backpacks and pairs of shoes they claim to have found abandoned in the forest. When Webber processes them, he will send over the details."

"The bags and shoes could be trophies." Bradford crossed her legs. "What do you think, Sheriff?"

" I don't think so. Up to now, the killer hasn't taken the victims' personal possessions with him as far as we know." Jenna's attention moved to Bradford. "We found the belongings of the other victims close to the scene. The Blythes remain on our list of people of interest until proved otherwise. They could be off the grid because they prefer to live alone. Being antisocial isn't a crime; neither is collecting things people leave behind in the forest." She sighed. "Or they are mass murderers. Right now we don't have enough evidence to haul in anyone."

CHAPTER FORTY-THREE

He heard the undertones of an argument as he strolled along the walkway between the bar at the Cattleman's Hotel and the main lobby. He slowed his pace, seeing the couple in a heated exchange in an alcove, and wondered what had brought the sheriff and her deputy to the hotel at lunchtime. As he moved closer, he realized they were out of uniform. His heart skipped a beat; perhaps they had discovered his identity.

The sheriff pushed her deputy hard in the chest and stormed toward the hotel foyer. Closer now, he stared at her face in surprise. The small, dark-haired woman was not the sheriff at all but could be a close relative. As she headed for the door to the restaurant, the man with her gave him a dismissive glance and followed her. Not a doppelgänger for Deputy Kane after all. This man was older, in his late forties, and had a slight paunch.

He headed for the restaurant and gave his name to the maître d'. An unfamiliar waiter approached and he requested a table at the back of the room adjacent to the arguing couple. He could see the woman's face clearly now, the way her eyes flashed with anger and the stubborn set of her chin. She flicked her dark hair out of her eyes, and at that moment, the overpowering desire to watch her die overwhelmed him. It came in an emotion so strong he had to squeeze his eyes shut to regain control. His hands trembled at the thought of her angry gaze set on him. She would fight—at first.

Once she came to the understanding she was part of a game, the fun would begin. He would allow her to run, just far enough before clipping her to slow her down. The hide and seek was the best part. He could always smell women's fear, and when he found them and dragged them back to their men, they put on a good show. Since his last kill, he craved for another. The instructions coming through his earpiece from the viewers' votes had heightened his experience to a new level.

Lilly had lasted longer than expected and he had enjoyed every moment. He opened his eyes, peering over the menu at the woman at the next table, and could see her dead, staring eyes superimposed over her face. The ceiling lights sparkled on the knife set so neatly on the pristine white tablecloth and shot the memory of Lilly's final moans to the front of his mind.

In fact, in the end, Lilly had looked darn right grateful. He did not want her thanks; he needed his prey to realize there was no escape and no God to save them. He was in control of every breath and heartbeat until he alone decided when they could die.

It was a damn shame Lilly's boyfriend had gotten away. The trail where he left her was isolated and the chances of anyone finding the couple's bodies would have been remote. From what he had seen on the news earlier, the sheriff and her team had finished their investigation in the forest and uncovered few leads. With the sheriff back in her office, he could plan another hunt straight away.

Hikers swarmed into town daily and most took the regular trails to take in the falls or the rivers. It was the couples, who went into the forest for some alone time, that he needed for his sport, and they came in droves at this time of the year. His choice of a dark-haired small woman was one thing, but haunting the local bars and restaurants in the hope of overhearing people's plans was making him far too visible. He glanced at the couple at the next table and decided to shadow them for a couple of days because they would be perfect.

The waiter arrived and he gave his order then took out his notebook and flipped through the pages, not reading a word. His attention had fixed on the couple's conversation. The woman, he discovered, was Mariah, and she called her companion Paul. He gathered from their chat Mariah worked as his secretary and they were away on a business trip, or dirty week, take your pick.

She was not happy. Apparently, he had offered her a scenic tour of the falls; their outing to the most popular area earlier in the day had almost led to one of Paul's business partners finding them in a compromising position, and Paul was a married man.

He listened for while, losing interest, but when the waiter delivered their meals, Paul was kind enough to ask if the waiter knew of any secluded places a couple could go to be alone in Stanton Forest.

He almost burst out laughing when the waiter suggested the old trail that ran past his cave. So enthusiastic to help the couple, the waiter came back a short time later with a tourist map and marked the trail with his pen.

Mariah seemed to be happy with the compromise and they made plans to rent the gear they needed to stay for one night in the mountains. As the conference they were attending wound up on Friday, they could head up the mountain on Saturday morning.

His meal arrived and the bottle of merlot he fully intended to consume to the last drop. He sipped his glass of wine and allowed the aromatic flavor to spill over his tongue. As it was Tuesday, he had plenty of time to set up his trail cams. The added bonus: He could visit his friends in the cave and discuss his plans with them—after all, they were such good listeners.

CHAPTER FORTY-FOUR

Wednesday, week two

Early Wednesday morning, Jenna received a call from Wolfe requesting a meeting to discuss his findings. No matter how much she insisted, he had refused to discuss anything over the phone. Since Lilly Coppersmith's murder had hit the news, the phones had been running hot with information, all of which had taken precious time to investigate. The killer was a ghost or blended so well into Black Rock Falls, no one had actually seen him moving to or from any of the crime scenes. Any leads they had run down had been a complete waste of time.

She waited for her deputies to take seats then smiled at Wolfe. "Okay, what do you have for me?"

"Plenty." Wolfe dropped a file on the table. "I've been working closely with the FBI's Cyber Division. They discovered a small thread of information about a syndicate running a pay-per-view site on the dark web. This site is disturbing; for instance, cannibalism. I found advertisements and some folks actually volunteer to be eaten."

"Oh my God." Bradford paled and covered her mouth.

Jenna glared at her. "Go on."

"We already know the dark web is used for every illegal activity across the spectrum. The problem is that they are virtually impossible to track. They select remote locations, which are difficult to identify." Wolfe opened the folder. "Until now." He handed images to Jenna and Kane. "These are stills from a fraction of video from the murder of Lilly Coppersmith." He cleared his throat. "Worse still, if you look at the bottom of the images, you can see an indicator and a corresponding list. I believe the people watching controlled what happened next. They voted and paid for the killer's next move."

"This is a first, a psychopath taking orders during a kill. Usually they are in almost a trance of self-centered bliss." Kane sifted through the images. "How much of this do you have?"

"That's it." Wolfe pushed a hand through his hair and gave Kane a weary look. "I used every technique I know but this organization is very smart; they broadcast then autodelete. This is why I only found a trace of the video."

Jenna's stomach clenched at the horrific shots and the realization of exactly what Wolfe had discovered. It wasn't long ago that she had been that woman, tied, naked, and helpless with a maniac hovering over her. This was her trigger, the scene that caused a chain reaction in her mind and sent her tumbling into a flashback. A wave of nausea washed over her and she thrust the memory to the back of her mind and replaced it with a butterfly perching on a flower. As her control dropped firmly back into place, she folded her hands on the table and took a deep breath. She was determined to catch this man before he could harm anyone else. "We at least know why he needed the trail cams now, and the body cam." She glanced at Wolfe. "No leads on the killer? No images of him at all?"

"Nope. He is using a voice distorter as well, and what we do have is fragmented; the FBI will see if they can clean it up but it's doubtful." Wolfe leaned back in his chair. "I do have information on the backpacks." He sifted through the photographs in the file. "I've uploaded all this information to the appropriate files. As we have at least three people, I named the file 'Backpacks' for an easy reference. I'll leave it to you to chase down what information I found on them, but at this stage I would assume they are deceased." He sighed. "Until you determine if they are dead or alive, we have nothing to investigate. However—" Wolfe pulled an evidence bag from his pocket and placed it gently on the table "—one of the bags had a small camera wrapped in a pair of socks. Unusual as most people use their cellphones to take selfies, but as luck would have it, I found images of a couple with Bear Peak in the background. They are in the file, and the FBI cross-checked the images on all available databases; the couple is from France and went missing two years ago."

"It's a Nikon." Kane's face held a puzzled expression as he peered at the camera. "Blythe senior said he hadn't sold anything from the bags; perhaps he was telling the truth."

Jenna stared at him in disbelief. "If he found valuables, he should have handed them in."

"Well, technically he did." Kane met her gaze. "He gave them to me."

"What else did you find, Wolfe?" Jenna reached for her coffee and sipped.

"The contents of each bag gave clues to the identity of the owners. Tags in clothes had names and we found a credit card inside a concealed pocket. Out-of-state and overseas visitors, all of them. Likely one woman and three men, going on the contents of the backpacks. The woman in the photographs has dark hair, which is significant. I found blood trace evidence on all of the bags, and it is degraded but it is human." Wolfe's lips formed a thin line. "People don't leave expensive cameras and credit cards behind. I found a similarity between these bags and the ones we took from the crime scenes. Someone or something covered these bags with organic material from the forest floor. From the rate of decomposition and fungi growth in the organic material, I believe someone attempted to bury them at one time."

"That would be hard to do in the forest with the number of animals foraging around." Rowley looked up from making notes. "They are inquisitive. A bear will tear a camp to shreds looking for a snack, same with a backpack. I'm surprised the bags are intact." He rubbed his chin. "I haven't seen bobcats bury things." He smiled. "Apart from their poop."

Jenna got to her feet and stared at the whiteboard. "What jumps out at me is the killer or killers are targeting hikers who are unfamiliar with the area."

"It also means we have more bodies in the forest." Kane's gaze moved over the evidence. "Depending on how far back the murders occurred, we will have a difficult time finding them."

"Don't forget Lilly Coppersmith came from Blackwater." Bradford leaned forward in her chair. "She should have been familiar with Black Rock Falls."

Jenna shook her head. "Not necessarily; this might have been her first visit." She stared at Colter Barry's name for a long second then tapped the whiteboard. "We need to speak with him again. I want to know how he happened to be on a remote trail and if he discussed his trip with anyone in town." She turned and looked at Kane. "Someone is watching these couples; they find out where they are heading, and if it is in a remote area, they set up the trail cams then kill them." She turned her attention back on Wolfe. "How long would it take to set up a pay-per-view?"

"If they have subscribers, as long as it takes to send a text." Wolfe's chair creaked as he leaned forward. "Live-screening is instantaneous. They would launch an app and there would be at least two people involved. The killer and a moneyman who does the grunt work, likely a black hat he is working with and trusts to a certain degree. Remember, in the world of the dark web, people are ghosts without faces, they are usernames or simply codes. I would say the moneyman

pays the killer a retainer or advance then a percentage of the take."
He sighed. "For the killer, it's a win–win situation. He gets the thrill
of the kill and a bulging bank balance."

"Untraceable?" Jenna huffed out a breath.

"Yeah, I'm afraid so. I can't even give you a heads up if they set
up again. They move the download mirrors and only the subscribers
get the link." Wolfe pushed to his feet. "That's all I have to report,
ma'am, and I need to get back to the lab. I'll call if anything significant
comes through from the samples we took at the crime scenes and
send my full report by email."

Jenna smiled at him. "Thank you. I appreciate the time you've
put into this, Wolfe."

"Just doing my job, ma'am." Wolfe pushed on his hat and headed
for the door.

Jenna sat down and sifted through the file Wolfe had left on the
desk. "Okay, this will take a couple of days to work through. Rowley,
I want you and Bradford to search for the backpack people and see
if you can find any reports on them. The first place to contact is
their embassy or local police. They would know if their families had
reported them missing and when." She tapped her bottom lip. "If you
come up empty, find out if they left the country and when. While
you're doing that, Kane and I will pay Colter Barry another visit."

CHAPTER FORTY-FIVE

At the hospital, Jenna greeted the deputy from Blackwater sitting outside the elevator on the secure floor. The Blackwater Sheriff's Department had supplied men for shifts around the clock, with Walters filling in where possible. "Thank you for your help. I gather three deputies are staying at the motel until we can get Mr. Barry to a safer location?"

"Yes, ma'am, and with Kane here making sure Aunt Betty's Café keeps us well fed, there won't be any lack of volunteers the next time you need assistance."

Jenna bit back a smile. "That's good."

She led the way to the hospital room with Kane close behind and smothered a gasp at Colter Barry's bruised and battered face.

"Good morning, Mr. Barry. How are they treating you?"

"I'm okay. I have drugs for the pain." Barry's bloodshot eyes settled on her face. "My folks came by to see me last night and I'll be going home as soon as the swelling goes down on my spine. The doc says there's no permanent damage but it was close."

"That's good." Jenna pulled up a chair and sat down. "We are going to arrange for you to stay in a safe house until we catch Lilly's killer. You are the only person who has seen him and he doesn't know you can't identify him."

"Okay. I guess." Tears leaked from Barry's eyes. "Do you know what it feels like to be helpless while some maniac kills the person you love?"

"Yeah, I do." Kane dragged a chair from the other side of the room and sat down. "You can't blame yourself and you can't change anything."

"I miss her so much." Barry's bottom lip quivered just slightly.

"I would say 'sorry for your loss' but it means nothing." Kane cleared his throat. "What gets me through is knowing their love will remain in your heart forever and they'll always live in your memories. Any time, day or night, you just have to think about them and they are with you again."

"Thanks." Barry blinked at Kane. "That is a lovely thing to say."

A love that lasts forever. His wife. Jenna glanced at Kane and swallowed the lump in her throat then turned back to Barry. "We came to see you because we need what you can tell us about where you went and who you spoke to before you went on the hike."

"Last Friday we caught the bus up the mountain for a look around. I wanted to find out from the checking station if there were any safe hiking places well away from the hunters. We hiked up to the falls. We stayed at the Black Rock Falls Motel. Caught the bus on Sunday and got put down near the old trail to Bear Peak."

"So, you found out about the trail from one of the wardens or a ranger?" Jenna took out her notebook and pen. "Do you remember his name, or can you give me a description?"

"No, not a warden. They were so busy they told me to take a map and keep out of the designated hunting areas." Barry sucked in a breath. "We missed the bus and hitchhiked, got a ride from one of the hunters. I asked him for the most secluded trails and he gave me an old map. He told me about the track leading to Bear Peak, how quiet it was away from the tourists. In fact, all the info we needed. He even gave us the bus information. He was a real nice guy."

Psychopaths usually are real nice people. Jenna and Kane exchanged meaningful looks. She smiled at Barry. "Do you remember where you put the map?"

"It was in the pocket of my jeans. The doctors cut them off me when I arrived."

Jenna sighed. The hospital would have incinerated them by now. "Do you remember what type of car he was driving?"

"Nope, it was the same as everyone's rig around here." Barry closed his eyes. "It was a dark color, I don't remember the make."

"What about the driver, was he from around here?" Kane leaned forward. "Or did he have an accent? Was he Caucasian, Native American?"

"He was white, wearing a woolen cap like yours, didn't see his hair or eyes—he was wearing shades. Can't say how tall he was either, he was sitting down." Barry shook his head. "He wasn't the killer—that man had a creepy voice like an alien."

"Did you see his hands?" Jenna pushed on. "Any rings, scars on his face or hands, tattoos?"

"Nope, he was wearing gloves." Barry sighed then moaned and pressed the morphine drip dispenser clutched in one hand. "He was a normal guy. He dropped us right at the motel. We ordered in for dinner and left town early Sunday to catch the bus. We didn't speak to anyone else about our plans." He closed his eyes and took a deep breath.

Jenna stood. It was pointless trying to question him now. She turned to Kane and waved him outside into the hallway. "What do you think?"

"If it was the killer, then it's more than likely a chance meeting because he is too smart to risk someone seeing him with the victims." Kane shrugged. "If someone did see him pick them up hitchhiking, Barry says he dropped them off at the motel. It wouldn't be evidence against him but as Lilly was the type of woman he enjoys killing, he used the information he gave Barry to set the scene for his next kill."

A shiver slipped down Jenna's back. "That easy? That scares the hell out of me."

"That easy this time maybe but not for the others. The chances of everything falling into place for him like that would be remote." Kane rubbed the back of his neck. "I figure the only possible way the killer finds his victims is once he sees a suitable couple, he stalks them to discover their movements. Let's face it, most couples who don't come here to hunt are looking for a romantic weekend or honeymoon."

Jenna leaned against the wall, running the information through her mind. "Stalking them would be difficult unless the killer works in the industry, as in at the hotel or even as a travel agent. How else would he be able to follow their movements or know their plans?"

"The killer could frequent the Cattleman's Hotel like most of the hunters in town; we know the first two couples stayed there." Kane shrugged. "We have two suspects who go there as well: Woods and Canavar. We have information that Canavar visited Black Rock Falls last fall and I would be interested to know if he took a room at the hotel."

Jenna chewed on her bottom lip. "Both men fit the description Barry gave us, but this scenario removes the Blythes. I doubt either of them go to the Cattleman's Hotel very often."

"They don't fit the description of the man who picked up Lilly and Colter. I wouldn't describe either of them as a—" Kane made quote marks in the air with his fingers "—'really nice guy.' Would anyone suspect a nice guy staying at the hotel who has a casual chat with them in the restaurant or at the bar? This is a friendly town, everyone chats to strangers."

Jenna nodded. "That's true."

"Then again the killer could have a partner who works where the old maps are still available. Psychopaths could be smooth-talking, good-looking men; he could have a woman for a partner. Remember there are women who are attracted to killers." Kane stared into space as if running scenarios through his mind. "The moment they come across a suitable couple mentioning hiking in a secluded area, they alert the killer and he stalks them until he discovers their plans. He sets up the pay-per-view and meets them on the trail."

Jenna gaped at him then the pieces started to fall into place. Everything Kane said made sense. No one would sit in wait for days in the forest hoping a couple matching his perfect type would stumble into a trap. "Yes, previous gaps between kills could mean he was waiting for the right couple to come along." She straightened. "As the Cattleman's Hotel is linked to two couples, and two suspects, we should head back to the office and split the workload. I want information on the owners of the backpacks as soon as possible. If any of them are missing, we need to find out if they stayed at the Cattleman's Hotel and when."

"Yeah, and I would like to know how many people inquire about the old trails. I'll make some calls and find out who has copies of the old maps available for tourists." Kane glanced at her. "We'll need to be told if anyone makes inquiries then alert them to the dangers."

Jenna headed along the corridor. "Let's hope one of the people we talk to isn't the killer's partner, or he'll know we're closing in on him."

CHAPTER FORTY-SIX

He arrived back at the Cattleman's Hotel in time for lunch. His business in town had not taken long, and after watching the local news broadcast, it was obvious Colter Barry had not been able to offer a clear description of the killer, described as Caucasian, between five ten and six feet tall, wearing camouflage gear. He chuckled. That description covered at least fifty percent of the men in town at this time of the year.

He passed Paul and Mariah on the way to the restaurant and headed for the stairs. He had discovered so much about them in a short time. Simply by following them into the hotel elevator and leaving on the same floor, he had their room numbers. Obtaining a pass card had been easy. He had "accidentally" tripped over one of the housekeeping staff and removed the card from the cord on her belt without her noticing.

Not a soul passed him in the hallway, and the excitement of entering Mariah's room made his hands shake. She had dressed in a hurry. Clothes littered the bed and it was easy to see which side Mariah preferred by the open book on the bedside table. He touched her intimate belongings and, staring at his reflection in the mirror, rubbed them over his nose, inhaling her scent. His expression showed an urgent desire to kill her—on a face none of his prey would ever see.

He lay on the bed, wishing housekeeping had not made up the room, and pressed his head in the pillow to leave an indent. Tonight, she would place her face there and maybe smell a hint of his aftershave. He swung his legs off the bed and reluctantly stood then selected a pair of silk panties from the drawer. After kissing them, he laid them on top of the old map on the nightstand then selected a lacy bra and draped it over the phone. Would she notice? Would she sense he had been there, would she feel his kiss on her underwear?

It took effort to leave and not hide inside the cupboard to watch her, but the fun was in the hunt. Killing her in the hotel was not an option, although he would have enjoyed it. He smiled to himself, imagining how she would react when he told her how close she'd come to dying in her bed.

After spending the night before viewing footage from his favorite hunts, he had great plans for the next kill—for Mariah especially. As he walked through the restaurant entrance, his mouth watered at the sight of the couple chatting over their meal. They were creatures of habit and dined here every day. Before he finalized his plans, he needed a little more information about his prey and wanted an excuse to get closer. As perfect as Mariah and Paul appeared, hunting people from out of state or overseas had always been a better option. It was often weeks before their relatives reported them missing. He turned to the maître d'. "Is that Sheriff Alton over by the window?"

"No, that is Mr. Benton and Miss Crane out of Washington and in town for the conference, I believe." The maître d' gave him a smile. "I must admit I did mistake her for the sheriff as well. They could be related but it's not worth my job to pry." He turned to a waiter. "Ah, Erik will show you to your table."

He smiled at Erik. "Is the table over by the window available? It's such a nice day."

"Of course." Erik led the way.

After ordering, he stared at the window, watching the couple in the reflection in the glass. *Paul Benton and Mariah Crane, enjoy your meal while you can.* He caught a few bits of their conversation but nothing more about their plans for the weekend. His only option would be to set up his trail cams ahead of time then wait and watch before following them to their camp. His heart pounded. Being so close to his prey yet unable to touch was excruciating.

His attention drifted to Paul; he would be no fun at all. A big man was always a threat but by hitting him in just the right spot in his lower spine, he would be paralyzed and under his control. He had become quite the expert on disabling his prey. Once he removed the male, the hunt could begin, although Colter Barry had gotten away. He would need to make sure he incapacitated them in future. He would show Paul how a dominant male should treat a sassy-mouthed bitch, then he would take him apart piece by piece. Or he might gain interest from his viewers by offering him as target practice. *Now that would be fun.*

He would leave Paul's remains for the bears. After all, they would enjoy a good meal before winter. The forest had such a useful ecosystem, so many critters ready and willing to move in and take out the trash. Leaving a trail cam hidden high in the trees to watch would be entertaining, but with the sheriff stumbling over his kills of late, it wouldn't be worth the risk.

With Paul as bear meat, Mariah would gain his full attention. She would be begging and trembling, just the way he liked his women. He stared into her reflection in the glass, imagining her torso dripping with blood. His skill of dissection would keep her alive and experiencing the delight of excruciating pain for as long as he decided. What would she offer him to stop? He grinned. *I never stop.*

His attention slid to the slash of red surrounding her white smile; the ripple in the glass distorted the color into a smear of blood. He bit back a groan; he could almost taste Mariah's mouth, cold and set in a silent scream, pressing against his lips. His cave would be close by and his friends would enjoy some female company. He grinned into his glass of red wine. *I'm going to keep her.*

CHAPTER FORTY-SEVEN

After hunting down places that kept the old maps, and making inquiries about anyone who had asked about the old trails, Jenna had taken down notes about a few vague memories but had found nothing of value. Armed with a list of the owners of the backpacks, Jenna set out with Kane after lunch to the Cattleman's Hotel.

As they stepped from Kane's rig, the wind picked up, swirling the fall leaves around their feet. Jenna looked up at the gray sky; the weather had been unpredictable of late with showers and sudden drops in temperature as if winter had made plans to arrive early this year. She glanced up at Kane. "I'm sure glad the fall dance isn't until next weekend. I'm not sure we could handle the workload right now."

"We're fortunate to have the Blackwater deputies assisting Walters to guard Colter Barry at the hospital." Kane's expression was grim. "I'll feel happier when we have him locked in a safe house."

Jenna walked through the glass doors of the hotel, almost colliding with Ethan Woods. He gave her a contemptuous glare, slammed a black Stetson on his head, and brushed past her. She stopped in the entrance and turned slowly to watch his progress to a black truck. "I can't believe the judge allowed Stone to post bail."

"Wolfe found zip at the barn to suggest he used the place to wash up after killing Lilly. We know he was in the area and have him on video, but so far we only have circumstantial evidence, he was involved in the murders. The trespassing charges are all we have on him." He smiled at her. "The judge had no choice but he is still on our radar. He fits the description Barry gave us, was in the area, and fits the profile."

"Oh, I figure he could be the killer, but being a nice guy seems a stretch of the imagination. I've only seen his nasty side." Jenna strolled to the front desk, noticing the display of maps and other brochures set in a holder.

In her periphery, she noticed Nigel heading their way. She offered him a smile. "I'm after some information."

"I'm at your service as usual, Sheriff Alton." Nigel cleared his throat. "As long as it doesn't contravene our privacy policy."

Jenna took out her notebook. "As you are aware, three murders occurred in Stanton Forest recently and we also have a cold case. We are aware that two of the couples stayed here; one couple stayed at the motel."

"That in itself isn't unusual; most people take rooms here." If Nigel had been a bird, he would have fluffed his feathers. "I hope you're not suggesting that is a reason for their murders?"

"Not at all." Jenna shrugged. "We figured as out-of-towners they must have gotten their information about the safe hiking trails from here." She leaned on the counter. "Do you recall Bailey and Jim Canavar asking about the old trails?"

"Well, I sure do." Nigel pressed a hand dramatically against his chest. "I gave them a map and showed them some of the old trails up near Bear Peak. Good Lord, you don't think I sent them to their deaths, do you?"

"No." Kane rested one hip against the counter and gave Jenna a meaningful stare. "Do you remember anyone else here at the time, anyone who could have overheard the conversation?"

"It was busy at the time. Yes, I do remember there being a line of people waiting. Some were annoyed because I chatted to them, but no, I don't recall anyone specific." Nigel's face paled. "Oh, and Erik asked me for an old map recently for one of our customers. He is one of the waiters in the restaurant." He glanced from one to the other. "It's not unusual for couples to head off on their own to the more remote areas. These old maps are in high demand. I gather tons of people prefer to hike in the remote areas and commune with nature."

Jenna drummed her fingertips on the wooden counter. "Okay, thanks for the information; we'll speak to Erik." She pushed her notepad across the desk with the list of names of the backpack owners. "We have reason to believe these missing people could have passed through town. They might be victims of the same killer. Could you check the records, going back a couple of years, and see if they stayed here?"

"If I don't, you'll get a search warrant, right?" Nigel peered at the list then tapped the names into the computer. "We have information going back seven years or so." He glanced at Jenna. "This might take a while." He pulled out four coupons from under the desk and handed them to her. "Complimentary cakes and coffee while you wait?"

"Well, I figure as I'm asking him for a favor, this can't be considered a bribe." She grinned at Kane. "I guess I'll have to force you to eat cake?"

"Well, we do have a good excuse. We need to talk to Erik." Kane's stomach growled and he looked sheepish. "I know it's only been two hours since lunch." He turned toward the restaurant then spun around and grabbed Jenna by the shoulders.

Jenna glared at him. "What are you doing?"

"Move." Kane's broad shoulders blocked her view.

Turned away and almost pushed into a corner, she glared up at him. "What the hell is going on, Kane?"

"Do you have a sister?" Kane's voice had lowered to just above a whisper. "Any family member that looks like you?"

Jenna shook her head. "No, I've told you before. I don't have any living relatives. Why?"

When Kane moved to one side, Jenna gaped at the woman strolling toward the elevator. After extensive plastic surgery to disguise her, she could resemble anyone. She looked up at him and whispered, "Oh, shit. Now I know where my face came from. I hope she isn't anyone famous." She walked back to the counter and Nigel glanced up at her from the computer screen. "That couple looks familiar. Who are they?"

"Paul Benton and Mariah Crane out of Washington for the convention." Nigel raised an inquiring brow. "Is she a relative?"

Jenna smiled. "I thought so but I don't recall her name. I might catch up with her later. How long is she staying?"

"I can't say for sure— the convention winds up on Friday but they do have the after-convention socials through to next Wednesday."

"Great, thanks!" She turned to Kane. "Let's go find Erik."

When Jenna asked the maître d' if Erik could seat them, he gave them a beaming smile and waved the young waiter forward. The restaurant was practically empty with only a few people lingering over coffee and cake. They took a table at the back of the room and waited for him to bring the cart with an array of delicious cakes and pastries. After making their selection, she brought up the information Nigel had given them. "Do you remember who asked you for a map of the old trails?"

"Yes, it was Mr. Benton and Miss Crane. They have been working so hard at the convention they said they needed a break away from everyone. I suggested the trail that goes way up along the res, then veers off along Bear Peak. They can see the waterfalls if they climb up to the plateau and the views are great." He served the cake and poured the coffee. "They planned to spend the weekend hiking." He smiled at them. "I'll leave the cart. The chef throws out leftovers at four so you might as well eat your fill. I'll bring you a fresh pot of coffee."

"Thank you." Jenna leaned back in her chair, taking in the look of concentration on Kane's face. "What are you thinking about? Not cake, that's for sure."

"I've figured out a plan."

CHAPTER FORTY-EIGHT

Unable to persuade Kane to discuss details of his plan in a public place, the moment they had finished eating, Jenna returned to the front counter to discover if the backpack owners had stayed at the hotel. Nigel confirmed that two of the three missing people had booked a room, and both in the fall of previous years. The coincidences between the victims were stacking up.

After they headed back to the sheriff's office, Jenna called in Wolfe and her deputies. Once they had taken their seats, she turned her attention to Kane. "Okay, no one can overhear us in here. What is your plan?"

"It would depend on the cooperation of Mr. Benton and Miss Crane." Kane's gaze swept the other deputies. "They are a couple staying at the hotel and Miss Crane bears a striking resemblance to the sheriff. Going on the last murders, Miss Crane is the type our murderer likes, and they plan to go hiking at Bear Peak at the weekend." His attention fixed on Jenna. "I believe there is a good chance they could be the killer's next target."

"Okay. So, you want to use them as bait?" Rowley leaned forward in his seat, pen raised above his notebook. "How do you plan to rope them into your scheme?"

Jenna cleared her throat, gaining everyone's attention. "We are not—I repeat *not*—using anyone as bait for a serial killer."

"Not *them*. I would never risk a civilian's life." Kane's eyes darkened and he turned into the highly trained iceman killer she had glimpsed before. "Us."

Jenna had spent time undercover during her time with the DEA and had escaped with little to spare, the result of which had landed her in Black Rock Falls with a new face and name. Placing herself in the direct line of fire and risking a lunatic dissecting her alive did not appeal to her in the least. She chewed on her bottom lip and considered the implications then met Kane's gaze. "I think you've lost your ever-loving mind but I'll listen. Lay it on me."

"Crane resembles you, and the couple are out of Washington like us, so the accents won't be a problem. She is the murderer's type of preferred woman, and from the intel on their movements this coming weekend, I figure we have two choices." Kane leaned on the desk, folding his huge forearms. "Get the couple the hell out of Dodge or get them to advertise their plans for the weekend far and wide then move them to a safe house and take their places. I'm pretty sure as the killer's main focus will be on the woman, I'll be able to pass as Benton at a distance, especially if I wear a Kevlar vest under my jacket to add the extra bulk." His attention moved over Jenna's face. "We are trained to take down this son of a bitch and we'll have backup."

"*If* he takes the bait." Wolfe's expression was grim. "We are only surmising he picks out couples visiting town then sets a trap once he knows where they're heading. He isn't going to be sitting up in the mountains on the off chance someone will stroll by, and not every woman is going to fit the type he prefers." He sighed. "I bet I could count on one hand the number of couples who venture up the old trails."

Jenna shook her head. "Not according to Nigel at the counter of the hotel. He informed us it is common for people to hike in the remote areas, and they pick up maps all the time." She shrugged. "This tells me we have two possible scenarios. The first: The killer could be either Woods or Canavar. As we haven't found a trace of

Canavar, he could be living off the grid somewhere in the forest, and we know Woods was prowling the area at night. If they set up trail cams on the more remote areas around Bear Peak, they could be monitoring the area. It wouldn't be difficult to get to a suitable target if they placed themselves in a central position. Secondly: If the killer is lurking around town and maybe stalking suitable couples, as Kane suggests, he'll take the bait."

"Assuming you're right, I would say the killer is planning another pay-per-view, and he will need time to set up the location. So once he is sure of the couple's destination, he will go on ahead." Wolfe's lips formed a thin line and worry creased his brow. "It's risky. We have to assume this man has considerable IT skills. If I planned this, I would set up a hidden camera in the hallway outside their room and maybe place a tracker on their vehicle." He glanced at Jenna. "That's another thing, we are assuming this is a single killer yet he manages to kill, clean up, and dispose of the victim's vehicles before we find the bodies."

"Yeah, but in the first murder, the wildlife took care of the bodies." Rowley lifted his chin and looked at Wolfe. "He was expecting the same thing for Bailey Canavar and John Doe. I figure he has gotten rid of their cars after the murders to give the impression they left the area. From what we know, most of the tourists rent a car from the airport. He probably leaves the car at the drop-off point and cabs it back to town."

"That would work as the vehicles are cleaned and sent out again." Wolfe rubbed his chin. "All trace evidence is destroyed but that situation wouldn't apply if we catch him this time."

Jenna leaned back in her chair and ran the scenarios through her mind. Kane had tactical experience and so did Wolfe as both had served in the marines. "Okay, so we wear the Kevlar vests; that's not going to help if he decides to take a headshot, is it?"

"Nope." Kane shrugged. "But it's not his MO. From what we've seen, he disables the male victims with a lower lumbar shot to paralyze him. My vest will cover me and we will deploy the rest of the team in high positions. With everyone dressed in camo, we will look like a normal hunting party, but we will all be carrying concealed weapons. Wolfe, Rowley, and Webber will be carrying rifles, and they'll look legit if they are seen by the killer." He leaned back and stretched out his legs. "Look at the area we have to work with; it's close to the mountain and we get to choose the location. We will have the advantage. We will know he is coming so he won't have the element of surprise. We will be armed and highly trained. It should be a walk in the park."

"I'll set up a few trail cams of my own as well." Wolfe looked at her. "You'll have trackers and coms just in case anything goes wrong."

"I don't think Jenna and I can risk trail cams or use coms." Kane turned his head to speak to Wolfe. "If he sees them, he'll smell a rat. He will likely be using a scope to bring down the guy, and from what we have seen so far, he is not careless."

A wave of dread closed in around Jenna; her deputies were talking as if this was a military mission: no emotion, no worries they might die. Kane and Wolfe threw ideas back and forth, and she listened, intrigued. Unlike her, they had been deployed overseas during their time in the marines. Kane and Wolfe had gained more experience in the field than she had. What they had planned was potentially a life-threatening situation, and when dealing with a psychopath anything could go wrong. She offered up a few of her own ideas but decided to take a small step back and defer to their skills.

"Okay. I want Kane to take the lead in planning the tactical, and Wolfe you'll lead in the field." She looked at him. "Make sure everyone is on the same page; our lives are on the line." She scanned the faces before her. "I'll speak to the couple by phone; we can't risk being seen with them. If they agree, we will arrange to switch places with them in the clothing store, Dowy's, the expensive one. It won't be busy early in the day. I'll send Maggie in with uniforms well beforehand, and Mr. Dowy will cooperate."

"It could work." Bradford wet her lips nervously and her eyes darted to Kane then back to Jenna. "Where do I fit in?"

Jenna smiled at her. "You'll be the lookout, and if Wolfe is busy, you'll be able to relay messages to the team via your com."

"What if we have to stay up there overnight?" Bradford picked at her fingernails.

"Then Wolfe will organize sentry duty." Kane's look was direct. "It's going to be cold and you'll be sleeping rough. Say now if you want to stand down; we'll understand."

"No, I've slept rough before, I'll be fine." Bradford lifted her chin. "I'm part of the team."

"And me, ma'am." Webber straightened and looked at Jenna and his eyes sparkled with excitement.

Jenna waved a hand toward Kane. "Kane will organize tactical."

Kane's chair creaked as he turned to look at Webber. "You and Rowley will join Wolfe as our sharpshooters. You'll be positioned up high to scan the immediate area for the killer."

"Roger that." Webber looked suitably impressed. "Who will take care of things in town?"

Jenna sighed. "Colter Barry will be in the safe house by the weekend. So I'll have Walters and Maggie here. They are quite capable of holding the fort at the weekend." She rubbed her hands together. "Okay, now all we have to do is convince Crane and Benton to set up a serial killer."

Kane's almost blank combat expression remained set in place. "And we have to hope the murdering SOB takes the bait."

CHAPTER FORTY-NINE

Thursday, week two

The outdoors store was busy and he waited in one of the lines to the counter, arms piled high with spare camo, two new pairs of hiking boots, and spare ammunition. He glanced sideways and straight into the eyes of Mariah Crane. She lifted her nose as if he smelled like old socks and turned to her companion. The same older man he knew as Paul Benton. As they shuffled to the counter, he could hear Mariah as clear as if she was speaking to him.

"For once I agree with you, Paul." Mariah fingered the thick hoodie over one arm. "We do need warmer clothes for the mountains. I'm so glad you persuaded me to go up to Bear Peak; that old Native American trail leads right to a plateau. I'll get some wonderful shots of the valley from there."

"Look here." Benton maneuvered his shopping cart to one side and took a map from his pocket. "We can drive here and leave the car. See – there are three trails: The one on the left is the old one; the other two lead to the falls. So if we take this one that follows a trail to a canyon with a spectacular ravine, it will be amazing to view from the top." He smiled at her. "I spoke to Nigel at the hotel; he told me it's colder up there at this time of the year. Most visitors take the trails lower down the mountain and visit the rock pools and rivers. It's well away from the designated hunting areas and the chances of us running across anyone from the conference will be remote. In fact, darn near impossible. I asked around and no one is heading up that way this weekend."

"I hope you didn't tell anyone where we're heading." Mariah pouted. "I don't want another day ruined."

"I'm not a complete idiot." Paul touched her cheek. "This weekend will be one to remember, I promise."

I promise too. He pushed the graphic images he'd conjured of Mariah's body after he'd finished with her to the back of his mind and focused. He waited a beat to present a calm exterior, dropped his purchases on the counter, and smiled at the sales clerk. "Great weather for hunting."

"Sure is. I think this has been our busiest season this year. Tons of new faces in town as well, and everyone is spending big. It seems like Black Rock Falls is becoming a top tourist destination." The man dropped the goods into a paper bag and gave him the total.

He used cash, much safer in case anyone decided to check out credit card receipts for his caliber ammunition. "I'll be well away from the tourists. I aim to bag me a ten-point buck. I spotted one yesterday heading right toward a hunting zone."

"Good luck." The man handed him his purchases.

He strolled outside and grinned into the sunshine. Some days it was worth getting out of bed. The players in his pay-per-view had just confirmed the weekend's schedule. He could not believe his luck. Rather than following them around for the next couple of days to discover their plans, he could finish any business he had to do in town, collect his gear, and head to the checking station closest to Bear Peak. His cover for being in the area would be secure. It was a long hike through the hunting area to the old trail they had mentioned, and fortunately close to his cave. He'd have plenty of time to set up then just sit back and wait for them to arrive. He dumped his shopping in the back of his rig, took out his burner cellphone, and sent a text to the organizer:

Saturday. Will give a one-hour countdown. Lock and load.

CHAPTER FIFTY

Saturday

In town, multicolored leaves blew across the blacktop and sat in drifts over the curb, giving the air the earthy smell that came with fall. It was a great day to be outside, sunny with clear blue skies, and the townsfolk and tourists were making the most of it. It was not yet eight thirty, but stalls selling everything from cakes to hotdogs lined the sidewalk. Kane slipped from Rowley's cruiser and followed him and Jenna to the clothing store. So far, everything had gone to plan. Mariah and Paul were more than happy to cooperate after discovering they could be the next victims on the killer's list. In fact, Mariah informed the sheriff she had the feeling someone had been watching them since their arrival in Black Rock Falls.

The couple had been enthusiastic in helping them trap the killer after Jenna had ensured their safety. Armed with one of Wolfe's tracking devices, to activate if threatened, and with a deputy on duty close by, the couple had visited all the locations that handed out the old maps over the past two days. They had made a point of publicly discussing their plans for the weekend in each store and at the Cattleman's Hotel. If the killer had stalked them, he would have all the information he needed.

They had planned the arranged changeover to the second. The couple arrived earlier to browse the range of goods for sale, more expensive than in the local outdoors store. Kane took out his notepad and paused to read his notes, to give the appearance he was on the job, then went inside the clothing store. He gave the owner a nod then went straight to the fitting room area, where he found Paul wearing one of his old uniforms and Mariah dressed as Jenna. "Okay, wait at the counter then go with Rowley. He'll drive you to a safe house—it's a ranch out of town. Deputy Walters will be checking on you by phone." Kane handed them a burner cellphone. "His number is in the contacts. Don't call anyone else at all. Understand?"

"Yes, the sheriff made it quite clear." Paul pulled the black woolen cap down over his ears and shrugged into a jacket.

Kane gave the couple a once-over and nodded. "You'll pass as us at a distance. Don't make eye contact with anyone, just go straight to the car."

The couple waited a few minutes then left with Rowley. He would drive them to the ranch then leave his cruiser in town. After changing into camo, he would collect Bradford and drive an unmarked rig to meet the rest of the team at Bear Peak.

Kane changed clothes and met Jenna at the counter. "All good?"

"Yeah." She handed over her folded uniform to the clerk. "Thanks for your cooperation, Mr. Dowy. We'll drop by on Monday and pick up our things."

"My pleasure, Sheriff." Mr. Dowy placed both uniforms in a large bag and pushed it under the counter. "These will be safe with me, don't you worry none."

Glad that Dowy was a retired cop and understood the meaning of secrecy, Kane grabbed the bags of spare clothes and ammunition they had stashed there and followed Jenna to Paul Benton's rental car. He slid behind the wheel. "That went well. I hope the killer took the bait."

"That was just a precaution." Jenna buckled up. "I figure the moment he discovered the couple's plans he would have hightailed it to Bear Peak to set up his macabre theater." She glanced at him as they headed out of town. "If not, this is all a waste of time."

Thirty minutes later, Kane checked his watch and pulled the rental into the parking lot near the falls. The success or failure of any mission was often in the timing. He called Wolfe for an update and listened in silence. "Roger that, we are moving out. ETA twenty minutes."

Wolfe and Webber had taken positions above the trail and each could cover a one-eighty-degree angle of the forest below. Rowley and Bradford would be along soon. The team had dressed in camo to blend into the forest, and from the moment the couple had agreed to their plan, he had drilled the team like a sergeant. They were as ready as they would ever be.

Agreed, his plan had more holes than a sieve, but if it was one chance in fifty of stopping the killer, it was worth it. The location posed a number of problems and gave the killer an advantage. The density of the trees would hide a man in camouflage but Kane had selected a small area for the couple to talk about and Wolfe and Webber could zero in on them in seconds if the killer attacked. He had confidence in the team but his priority would be keeping Jenna safe. She was the killer's main target and he was just window dressing.

As they climbed from the car and collected their backpacks, he glanced at her determined expression and an unusual trickle of worry ran down his back. She had jumped in boots and all to take down a killer who would dissect her alive. That took guts. Oh, yeah, she could fight, and if he went down, she had superior skills plus the backup of three good men with sniper rifles. *I don't plan on going down.*

"You know, I can tell when you're worried." Jenna shrugged into her backpack and slid one hand inside her jacket to check the Glock in her shoulder holster. "You pull this face, like you've been turned to stone or something."

"Yeah? I've been trained to turn off all external stimuli and concentrate on the mission." He slid the handle of the bag carrying supplies over one shoulder then adjusted the straps of his backpack. "I didn't think it was that obvious."

"It is." She smiled at him and slid on her sunglasses. "The killer could be scoping us right now, and you're supposed to be a married man out with your secretary for a dirty weekend. Lighten up a bit." She slid her hand into his and dragged him toward the trail. "Walk slow— you're meant to be out of shape."

"With the metal plate Wolfe added to my backpack for extra protection, I won't need to act." He grinned back at her but the smile did not reach the eyes peering at her over the top of his sunglasses. "Stay alert."

"I'm always alert." She led the way down the narrow path then took the trail to the left. "Here we go."

CHAPTER FIFTY-ONE

He leaned against the moss-covered wall of his cave, an iPad balanced on his knees. Using his cellphone as a wireless hotspot, he brought up the images from his webcams and smiled. Exhilaration at seeing Paul and Mariah heading in his direction made his heart pound. He watched them weave between the trees, picking them up again as the trail brought them along the face of Bear Peak. He looked up and grinned at his friends; all looked back and their black eye sockets gave them a wide-eyed appearance. He liked the way their flesh-peeled skulls smiled at him. "Here they come. He turned around the screen to show them. "Do you like her? I chose her just for you. I'll bring her here soon enough to keep you company."

It had not taken him long to set up his webcams then hike back to the designated hunting area. He waited for a couple of strangers to come by then made up a story about seeing two black bears heading toward Bear Peak. He voiced his concern that the tourists visiting the falls might be in danger. As he expected, the older of the two called in the sighting to the checking station to warn hikers to avoid the area. He had waved them goodbye and headed back to his cave for the night.

He enjoyed making camp in his cave. Most men would worry about the smell but he found it stimulating and the way his friends changed fascinated him. It surprised him how they moved as they decayed. He had wrapped them so tightly in plastic, he would have thought it impossible, but he would come by and they would be lying down or collapsed into a heap of bones. He sighed and turned his attention back to Paul and Mariah. They had reached the main trail and the forest gave way to a few small clearings. Areas big enough to pitch a tent or safely build a fire. In fact, many had fire circles of rocks left by other hikers. If they followed the normal pattern, Paul and Mariah would make camp soon and rest a while, perhaps eat, then he hoped they would venture out to walk the surrounding trails.

He might wait for them to return from their adventures before he struck. They would be tired and Paul would be exhausted after hauling his bulk up the mountain. Paul would be easy prey and no fun at all but *Mariah*. Excitement at thinking her name made his hands tremble. He stared at the screen. "Mariah, will you run? Will you scream?" He ran one finger over the image of the woman getting closer by the minute. "Will you beg?" He moaned. "I so want you to beg, Mariah."

She would be hot from her walk, cheeks pink and her body coated with sweat and fragrant. The hunt would be slow. He wanted to stalk his prey and watch the fear in her eyes before he disabled her and took her back to Paul. He had messaged his online associate a list of what he planned to do to Mariah and already the votes and payments were coming in. The thrill would be in what order his viewers wanted him to kill her. From the last pay-per-view, they all enjoyed a slow kill, just like him.

CHAPTER FIFTY-TWO

Jenna led the way through the forest and they had been walking for some time before Kane tugged on her jacket. She turned to face him and he pulled her into his arms and nuzzled her neck. Surprised, she relaxed against him then heard his voice close to her ear.

"He took the bait and we've just entered the danger zone." Kane cupped the back of her head and stared into her eyes, his voice just above a whisper. "Trail cam at two o'clock. When I spin you, scan the trees on the other side of the trail. They could have audio so be careful what you say and stay in character." He lifted her and twirled her around laughing.

Jenna put her arms around his neck, and when he lowered her to her feet, she stared into the lens of another camera. She grinned at him and kept her voice low. "I see another. We are in the lion's den. Hold my hand and squeeze if you see anyone or a trail cam."

"I think we'd better find somewhere to make camp. There should be a place close by." Kane took her hand and led the way, stepping with care over the uneven ground littered with tree roots. "Ah look, a clearing with firestones. Perfect." He pulled her into the clearing and dumped his bags onto the floor. "I'll pitch the tent. You gonna fix us something to eat?"

"Okay." Jenna shrugged out of her backpack. "We'll have the sandwiches I picked up from the café and there's hot coffee in the thermos. We can collect some wood and light a fire later." She sat on a convenient log set beside the ring of firestones and went through one of the bags.

Behind her, Kane worked fast and had the tent up in minutes then vanished inside with the sleeping bags. Hidden inside, he would contact Wolfe and make sure everyone was in place. She pulled out the thermos, cups, and the bag of sandwiches. It took an effort to appear relaxed when every muscle had tensed so hard they ached. Jenna pushed her sunglasses up the bridge of her nose and moved only her eyes to do a visual reconnaissance of the immediate area. She spotted another trail cam set high on a tree leading away from the campsite. Her skin crawled knowing a violent, vicious killer was watching her and planning how to make her suffer like his other victims. Glad Kane was close by and they had deputies watching over them, she tried to relax. *Get it together, Jenna.*

"You okay, honey?" Kane stepped over the log and sat beside her, his sunglasses masking his expression. "Or are you just bored with me already?"

The unfamiliar term he used for her surprised her for a moment before she realized he was acting the part of Paul Benton for the benefit of anyone listening. "Nope, I'm just starving." Jenna smiled at him. "So, what's next on the agenda after we eat?" She poured him a cup of coffee.

"We can head down the mountain and take a look at the ravine, collect some firewood, and come back." Kane took a sandwich from the bag. "We'll get a fire going and get cozy then in the morning we'll hike up the mountain to the plateau so you can take photographs."

"That sounds great." She leaned into him and did her best to play the role of Mariah, a secretary having an affair with her married boss. She added a slight whine to her voice. "I like being alone with you, Paul. I hate it when we have to go back to work. When are you going to tell your wife about us?"

Kane's sunglasses slipped down his nose and he peered at her cross-eyed. Trust him to make a joke when a violent criminal intent on killing them was close by. Jenna smothered a laugh with a cough and bumped his shoulder. "Well? Cat got your tongue?"

"Nope." He cleared his throat and Jenna almost believed he was Paul Benton. "It's complicated, you *know* that, honey."

"Well, I won't wait forever, Paul." Jenna brushed the crumbs from her hands. "Tons of guys in the office want to date me."

"I know and I'll fix things, you'll just have to be patient." Kane gave her a squeeze. "These things take time."

Wow, he is acting the part. She finished her coffee. "Ready?"

"Five more minutes." Kane chewed slowly and washed down each bite with coffee. "I'm exhausted after that long hike."

Jenna pulled items from their backpacks and tossed them into the tent. "We'll leave most of our things here. I'll take water and a couple of energy bars."

"And the first aid kit." Kane smiled at her. "Put everything in my bag, I don't want you overtired for later."

Jenna gave him a wide smile and stood, handing Kane his backpack. "Which way?"

"Downhill." Kane unfolded the map and made a show of pointing the way. "The switchback is not too far but it will be uphill on the way back." He pocketed the map then shrugged into his backpack and held out his hand. "Come on, it will be fun and we might see some squirrels or even a deer."

Jenna's self-preservation instinct kicked in and the idea of walking into danger lifted the hairs on the back of her neck. With her nerves on a knife's edge, she followed Kane's lead along the narrow, uneven pathway. As they ventured deeper into the forest, the temperature dropped and every shadow they passed seemed to carry a potential threat. A glance into the branches as they walked revealed the killer's trail cams placed in strategic positions. This was his killing ground.

The wind moved through the trees in a cool caress, lifting the leaves on the trail and sending a rush of dread through her. He was out there waiting to make his move. The beauty of the forest faded into the background, leaving behind the threat of a frightening trap. The location alone gave him the advantage. It was fall and every shade of green, brown, and amber on an artist's palette painted the forest. A man wearing camouflage gear would vanish into the background like a tiger in the jungle.

Acutely aware of the groans in the tall pines as they swayed from the wind, she glanced behind her, scanning the immediate area. The woods played their own music, from birdsong to the chatter of squirrels and the sway of branches; all these sounds would disguise the killer's footfalls. *Will he strike now or tonight when we are in the tent?*

She tried to smother the rising uncertainty, but night would come soon enough and the day's beauty would turn quickly to a shadowed feeding ground for the forest's nocturnal inhabitants. The trees would become lines of black posts shutting her inside and preventing her escape. The moon would offer little light, and every boulder would loom out of the forest like some hideous gargoyle. She tried to swallow the rising panic creeping into her mind. *He's coming and I'm the target.*

CHAPTER FIFTY-THREE

He checked his watch then removed it and left it in a backpack; he did not want it covered in DNA. The time he had planned to make his first move would be perfect. The sun had already dropped in the sky. One more weapons' check and he headed out the cave and down the mountainside, moving with stealth through the dense undergrowth along the narrow animal paths he knew like the lines on his palm.

Paul and Mariah had chosen a perfect spot for the hunt. One hundred yards from their current position, the trail fell away on one side to a canyon with a rocky ravine dug out of the mountain by a prehistoric glacier, and only a fool would risk running down there. The track ended in a switchback forcing the hikers to double back; in other words, his prey would be running around in circles. He would position himself in the middle and have a clear shot to bring down Paul in full view of the trail cams.

His cellphone vibrated and he glanced at the screen. The viewers had voted for his first move. He chuckled. They were like a medieval bloodthirsty crowd waiting to watch someone hanged, drawn, and quartered. He tied the bandana around his face and put on his sunglasses. The cap covered his hair, and dressed like this with the voice changer app turned on, no one would recognize him. His earpiece and mic were in place and ready to live-stream. He turned on his body cam and spoke to his viewers. "Moving out. Come on, you sadistic assholes, make me work for it. I want to take my time and enjoy killing the bitch."

CHAPTER FIFTY-FOUR

Bradford listened to Wolfe's instructions in her earpiece and glanced at Rowley, positioned a few feet above, on the plateau. The sun was dropping and the team was moving down the black rocky slopes and into a better position. She trembled at the thought of being alone so close to the bottom of the mountain; the place Wolfe had sent her was only a few feet from the forest floor. She would have to run through the trees then dash twenty yards along an animal track before climbing into the safety of the crevice. The idea of being so close to a potential killer scared the hell out of her, and to make things worse, she had seen a bobcat earlier. In an effort to calm her nerves, she took one last look around then contacted Rowley. "Is it safe for me to move out?"

"Yeah. I've scanned the immediate area and can't see any movement. If the killer is stalking the sheriff, he'll be way down the other end of the trail by now. The bobcat disappeared into the undergrowth and shouldn't bother you. You're good to go." Rowley's voice was confident. "Move out, I'll watch your back."

She clambered down the rough pathway and headed for the trees. With her back to a tree, she searched all around then bolted for the small incline that led to the crevice. After being in the sunlight, the pathway through the tall pines was dark and claustrophobic. She pushed her way through the undergrowth, searching for the animal path Rowley had insisted was there. A flash of green caught her attention and she stumbled to a halt. Not green but the reflection from cat's eyes. She bit back a scream as the bobcat sprayed his scent over the closest tree. The cat lifted its head and his eyes fixed on her, but only the tip of its tail twitched.

Heart pounding against her ribs, she turned and ran for her life, stumbling over branches. The com link had fallen out of her ear and tangled around her legs. She ripped it free and ran through the forest, heading down the first trail she found. She heard the sound of something big behind her then a huge weight slammed into her back and she crashed to the ground. The wind rushed out of her lungs and she gasped painfully for breath waiting for the cat to bite. She heard a disjointed chuckle as someone rolled her onto her back then fell on her, crushing her ribs. It was not the scent of a cat or its sharp claws but a man.

Terror slammed into her, cutting off the protest in her throat. A skull looked back at her, the eyes covered with mirrored sunglasses. She tried to move but the large man had her arms pinned under his knees, and with his weight on her chest, she fought to suck air into her lungs. His head turned from side to side, as if evaluating her.

"Get off me." Her voice sounded high pitched and breathless.

Before she had the chance to inform him she was a deputy, he gripped her throat and squeezed. She could do nothing but stare into her own terrified reflection in the lenses of his sunglasses. Anger welled inside her. If he intended to strangle her, he would have a fight on his hands. She kicked hard with her legs then dug the heels of her boots into the leaf mold in an effort to push him off her. His reply was to squeeze her neck so tight, her vision blurred and she gasped for air.

"We have an unexpected bonus." The voice was strange, almost mechanical. "Why are you out here all alone?"

"I was taking a shortcut back to the hunting area to meet my husband." Bradford grunted. "He's not far away."

"Really? I didn't see anyone." His voice made her skin crawl.

The grip around her neck decreased slightly and she nodded, in the hope Rowley would be following her movements in his scope. The killer had found her, and without Rowley's help, she would become his next victim. She had to get away from him but he was so strong. Somewhere in her confused panic, she remembered Kane talking about how psychopaths liked their victims to scream and fight back. In an effort to gain a precious few minutes, she forced her tense muscles to relax. The man noticed immediately, and keeping a grip on her throat with one gloved hand, he used the other to unzip her jacket. He slid out her service weapon from the shoulder holster and waved it in front of her eyes.

"You should have drawn this when you saw the bobcat." He ran the muzzle of the gun down her chest between her breasts. "A couple of shots in the air and the cat would have taken off. Yet you decided to run. Cats like to hunt. You ran and made it a game for him and me." He stared at her. "Most girls would be begging me not to hurt them about now. Are you very brave or are you trying to psychoanalyze me?"

She shook her head, refusing to speak to him.

"I'll give you a heads-up: I never negotiate and you're about to die." He gave a snort of mirth. "Open your mouth."

Tremors wracked her body but she complied. He ran the muzzle of the gun across her cheek then pushed the barrel into her mouth. Cold metal pressed against her tongue and the taste of oil spilled across her taste buds. She could not believe how calm and in control he was. Not the crazed, slashing maniac she had envisioned. Staying calm was her only hope, and Rowley would come crashing through the bushes at any moment.

"Give me the figures." He spoke into his mic and nodded as if getting instructions via his com then moved the gun back and forth in her mouth. "Where are the others now? Okay, I'll get into position after I've dealt with this one."

He paused as if listening, and her eyes swiveled to notice the body cam and com pack he was wearing. He was awaiting instructions for his pay-per-view. *Oh, Jesus, help me.*

"Oh, I like that and then I'll be on my way." His attention moved back to her. "If we had met at another time, we could have enjoyed this so much more." He leaned to one side and she heard a swishing sound.

Then she caught sight of the knife.

CHAPTER FIFTY-FIVE

Kane wanted to protect Jenna. If the killer planned to aim a bullet at him, he could not risk him missing and hitting her by mistake. He gave Jenna a friendly push in the back. "You go first and watch your step. According to the map, the canyon is on the right; the edge is probably covered with vegetation and there is a ravine at the bottom."

"Sure, I guess if I slip you'll grab me in time?" Jenna glanced at him over one shoulder.

"You know I will." Kane moved closer and rested one hand on her shoulder. "Is that better?"

"Much." Jenna's muscles tensed under his grip. "The sun is dropping fast—how late is it?"

Kane glanced at his watch. "Getting on for three."

They moved off again, looking like elephants linking trunks. Kane had picked this particular trail for the canyon that split the forest with its bottomless ravine. The killer could only come at them from one side, and he figured if an attack came, it would be on their return to camp and from the rear. So far, the killer had used the forest to his advantage, and on the way back they would be traveling uphill, and be slower targets. If they heard him, which he doubted, and turned to look at him, they would be looking directly into the sun and would not see him coming.

His phone vibrated in his pocket. He waited. If Wolfe needed to speak to him, it would stop and start up again. If the team had laid eyes on the killer, it would keep on going. It stopped then started up again a few seconds later. He squeezed Jenna's shoulder. "Hold up. Nature calls."

"Me too." Jenna darted into the undergrowth.

It was a planned move. They had noted the position of the trail cams and made sure they were out of sight. Kane walked into the forest, leaned against the widest trunk he could find and scanned the area. Sure that no one could see or hear him, he took out his cell. He needed to keep it short and get back to Jenna. "There are trail cams set out along the path. He's here, I can almost smell him."

"If he is, we can't see him." Wolfe sounded tense. *"It's later in the day than we reckoned and the sun is blinding us. Right now, he could pick up a reflection from the scopes. I'll move lower down the mountain but it will take time. I've sent Rowley to the plateau and Bradford to the crevice on the far right. They'll be able to cover you, but when sun drops lower we'll need to reposition again."*

"Roger that." Kane disconnected and hurried back to the trail.

He glanced around and worry cramped his gut. Jenna had not appeared. "Mariah, where are you hiding?"

"Right here." Jenna pushed out of the bushes. "I need the wipes out of the backpack. Peeing in the forest is gross." She opened a flap in his bag and pulled out the wipes.

Kane bent and pretended to nibble her ear. "The team is moving. We are on our own until they relocate so take it slow."

"You say the sweetest things." Jenna wiped her hands then glanced behind him. "I guess we better keep moving."

He looked at her and his heart skipped a beat. Had he made a fatal mistake by risking her life? The canyon loomed out of the forest and he paused to take in the scenery. Pine trees marched up each side and he could see the tops of some. The ravine at the bottom of the canyon must be over 100 feet deep. A multitude of bushes covered the bottom and he wondered what lurked down there. He touched

Jenna's arm to slow her. "I know you're anxious to get back but I need a rest. There's a log over there—let's take five before we go on."

"Okay, I need a drink." Jenna dropped down onto the log. "It's beautiful here. I didn't know there would be so many varieties of birds in the forest, and look over there, squirrels scampering up the trees."

"Yeah, it is, now I guess you're glad you came hiking with me?"

"Hmm, one weekend will probably be enough for me." Jenna brushed ants from her boots. "I don't like the insects, and if we run into a bear, I'm running all the way back to the car."

The fallen tree was on the edge of the canyon and Kane figured that if they kept their backs to the drop, they could keep watch for the killer. He shrugged out of his backpack and pulled out a bottle of water then handed it to Jenna. He rolled his shoulders and leaned back as if closing his eyes, but beneath his sunglasses, he scanned the forest from one side to the other. Nothing. Oh, the killer was good. If he was close by, he had the skills of a Navy Seal.

A high and piercing sound cut through the peace and sent birds rising in flocks. The noise made his heart pound but it shot Jenna into combat mode. She swung around and stared up the pathway, one hand going to the zipper on her jacket. In a moment, she would pull her weapon and the killer would disappear like an ice cream on a hot day. He rested one hand on her arm. "It's okay. That could be a bobcat some ways away. They are territorial and a rival has probably walked by or challenged him."

The screech came again and Jenna stiffened beside him. "That sounded more like a woman screaming than a cat." She shuddered. "I've heard stories about forests at night. All sorts of supernatural creatures roam around. It might have been a banshee or a spirit bent on revenge."

Oh boy, Jenna is playing her role to the hilt. Kane pulled her against him. "Don't worry; I'll protect you against banshees and ghosts." He leaned in then dropped his voice to a whisper. "Stay in front of me once we hit the switchback. If he is planning on hitting us before we get back to camp, it will be soon." He wanted her some distance away from him and glanced around, taking in the trail cams.

"Okay." She turned away and strolled ahead. "Coming?"

Kane smiled at her. "Yeah." He continued down the path at a leisurely pace.

Sometime later, Jenna stopped and turned around to look at him.

"You are slow." Jenna pulled a face. "It's taken us over ten minutes to walk a hundred yards." She turned and walked away.

He grinned and raised his voice. "I'm not as young as you."

Pain shot through his head in an explosion of agony and the forest went out of focus. He lifted one hand to his head and stared at the blood on his fingers. *I've been hit.*

CHAPTER FIFTY-SIX

The loud scream Rowley heard worried him; it could have been the bobcat but Bradford could be in trouble. After trying without success to contact her via her com, he used the scope on his rifle to scan the area between her last position and the crevice. The thick vegetation hampered his view but he could see the trail she had headed down earlier, and nothing moved in the immediate area. She should be safe by now and had only been out of his sight for a few yards before she reached the crevice. *Why isn't she answering her com?*

His job was to watch for the killer and protect the sheriff and Kane from a surprise attack during the time it took the sharpshooters to move into a better position. He scanned the forest again then reached for his cellphone, breaking Kane's instructions to remain silent, and called Bradford. The call went to voicemail and he cursed under his breath. *Where are you?*

Unable to leave his current position, he contacted Wolfe and explained the situation.

"*There is a chance her signal is blocked by the crevice. We are climbing down the rock face now and should be in position in about five minutes.*" Wolfe was breathing heavily. "*Do a visual scan of the sheriff's position and the surrounding areas for the killer. If all clear, make your way to the crevice, but if you see the killer, follow the plan. Call the sheriff and we'll drop to the forest floor and surround him. We heard the scream. Stay alert. If there is a bobcat down there guarding its territory, it's likely there is more than one male prowling around.*"

"Roger that." Rowley checked the area again, peering through the trees in the direction of the canyon.

The sheriff and Kane should be nearing the switchback by now and out of sight, but would be visible again once they hit the straightaway trail back to camp. Satisfied the killer was nowhere near the sheriff, he stood, placed his rifle over one shoulder, and headed down the steep pathway to the bottom of the mountain. He passed the place Wolfe had first positioned Bradford and jogged into the bushes. He found the path she had taken and after a few minutes spotted the curly white cord to her com pack. From his location, he could clearly see the crevice bathed in sunlight and one quick look through his binoculars confirmed it was empty.

A chill crept up his spine. Had the bobcat spotted her? He moved deeper into the forest, peering into the shadows, and the smell of cat urine hit him like a brick wall. *Oh, shit.* She was no fool but would she have panicked and run? He glanced around, searching for a clue, and found a boot mark in the soft ground heading away from the mountain. She had run in the sheriff's direction, and if they had lured the killer to the area, she would be in great danger. He got back on his com. "Wolfe, we have a problem."

CHAPTER FIFTY-SEVEN

Jenna took ten or so paces along the track then looked over one shoulder at Kane. She heard a *putt* not much louder than a twig breaking, and a spray of blood exploded from Kane's head. She gaped at him in astonishment then a *putt* came again and a tree branch exploded beside him. Holy hell it was the sound from a sniper rifle with a suppressor and Kane was the target. The shooter could be up a tree hundreds of yards away or on the ground with a clear view through the trees. She dived to the ground and rolled into the bushes but Kane remained on the path, staring into space with a dazed expression. She waved to get his attention. "Get down."

Terrified at the amount of blood streaming down his face, she belly-crawled toward him through the trees. This should not be happening. Nothing was going to plan. Another bullet whizzed past Kane's head, hitting a tree beside the path, and he just stood there as if transfixed. Something was terribly wrong. Kane's combat experience would normally make him react instinctively and move into cover. She edged forward again, wriggling toward him, but he was ten or more yards away and she dare not call out and give the shooter her position again.

When Kane staggered and dropped to his knees inches away from a steep drop at the side of the canyon, her stomach cramped in panic. The words tumbled out of her mouth before she could stop them. "Be careful, you'll fall."

After a feeble attempt to drag himself up, he lurched forward then to her dismay rolled over and tumbled into the canyon. Stunned, she crawled on all fours to the edge and stared in horror as his body bounced down the slope like a rag doll then snagged at the base of a tree. The surrounding bushes hid most of him from view and she could only make out one arm hanging over a log. He was not moving. *Kane. Oh, dear God.*

Shocked and horrified, she gaped at him in disbelief—she had to get to him, but inside the truth gnawed at her. She bit back a sob of grief. The son of a bitch had killed Kane. Her first instinct was to run into the canyon after him, and she hovered on the edge deciding how to descend the steep fall. The squawk of an eagle overhead, as if in warning, brought her back to reality.

There was a still a chance Kane was alive and she could not help him if the killer shot her as well. *Take cover and contact Wolfe.* She moved back into the forest then got to her feet, placed her back to a tree, and pulled out her cellphone. Another muffled *putt* and the screen shattered. Pain shot through her fingers and she fell hard, crashing to the ground. She lay winded for a few seconds trying to catch her breath. A bullet had passed through the cellphone and torn a six-inch split across the left side of her jacket. The shooter was using a suppressor and her team would not have heard the shot. He had her pinned down and was well hidden. She considered the angle of the shot. *He is in front of me and on my right. How far away is he?*

Heart thumping in her ears, she scanned her immediate area. The bushes offered her protection for now. *I have to get to Kane.* She unzipped her jacket and with tingling fingers slid the Glock from the shoulder holster then crawled to the edge of the canyon. Under cover of the long vegetation, she slid toward the edge like a snake. She would have to move with care and not give her position away. If she waited for each gust of wind before belly-crawling through the bushes, he would not see her. Under her, the rough gravel, tree roots, and debris tore at her jeans but the Kevlar vest offered her chest protection and had saved her from injury.

The images of Kane's head exploding in a spray of crimson replayed in her mind. *Be alive. Please, God, let him be alive.* Realization slammed into her. If by some miracle he had survived the headshot, he could have broken his neck in the fall. One way or another, she had to get to him. *Dammit, where is my team?* Her hand trembled on the grip of her pistol. She took a few deep breaths then rolled onto her back and listened. Anyone coming into the canyon would dislodge a good amount of rocks and she would hear them, but only the sound of her heavy breathing broke the silence. After sliding her weapon back into the shoulder holster, she got onto all fours and headed toward the nearest tree.

She stood in shadows with her back pressed hard against the trunk and peered down the slope. Kane's gloved hand hung over a low branch but his fingers had not moved. She swallowed the lump in her throat and tried to access her professional façade but desperation seeped into her. A salty wetness coated her lips and she brushed away the tears streaming down her cheeks. Loneliness and despair engulfed her. She was the target, not Kane. How had this happened?

CHAPTER FIFTY-EIGHT

Euphoria bubbled into a chuckle as he moved like a ghost between the trees. He had often traveled the pathways made by animals walking to and from the canyon. The com in his ear was buzzing with the excited voice of his contact. The headshot on Paul had blown their minds and his associate was replaying it in slow motion on the pay-per-view. A trail cam had picked up Mariah's shocked expression and his shot to take out her cellphone. A double whammy: Her cellphone was toast and the bullet had sliced a path across her ribs. That kind of shooting took skill. He grinned and paused to watch the slow-motion rerun of both Paul's head exploding and Mariah sprawling on her ass.

His contact assured him Paul had fallen into the ravine at the bottom of the canyon. His body would be dinner for the critters living in its fathomless depths. Without Paul to worry about, he had all the time in the world to play with Mariah, and he wanted this one to last. After all, winter would be here soon and the snow would force him to lay low until spring.

He licked his lips. Mariah, his prey, was already on the move; the blonde had merely whetted his appetite. The viewers had changed his usual game but, hey, now he could concentrate on Mariah. After posting a list of his favorite moves for them to choose from, they had voted for him to rape her then cut her. He enjoyed the torture. It taught the bitches how to behave in his presence.

His skill with a blade had become an art form, knowing how deep to cut without killing them. Once he had satisfied his viewers' bloodlust, he would strangle her just enough to subdue her before he took her to his cave. She would figure her time with him was over and then she would wake up and he could start over.

He approached the switchback and blended into the forest. She was close; he could almost smell her fear. He pulled out his knife and grinned. *Run, run as fast as you can, Mariah, but you will never escape me.*

CHAPTER FIFTY-NINE

"Orders, sir?" Rowley scanned the forest in wide sweeps. "I can smell a cat but nothing is moving down here. I can't risk calling out to Bradford. It would alert the killer I'm here."

"We are on the plateau and the sun is still obscuring our vision. Do a recon of the immediate area, say a hundred yards along the trail you assume she went, then call in if you find her or not." Wolfe let out a long sigh. *"We'll head down now. It's getting late, and if the sheriff or Kane had eyes on the killer, they'd have alerted us by now."*

Rowley slid the rifle from his shoulder, cocked the hammer and held it shoulder high. No way was he risking taking on an angry bobcat or a lunatic without a weapon in his hand. He headed along the trail. "Roger that."

He had lived in Black Rock Falls all his life and spent many hours in Stanton Forest. It had been a retreat from school and later, a place to relax with friends, fishing or hunting. Of late, the place held memories he would rather forget. As he moved with caution, stepping through the zebra shadows across the path, his mind went to one of his new friends. After meeting Atohi Blackhawk, they had spent a great deal of time together. Atohi had offered him a different outlook on life and had eased his apprehension about venturing into the forest again. Atohi had insisted the forest was not to blame for the atrocities of man, and in fact, the beauty of the trees and all the forest held would heal the sorrow he had inside him. *I hope so.*

The sound of crows and the flapping of wings as birds gathered in the branches made the hair on the back of his neck stand straight up. He had seen the signs of death before, and as sure as his name was Jake Rowley, crows gathering was the first sign. The breeze held the smell of blood and he stopped midstride and listened. Nothing, only the rustle of the leaves and the crows arguing as they watched from the branches. He stepped away from the trail and moved slowly from tree to tree, expecting to disturb a killer.

Sweat ran into his eyes and a pulse pounded in his ears. With each step, the unmistakable smell of death increased. He closed his eyes for a second and prayed it would be an animal. With every instinct screaming at him to turn around and head back to Wolfe and Webber, he gripped his rifle and moved to the next tree. The smell had gotten bad. He swallowed his fear and turkey-peeked around the trunk, but one quick look was enough. *Oh, Jesus.*

He fumbled for his com mic and depressed the button. "You need to get over here. It's bad."

"Details, Rowley." Wolfe's orders came through loud in his ear.

His hand trembled. "It's Deputy Bradford and there's a lot of blood."

"On our way. Check her vitals."

The forest closed in around him. The killer had a million places to hide and watch his reaction, the sick son of a bitch. He dragged up his last ounce of courage and walked toward Bradford. At the sight before him, his chest constricted and he could not breathe. He wanted to look away and had to force his eyes to take in the gruesome scene before him. There would be no need to check her pulse.

CHAPTER SIXTY

The rough terrain ripped at Jenna's jeans, and bushes whipped across her cheeks, but she pushed on, sliding and slipping down the steep canyon. With only her inbuilt sense of direction to guide her, she kept low and made her way toward Kane's position. Time was ticking by, and every second could mean the difference between life and death for Kane. She bit back a sob of frustration as the loose gravel underfoot hampered her speed. Without her cellphone, she had no contact with her team. She had a tracker ring, which in an emergency sent a message to Kane's phone. Damn lot of good that was with Kane down. If she could get to him, she could use his cellphone to call for backup.

The ground underneath her feet shifted, bouncing her in an uncontrollable slide into the canyon. In desperation, she looped one arm around a bush to slow her descent and grasped at clumps of grass to crawl to the base of a tree. She sat, gasping for air for a few seconds, then glanced up to check for any movement above her. *Where is the shooter?*

One thing for sure, the killer was up there and would be running through his trail cam footage to find out where she was heading. With half an hour to the next check-in time, her team would have no idea their plans had gone to hell. With the sun blinding them, they would be ignorant to the fact the killer had shot Kane and she was in danger. The moment Kane missed a check-in and neglected to answer his cell, they would move in. In the meantime, she had to outsmart a psychopathic killer and get to Kane.

She glanced around to get her bearings but the direct route to him would place her out in the open. *I'll have to find another way.* The canopy of trees would cover her for a few more yards and she jogged along an animal path through the trees, lifting her knees to avoid the tangle of dry grass and ivy. When she came to the clearing, she could see Kane's arm draped over a log twenty yards away. To avoid crossing the open patch to get to him, she would have to negotiate a small part of the perimeter of a fifty-foot drop to the bottom of the ravine.

With the urgency to get to Kane front and center in her mind, she pulled up her gloves, gripped the woody stalks of bushes, then lowered herself feet-first over the edge. Her legs hung in midair and her heart thundered in her chest as she felt around the crumbling rock wall for a suitable foothold. Gravel tumbled down behind her, sounding like rain as it peppered the bushes below. She chanced a look down and her stomach cramped. Fear held her motionless for a few long seconds, then grinding her teeth, she edged sideways, gripping the bushes and moving one careful step at a time.

The scrub moved under her grasp, threatening to uproot and plunge her to certain death. Shoulders aching with overexertion, she forced onward, edging along the perilous drop. Aware of the time her painfully slow progress was taking, she sucked in a sob of relief when shadows closed around her. The muscles in her arms screamed in protest as she dragged herself out of the ravine and lay panting in the grass. Not allowing herself a moment to recover, she belly-crawled into the cover of the tall pines then took in her surroundings. Kane was lying face down, legs sprawled. One arm hung over the fallen tree and he was still wearing the backpack. He had not made one twitch of a finger. Pushing down her instinct to run to his side, she scanned the area, making sure a shooter looking down from above would not see her, then moved closer.

Panic gripped her and she tried desperately to steel herself to deal professionally with what she would find. From the spray of blood from Kane's head wound and the fall into the canyon, the chances of finding him alive would be close to zero but she had to be sure.

She moved from tree to tree, taking care to remain hidden, then belly-crawled to Kane's inert body. Blood covered his hair and soaked the back and shoulder of his shirt. She removed her sunglasses and stared at the wound in surprise. The injury was not the gaping hole she expected and was bleeding profusely in a sign of life. Her survival training fell into place like a shield against her welling emotions of finding him alive. *I must stop the bleeding.*

The bullet had gouged a four-inch path across his scalp just above the right ear, exposing the titanium plate in his head. She shuddered at the sight of the dented metal. *How close did he come to dying?* She removed one of her gloves and slid her hand under his neck to check his pulse. Under her fingers, she felt the *thump, thump, thump* of strength, not the weak flutter of someone bleeding out. Relieved, she went through his pockets to search for his cellphone, dragged it out, and groaned in dismay at the shattered screen. With Wolfe only a call away, Kane would have gotten the expert care he needed. She glanced up the canyon to the top. Nothing moved through the long grass or disturbed the loose rocks. The killer hadn't found her yet. "I figure it's just you and me, Dave."

With gentle care, she ran her hands over his arms and legs, checking for injuries. She found no broken bones but blood pooled around his left knee and he could have damaged his spine. She eased off his backpack and moved his arm from over the log. With the trees hiding them from above, she could tend to his head injury without the killer seeing her. Apart from energy bars and water, Kane made a habit of carrying a Combat Lifesaver Kit complete with wound stapler. At least she could stop the bleeding. She pulled out the kit and went through the supplies. After pulling on surgical gloves, she trimmed away the hair, cleaned the leaves and other debris from Kane's wound, irrigated it, then stapled the edges together. After dressing the wound, she stared at him, willing him to open his eyes.

He had bruises all over, and deep scrapes and scratches on his face. Not wanting to move his head, she dabbed at what she could reach then turned away to pull a blanket from the backpack. As she turned back, Kane lifted one arm and had her by the throat. She stared up into the eyes of a man she did not know. Cold and intimidating, they bore into her, examining her face. He weighed a ton and she gasped for air. "Get off me."

"Who the hell are you?" Kane touched his head and winced. "You sure made a mistake trying to kill me, lady."

She gaped at him, trying to inhale under the weight of him. "I'm Sheriff Jenna Alton and your superior officer. We are chasing a serial killer and *he* shot you."

"I wouldn't be anyone's deputy, not in this life." Kane's fingers tightened around her throat. "Think again and I might allow you to live."

Jenna tried to think back to the stories he'd told her about working for POTUS. "Calm down and I'll tell you what I know. You're off the grid and I know you as Dave Kane." She looked into his eyes but not one glimmer of recognition showed there. "You told me once one of the agents guarding POTUS left his com on when he went to the bathroom for an explosive visit. You had to listen and guard POTUS without laughing."

"Go on." Kane's grip loosened.

Desperate to get him back on her side, she gave him an abridged version of his life. "Your wife's name was Annie and she was killed in a car bombing. You have a plate in your head because of that attack and ended up as my deputy in Black Rock Falls."

"I don't remember you or being a deputy." Kane's troubled gaze scanned her face. "The rest was yesterday. What's the date?"

Jenna told him then pushed her hand into her pocket and pulled out her creds. "Here, look. I am who I say." She waited for him to examine her ID then gave him a quick rundown of their situation in the hope it would trigger his memory. "We've been working together for a year. You live in a cottage on my ranch. You have a dog named Duke, a bloodhound."

"I don't remember but you check out and we are in the forest, so I guess I'll have to believe you." He rolled off her then grunted and his face paled to sheet-white. "Dammit, my knee is shot." He pulled himself onto a sitting position behind a tree and peered at a ripped hole in his blood-soaked jeans. "Smashed my kneecap."

"Let me take a look." To keep his mind off his injuries, Jenna gave him what information they had on the killer and what had transpired in the last hour. She dragged over the medical kit and bent over his leg. "You'll need this tended by a doctor. I stapled the cut on your head but this needs a specialist. All I can do is clean and dress it for now."

"Do it but I don't have one chance in hell of climbing up that slope." Kane winced as she poured antiseptic over the wound. "Have you called for backup?" He reached inside his jacket, checked his cred pack, then removed his weapon and searched his pockets.

"No, the cellphones are smashed." Jenna noticed how slow he was moving and frowned. "Any other injuries?" She took bottles of water from the backpack and handed him one then sipped the other.

"Too many to count." His glance was softer this time.

She finished dressing the wound and looked up at his pale, drawn face. "There's morphine in the kit."

"No, I need to be alert." Kane frowned then searched her face again. "We have to move. Now! If the killer saw me fall, he knows my position and could be on his way." He shrugged on the backpack then dragged himself up using a tree. "Hand me that branch, I'll use it as a cane."

They moved a few yards into the canyon in deep shadows before Kane needed to halt. Jenna could almost feel his agony but he had not made one complaint. He hung, panting, to a pine and she walked a few yards away and looked up to get her bearings. The branches shattered beside her as a shot whizzed past her head and struck the trunk of a sapling. She dropped and rolled behind a huge boulder. Fear clutched at her, speeding her heart rate; the killer had given a warning he was on his way. He wanted her terrified to increase his pleasure. *He is hunting me.*

She crawled to the other side of the boulder and found Kane dragging himself toward her. After helping him into a sitting position, she removed his backpack. "There is water and energy bars in there and a thermal blanket."

"Okay." Kane gave her a quizzical stare; the bruises on his face had turned a nasty purple and blood trickled from under the dressing on his head. "You planning on leaving me here for the bears?"

"You can look after yourself for a while. You have plenty of ammo and I've seen you shoot." She crouched down in front of him. "Listen to me, Dave. I'm going to lure the killer away from you. If he enters the canyon, we'll be more vulnerable; no one knows we're here. We've missed the check-in time and our team will know something is wrong by now and be moving in up there on the trail. I'll just have to avoid being caught by him before they arrive."

"No way." Kane's brow wrinkled. "If this is a serial killer, a psychopath, no one really knows what's in his mind; he could get mad and kill you just for the heck of it. I won't let you do this, Sheriff. Stay here and we'll fight him together."

The cold way he looked at her, it was like a stranger had taken over his body. "We don't have a choice. With your injuries, like it or not,

Dave, he'll have the advantage. If I leave you here, I will be able to draw him away. He is not interested in you, and I figure he already believes you're dead. I sure did." She looked into his bloodshot eyes. "You profiled this killer and I'm the type of woman he murders. The men he kills are superfluous to his needs."

"It's too dangerous." Kane gripped her arm. "If we stay here, the moment he walks into range, I'll take him down. The shots will alert your deputies and they'll come running."

She wondered if he had all his faculties after his head injury and shook her head. "I know that's the way you are used to working, Dave but we do this by the book. There are hunters all over the forest and anyone could be down here and walk into range. We have to be sure it's the killer before we shoot. You can't just kill the first person who walks in here; he has to pose a threat."

"I figure he's already posed a threat to me, ma'am." Kane's mouth twitched up in the corner. "Say I go along with this madness. What's your plan?"

"If I dart into the open, for just a second to gain his attention, I can move into the shadows and climb to the top of the canyon. The team is scanning that area. They'll spot me, and come running. This is the only option we have. Like I said, they have no idea we are down here." Jenna shrugged. "If I stay, we will be playing the killer's game. The lunatic up there doesn't want to kill me outright; he prefers to torture his victims and we can use it against him."

"And if he disables you?" Kane sipped the water from his bottle and winced. "Say he shoots you in the arms; you won't be able to fight or use your weapon. Your team won't be there in seconds, will they?" He gave her a long look. "He is using a high-powered rifle and from what I have witnessed so far is a marksman. He could take the team out before they know what's happening."

Jenna shook her head. "Not my team. For heaven's sake, you trained them and we have Wolfe up there in command. He is like you, an ex-marine. He won't let us down."

"If you say so, but I'm your best protection even with a busted knee." Kane's gaze narrowed. "If you know me as well as you say you do, you'll understand."

"I do but right now, I need to protect you. This is the best option. I have to trust in our team." She squeezed his shoulder. "Stay safe. I'll deal with this son of a bitch then send Wolfe to help you, I promise."

Refusing to argue with him, she replaced her sunglasses, pushed the bottle of water into her pocket, then turned and sprinted out of the forest across the sunlit area in full view and back into the shadowed tree line to the steep canyon wall. She dove into the undergrowth and headed slowly up the side of the chasm. Above her, she heard the sound of a rifle with a suppressor shooting in rapid succession; the killer was firing all around her as if herding her. A wave of panic hit her. *The game has changed. I'm playing by his rules now.*

CHAPTER SIXTY-ONE

His day could not get better and now his prey had marched right out of cover and into his sights. He chuckled and aimed a few more shots to her right. "Come on, get back on the trail. I am waiting to play with you." He leaned over the edge, watching the bushes move as Mariah climbed up the steep incline.

She would be exhausted by the time she reached the top, and with the sun dropping fast, he didn't have too much time to allow her to rest before he concluded his hunt. He glanced at his watch. He had maybe an hour of good daylight left. He wanted the chase; seeing her run frantic then knowing she could never escape fed his need. The votes were in on how he would kill her, but herding her closer to his cave was his main objective. He wanted to savor her in front of his friends. After all, it had been years since some of them had seen a woman.

He quivered with excitement at the thought of her reaction when he switched on the lamps in his cave. She would scream, horrified at his friends' expressions. He doubted many people would appreciate their rate of decomposition like he did. His friends would smile at her and he would feed off her terror. His heart would beat so fast and yet he would be calm. He did so like to take his time with his prey and savor each delicious moment.

He waited for her to pop out of the canyon and bolt down the trail, heading toward her campsite. Taking his time, he strolled after her; she was moving at a slow pace and it would be easy to keep up with her. He followed, then to his surprise, she stopped walking, stood in full view, and took a long drink from a bottle of water. He raised his rifle then placed two shots into a tree on her left. To his surprise, she did not run screaming into the forest but turned slowly to face him. He stepped into the open and pointed his rifle at her. He had distorted his voice and it should terrify her. "Run or I'm going to kill you where you stand."

"What? You're planning on shooting me in the back?" Her loud voice came out in a confident sneer and it was strangely familiar. "Big man, with a big weapon. You are just a weakling son of a bitch using a high-powered rifle against an unarmed woman. A real man would at least have the guts to fight me one on one." She lifted her chin. "What? Am I too big for you to take on? Go home to Mommy, little boy, and stop wasting my time."

Anger flared and he dropped the rifle and unsheathed his knife. "I'll make you sorry you said that to me, bitch."

CHAPTER SIXTY-TWO

Desperate to gain time, Jenna waved her arms at him. "Bring it on, you little worm."

Her bravery came from the movement ahead on the trail. Her team was closing in and her raised voice would have caught their full attention. The man before her was tall but not as big as Kane, and covered from head to foot. A hideous skull-print bandana masked his face, and sunglasses covered his eyes. He was just as Colter Barry described. She stood feet apart and shoulders straight to make him come to her. Kane's profiling on this lunatic filtered into her mind; the killer fed on fear and likely enjoyed his victims to beg for their lives.

Adrenaline pumped through her and she wanted to fight him as if the notion of a woman bringing him down would put everything right. She heard him speak but not to her; he was communicating through his com. The idea he might have accomplices had not entered her mind. Unease slid over her. He was advancing and tossing the knife from hand to hand as if he had all the time in the world.

"I'm going to kill you slowly and make you scream for mercy but I never give mercy." The killer moved toward her in slow, deliberate steps. "You're mine now, Mariah. There is no escape."

Desperate to show no fear, Jenna laughed at him. "My name is not Mariah."

She could hear people crashing through the bushes in the distance behind her, but was it her team or the lunatic's accomplices? Taking action was her only choice. "Drop the knife. I'm Sheriff Jenna Alton and I'm not alone."

The killer stopped mid-stride then, to her surprise, chuckled. "Ah, the ultimate prize. So, I gather I took Deputy Kane out earlier. Well, you had me fooled but then you resemble most of my victims, don't you? There is no one here to save you, Jenna. I have eyes everywhere and if that cute blonde was part of your team, well, I'm afraid she lost her heart to someone else." He stalked toward her in measured steps. "No one will get to you in time. It's just you and me, like it should be."

Worry for Bradford's safety flitted through her mind. How could he have gotten to her with three deputies watching her back? She lifted her chin. He did not know she carried a weapon under her jacket, and from what she could make out, he only had a knife plus a degree of insanity on his side. Reasoning with him might still be an option. "You didn't kill Kane. I'll give you one more chance to surrender peacefully."

"Are you crazy?" He tilted his head to one side. "I would die before I surrendered to a woman, especially *you*." His pace quickened as he moved toward her down the trail.

Without taking her eyes off him, Jenna unzipped her jacket and reached for her weapon. Holding it in both hands, she took aim. "Halt or I will shoot."

The killer laughed maniacally and kept on coming. Jenna squeezed the trigger, aiming for his right arm. The man staggered under the force of the bullet but held onto the knife as if he was impervious to pain, and his steps did not falter. He was less than ten yards away and closing fast.

"Bad, Jenna. Head or heart, sweetie." He shook his head like a dog then increased his speed. "Or did you miss? Not so confident now, are you, bitch?" He lunged toward her, knife raised.

Without a second thought, Jenna stood her ground, took aim, and fired. His kneecap exploded and he howled in pain, hitting the ground with a massive thud. She waited a beat, hoping he would give up. If she killed him, they would never know how many people he had murdered. When he roared in anger and waved the knife at her, fear trembled her hands and she gaped at him in terror. As if with superhuman strength, he gave her a satanic grin and dragged himself toward her.

"You're next, Jenna."

Jenna's finger dropped to the trigger of her Glock once more. "Oh, I don't think so."

"Hold your fire." Wolfe came crashing through the forest and onto the trail with Rowley and Webber close on his heels.

Before Jenna had a chance to issue orders, Wolfe kicked the knife from the killer's hand and cuffed him. She stared at the deputies. "You took your time. Where's Bradford?"

"She's dead." Rowley's eyes filled with sorrow. "By him, I figure."

Grief rolled over Jenna but she swallowed it and nodded. "He admitted as much to me. Get a rescue chopper out here. Kane is in the canyon and needs urgent medical attention. This asshole can wait."

"Leave the chopper to me. Where is he? I'll go down to him." Wolfe turned his attention to Jenna and waited for directions. "Webber can tend to the prisoner's injuries."

Jenna gripped Wolfe's arm and led him to one side. "Kane has been shot in the head and is suffering partial memory loss. He didn't recognize me. You'll need to be careful approaching him. He'll shoot first then ask questions later. He's gone back to just after the accident." She lowered her voice to just above a whisper. "The car bombing."

"He'll recognize me." Wolfe turned away and headed down the canyon.

Jenna walked back to stare down at the prisoner.

"You should have killed me." The killer lifted his head.

"I wouldn't have given you the satisfaction. I hope they keep you in jail for the rest of your life; lethal injection is too good for you." Jenna bent over the killer and ripped off his disguise then gaped at him. It was not Ethan Woods as she had expected. She blinked, confused at the face staring back at her. "James Stone."

EPILOGUE

So many things had happened to Jenna in the weeks since a military rescue helicopter winched Kane out of the canyon. Instead of flying him to Black Rock Falls Hospital, they went to the Walter Reed National Military Medical Center in Bethesda. When Wolfe had informed her Kane required a secure environment to recover, she figured he would not be returning to Black Rock Falls anytime soon, if at all.

So the call from the hospital came as a surprise. Kane wanted to see her. Worried what he would say to her, she chewed on her fingernails, figuring out what to do. The person who called informed her she could visit him a few days after his next round of surgery, but she wanted to be there for him and could not wait another second. She had to know if he intended to return to Black Rock Falls.

The flight to Washington gave her time to think how close she had come to being a victim of James Stone. She had been on dates with the man. Who would have thought a person who defended people for a living could murder in cold blood? She stared out the window at the clouds and allowed the case to settle in her mind. Kane would want all the details.

The days following the capture of James Stone had been harrowing. Without information on Kane's condition, other than that he was alive, her nerves had shattered. She called the hospital daily with the same result. Not being a relative, they refused to give out any information. Rowley and Wolfe had supported her the best they could, and Emily spent the weekends telling her gory tales to keep up her spirits.

She had shipped Bradford's body back to her family in Helena then thrown her team into unraveling the dark side of James Stone. After sifting through hours of horrific video footage of his murders, they discovered his cave at Bear Peak. Inside they found the body of Jim Canavar. Stone had documented Jim Canavar's death, clearing him of any involvement in the crimes. Jim sat alongside a line of unknown victims. Jim Canavar's ex-girlfriend and her boyfriend were not amongst the bodies in the cave, nor were the owners of the backpacks, but they found footage of the murder of cold case victims Paige and Dawson. It was a relief to close the cold case file and to know their killer would be behind bars for a very long time.

After tracking down missing Asian tourists, the FBI identified John Doe as Lee Pu, a Chinese national who had transferred huge amounts of cash from his bank account on the day before he left China. The FBI could find no trace of the off-shore account but assumed it was a payment to Stone to be involved in the murder of Bailey Canavar. Even though the payment for the new rig Stone owned came from an overseas bank account, Stone denied knowing Mr. Pu.

With Wolfe working alongside the FBI's Cyber Division on Stone's computer, they located and shut down Stone's site on the dark web. The details of his scheme had horrified her. Stone spent his vacations murdering all over the state and driven home with one special corpse as a souvenir but offered no names of his victims. He admitted to moving the body of his suitable friend through the forest on horseback to join the others in his cave. As Mr. Pu was obviously a client, the FBI were looking overseas for possible DNA matches for the other victims and hunting down possible cold cases throughout the state. Stone obviously derived a thrill out of taking his client's cash then killing them and once identified, the victims' bank details would be investigated by the FBI for any huge withdrawals from their accounts just prior to their disappearances. Even with all the FBI's expertise, they were still unable to trace his co-conspirator for the pay-per-view, or any of his online clients.

The extensive interviews with Stone carried out by an FBI profiler revealed that after Stone's family died in a house fire, a couple had adopted him. Not six months later Stone claimed to have discovered the couple bludgeoned to death in their bed. The police never considered Stone a suspect at twelve years old but the kill had whetted his appetite for more.

As the aircraft made its descent to the runway, Jenna shuddered at the memory of watching James Stone's interview. He had divulged his many kills with obvious glee but implicated no one. It was as if he enjoying reliving the macabre tale from killing his foster parents to a list of murders going back years, but hearing James Stone's final statement chilled her to the bone. He said she was his reason to kill the dark-haired women, and the men were collateral damage. His words ran through her mind in an endless loop.

"It was Jenna's fault; she made me do it. I tried to be nice to her but she treated me like a lowlife. She was no better than all the others. I was not good enough for the high and mighty sheriff. All I wanted was a relationship with her." Stone had turned and stared into the one-way glass as if he could see her. *"I had to make you pay for disrespecting me, Jenna. I had to make them all pay."*

The incident had happened a year ago, and no matter how many times she refused him, Stone had become a pest and when Kane arrived in town, she had asked him to warn Stone off. Stone had finally got the message and left her alone and she figured his fixation on her was finally over. She had no idea his hostility toward her had gone on for so long. The thought that women had died because they resembled her made her sick to her stomach.

After taking a cab to the hospital, a nurse directed her to a sterile, cold waiting room. Worried beyond reason, Jenna paced up and down. Kane had been under the knife for hours. She let out a sigh of relief when the double doors to the operating area swished open and a man wearing surgical scrubs strolled toward her. He held out his hand.

"Sheriff Alton, I believe? I have Mr. Kane's permission to give you an update."

Jenna shook his hand and nodded, fighting for words. "Is Dave okay?"

"It took three surgeries to repair his injuries and he'll need rehabilitation but he'll be okay." The doctor narrowed his gaze. "The plate in his head saved his life but it was extensively damaged and we replaced that when he arrived. The knee required two surgeries and he'll be on crutches for a time but he is tough; this won't hold him up for long."

She swallowed hard, fighting back tears of relief. "What about his memory?"

"He has blank spots but they'll return in good time." The doctor smiled at her. "Do you want to see him? He is out of intensive care and back in his room now."

Jenna nodded and her stomach squeezed. Perhaps this would be the last time she would see Dave Kane. The government would whisk him away and give him a job in another state. She followed the doctor along a corridor and he indicated to a room with a secret service agent posted outside. She showed the man her ID then stepped inside and held her breath. Kane was flat on his back with machines attached everywhere, and a large frame covered his knee. He looked pale and a large, red scar ran down one side of his shaved head. She edged to his bedside and touched his hand. "Dave, it's me, Jenna."

"Jenna?" His eyes opened and he stared at her. "You came all this way to see me?"

She sat on the edge of his bed and touched his arm. "They wouldn't let me to come earlier. It seems you are pretty special around here."

"You've been busy. Wolfe called before I went into surgery and brought me up to date."

Jenna wet her lips. She wanted to find out everything that had happened to him but he was in no shape to talk right now. "I'm glad you recognized Wolfe when I sent him down to help you in the canyon."

"I would have shot him but he used his codename and mine." Kane gave her a sleepy stare. "He was my handler when I was in the service. Ah, I guess you didn't know that, did you? Darn, now I'll have to kill you." He chuckled deep in his chest then groaned. "Oh, Lord, Jenna, don't make me laugh, it hurts."

She frowned. "Wow, the drugs are really messing with your head. You know, I'm sworn to secrecy, same as you, or have you forgotten?"

"I remember you fine. I was just lightening the mood. You look so worried." Their gazes met and Kane cleared his throat. "My timeline is muddled, is all, and the doc says in time, it will all fall back into place."

Jenna looked down at his bruised and battered face. "I'm so glad you're going to be okay."

"Enough about me. You caught the killer, James Stone, the super lawyer. Who would have picked him?" Kane frowned as if he had something difficult to say. "You are one hell of a sheriff. It took guts to take on that maniac alone."

Jenna's chest constricted. He was going to tell her he was not returning to Black Rock Falls. She swallowed hard. "I couldn't have done it without you."

"You did just that." Kane sounded as if he was fighting to stay awake.

Jenna cleared her throat. "Duke misses you. He sits by your rig and howls. I had to drag him into Rowley's house before I left. His eyes were so sad. I did tell him I'd be back soon."

"I miss him too." Kane shut his eyes. "Thanks for looking after him and the horses for me." He turned his head away as if not able to meet her gaze.

"It was no trouble. Duke is like family now." She could not prevent a tear from running down her cheek. "Something is worrying you, Dave. Just say it and get it over with."

"Okay. I *do* need to ask you something." He turned his head to peer at her through his lashes and his voice lowered. "Come closer, the meds are kicking in again."

As she leaned over him, Kane's voice came out in a sleepy whisper. "When are we going home?"

A LETTER FROM D.K. HOOD

Dear Reader,

I am delighted you chose my novel and joined me once again in the exciting world of Jenna Alton and Dave Kane in *The Crying Season*.

If you would like to join a mailing list for alerts on my books, please sign up here. You can unsubscribe at any time, and your email address will never be shared.

www.bookouture.com/dk-hood

Writing this story has been a thrilling adventure for me. Delving into the lives of ex-secret agents and serial killers was a dream come true. I enjoyed researching every aspect of the crime scenes.

If you enjoyed my story, I would be very grateful if you could leave a review and recommend my book to your friends and family.

I would love to hear from you, so please get in touch on my Facebook page or Twitter or through my website.

Thank you so much for your support.
D.K. Hood

 DKHood_Author

dkhoodauthor

www.dkhood.com

dkhood-author.blogspot.com.au

ACKNOWLEDGMENTS

I spend a good deal of time doing research before and during the writing of a novel. I want to make sure my stories are "real." In *The Crying Season*, I required some hands-on expert advice. My go-to person was Daniel Brown. I really appreciate his patience dealing with my constant questions. His explanations and suggestions have been priceless.

I must acknowledge the amazing team at Bookouture, who work so hard to make my books as good as they can be. Helen Jenner is incredible to work with and guides me along the right path. My stories pass through many very experienced hands before publishing. The editing, the fantastic covers, the audiobooks, and the promotion. Many thanks to everyone involved.